LOST

IN MANHATTAN

ALSO BY MOREEN LITTRELL

(Contributing Author)

Women's Comedic Monologues that are Actually Funny (Applause Books)

Teen Girl's Comedic Monologues that are Actually Funny (Applause Books)

LOST
IN MANHATTAN

A NOVEL

MOREEN LITTRELL

DEMILOCA

LOS ANGELES

DEMILOCA

Published in the United States of America by
Demiloca in 2021.

ISBN-13: 978-1-7366107-0-1 (Paperback)
ISBN-13: 978-1-7366107-2-5 (Hardcover)
Ebook also available at retailers worldwide.

Grateful acknowledgments are made to author Maggie Scarf
for permission to reprint excerpts from her article titled,
The Man Who Disappears © 2011 Maggie Scarf;
and to authors Joost Elffers and Gary Goldschneider
for permission to reprint an excerpt from their book,
The Secret Language of Birthdays by Gary Goldschneider and Joost
Elffers. ©1992 by Gary Goldschneider and Joost Elffers. Permission
to reprint granted by Joost Elffers Books LLC.

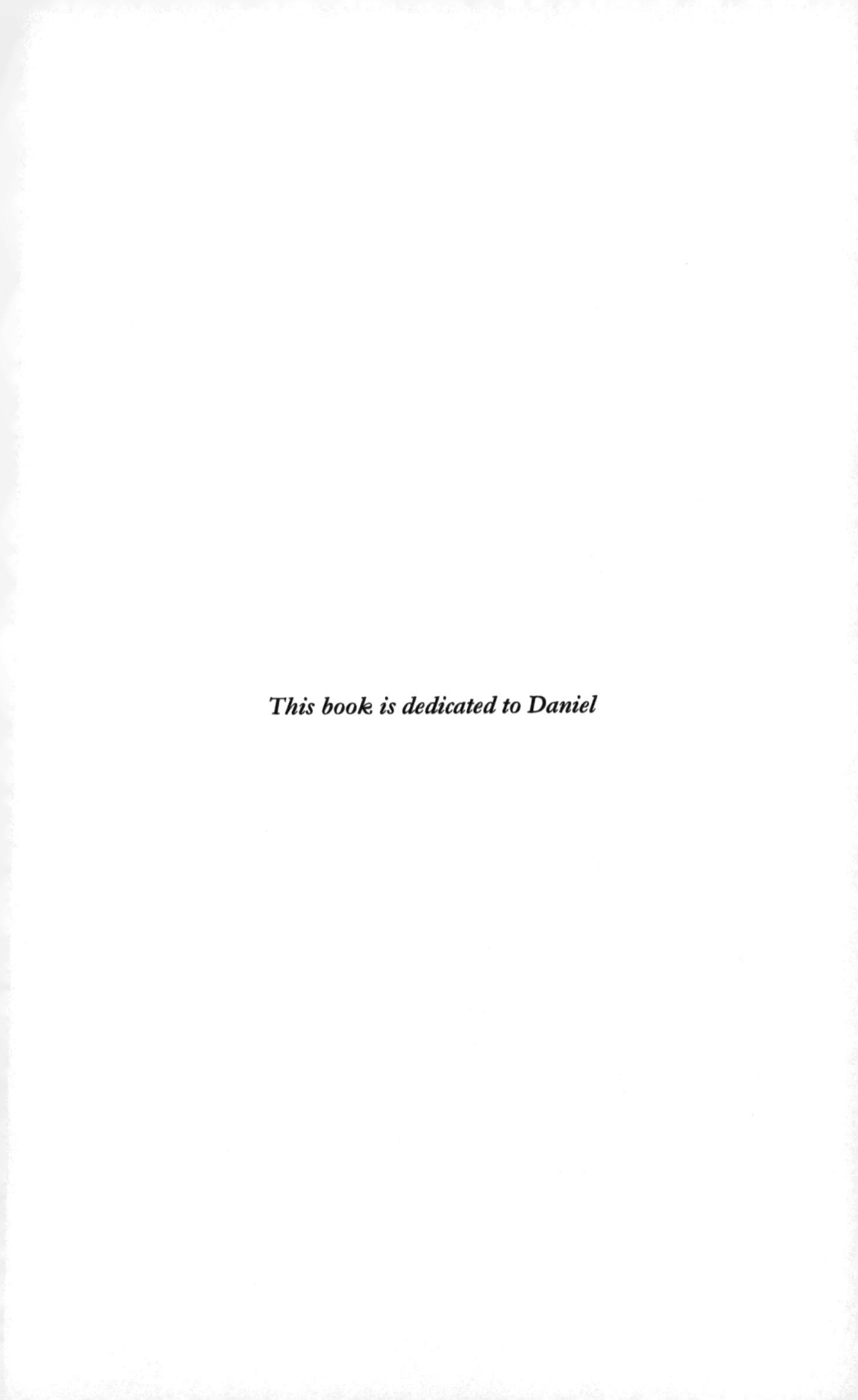

This book is dedicated to Daniel

LOST

IN MANHATTAN

AIRBORNE

I sit suspended midair, braving the heavens, staring out the airtight window of a SunJet 747. The sky is sunless and moonless, a funereal ash grey and I can't see a thing save for the flickering white light on the wing, but I look anyway, for *something*.

I am just one among several people who have purchased a seat on the cheapest, midsummer flight from Los Angeles to New York City during peak travel season, otherwise known as the blackout period. Mine is a one-way ticket. Now that it's an hour into the flight, and the City of Angels has receded to a vanishing point and the City that Never Sleeps looms, I suppose I should consume a Cape Cod (something red) to ingratiate myself into the impending landscape, but I have more important things to do like plan my life.

Planning of course never works. Planning is nothing more than a futile endeavor, albeit consoling notion, tantamount to wishing upon a falling star. For even if a plan or a wish for one's life could be fulfilled, the planner/wisher must, at the very least, have a beginning and end point from which to plot a plan or wish a wish. And today I have neither. No points to plot. No falling star upon which to wish. Once this plane lands at Newark International Airport, I haven't a clue what to do. I've never been to Manhattan, have no idea where this airport is in relationship to it although I understand it's in New Jersey, a state away. I know not a soul in the city (technically speaking), nor do I know where I will be sleeping my first night let alone any night thereafter. I have more scientific preoccupations, *a la* Darwin: *Survival.*

Actually, I am rather calm... *considering. Or am I... flatlining? Or am I unwittingly internalizing? Or am I wittingly internalizing? Or is la Cote-du Rhone Rouge working?* Imported into California the same year I was! Our fates inextricably linked (inexorably doomed), conspiring to bring us to the same altitude in time. As the last drop of wine nosedives into my circulatory system, I half expect the plane to similarly plummet.

"So, what brings you to New York?" asks the forty-something man seated beside me in front of a chicken entree. He has been reading the *Wall Street Journal* since the flight attendants first began their routine doomsday prep spiel about what to do in the event of "sudden loss of cabin pressure." I hadn't paid any attention either. *What could it possibly matter?*

"Long... story," I say, stretching out the words so as to subdue a moan lest it rip a hole in the fuselage and imperil innocent people.

"Would you like to watch the in-flight movie?" inquires a Doris Day-coiffed blonde, red-lipsticked flight attendant as she dangles two cellophane packages of headsets over our heads. I eye her contemptuously for I cannot believe the insensitivity of her to be thinking of entertainment at a time like this. *The nerve! As if the show must go on!*

"Sure, I'll take a pair," says my seatmate, exchanging his entree for a headset.

As the devil-may-care flight attendant ascends the aisle toward business class, dropping headsets left and right like Little Red Riding Hood tossing breadcrumbs, my neighbor releases his seatbelt, reclines his seat, and untangles the headset cord – preparing to be entertained. "Do you know what the movie is?" he asks me. An afterthought.

I shrug *sorry*, and he shrugs *no matter* and turns his eyes toward the overhead television set as mine drift back towards the window. As the cabin lights dim for previews of coming attractions, and a certain audacious flight attendant returns to shutter my window, leaving the cabin illuminated only by the red glow of the emergency exits and the white light of the occupied bathrooms, I look towards the screen. It is the first time since boarding that I have looked away from the window for longer than a glance only to exchange one form of escapism for another. But it's just as well. The inquiring man with the chicken wasn't really looking for a long story, certainly not a heartfelt saga from a twenty-four-year-old girl who couldn't possibly have a saga, certainly not one that could rival that of a forty-year-old man let alone merit attention away from poultry nor the feature presentation. No, at most, his question was extended solely to oblige the customary reciprocation, *'And so what brings you?'*

So what brings me to New York City…

By all appearances, I am the prototypical twentysomething on her way to the Big Apple for a fun-filled adventure. No, no one would think me troubled, certainly not while dressed in head-to-toe Gap. Outfitted in faded jeans, a black-and-white striped boatneck shirt, and camel mules that, overall, make me look *le Gap*, I am of no concern to the SunJet staff. Besides, everyone knows that troubled girls read Sylvia Plath, not the literary works of Condé Nast. No, there aren't any indications that I am heading for anything but a vacation.

"Peanuts?" asks the flight attendant, her face… *green? From the reflection of the screen?* "Honey roasted," she adds, extending the bag with her red polished talons.

"No thanks," I respond. But she must not have heard me because she tosses the bag at me anyway.

Just then the cabin fades to black, the flight attendant's face pales and the in-flight movie begins. *The Feature Presentation.* I pop in a peanut. *Mmmm.* Honey roasted. *When in Rome…*

PACIFIC TIME

1. PARTY CRASHER

It was supposed to have been a party. Just six weeks ago. Friday, June 24th. I was due at the Beau Rivage, a Mediterranean restaurant in Malibu, at eight o'clock for an intimate dinner for seven. It was my boyfriend (of six weeks) thirty-eighth birthday and cause for celebration.

As I drove north along the sinuous Pacific Coast Highway from my apartment in Playa Del Rey, the orange sun was about to submerge into the blue ocean, streetlamps were struggling to illuminate, and the coastline of double-decker condos was fast becoming a veritable parking lot. And, as I gained on an address in the twenty-six thousands and evidence of lives far more gratifying than mine mounted, I couldn't help but dwell on how full the lives of the rich were.

There they were at intersection after idyllic intersection – the beach bourgeois – tan and taut bodies packing ice cold beer and fresh ocean fish in carefree, barefooted stride, only a few days away from returning to their stable jobs, trust funds, and daddy-doled autos. How at odds I felt. How evidently counter-culture I was. I wiped away the tears and Lancôme's Black Noir mascara pooling in my lids, deciding it was best not to think of unpleasant things like the pleasant lives of others, lest I recall the severance check handed to me this morning. Unemployment is a sure-fire party killer. And worse than being unemployed is being a party killer.

I ARRIVED at the Beau Rivage, a lone, shrimp-pink villa juxtaposed against palisades, forty minutes late. I turned off the ignition, drew a deep breath as the engine died, conducted a final mascara check in the rear-view mirror, opened the door, and pressed my strappy black high heels to the gravel lot, wondering why I'd come at all.

I opened the stained-glass front door tentatively, hesitant to engage my own reality let alone a crowd-full. But there was no entering without detection. The door rattled as I opened it, (chimes suspended from the corner of it) and slammed shut behind me from a wind out of nowhere. I stood in the dark doorway as several sets of unfamiliar eyes from the bar settled upon me as if I were roadkill.

"He didn't think you were going to show," confided the dodgy-liquored breath of a man towering above me.

Before I could register who was speaking so close to me that sweat beads were forming in my inner ear, I saw Pavlos, the birthday boy, cupping a tumbler as he sat slumped on a barstool ten feet away, making no move to greet me. It was then that I noticed a petite, Donatella-esque blonde standing beside him who, I presumed, was beckoned to replace me in my supposed absence, my body barely cold.

"She's gorgeous!" exclaimed the blond in question, jumping off her barstool and approaching me, her arms outstretched. *"Mwah, Mwah,"* she said, kissing my cheeks, instantly endearing me to her, whoever she was.

Only when she pulled away did I realize it was Anthea, the mid-thirties artist and longtime girlfriend of Red, the former CEO of a music conglomerate standing beside her. And that was Chuck, the mid-fifties Bogey-esque drinker who whispered to me at the door, and there is Fabrizio, Malibu's favorite and most handsome thirty-year-old Sicilian-imported bartender. It was the same group I'd met the night I met Pavlos, the same group I'd spent the previous weekend with at their home just a few miles from here in Point Dume. Out of tank tops and shorts, and into evening attire, I hadn't recognized them.

"Happy Birthday," I said to Pavlos, pecking him on the lips as the others looked on as if awaiting the results of a taste test.

"I didn't think you were going to come," he said with wounded, puppy-dog eyes.

"How could I miss your birthday?" I responded consolingly, like a mother reassuring her child, as if the thought had never entered my mind. Pavlos then buried his head into my chest, completing the *Madonna and Child* configuration.

"Is your party here?" asked the *maître d'*, drawing menus from the podium.

"Yes, the party is here," said Pavlos, kissing me. He pressed his hand to the curve of my lower back as we, the party of seven, moved *en masse* to a candlelit table in the center of the room. The *maître d'* seated me in between Pavlos and George, Pavlos' best friend since elementary school in Greece who I was meeting for the first time.

"I'm so glad you showed," whispered George. "I didn't want my best friend sad on his birthday."

"I was just running late," I said, my ego buoyed by the notion that my presence or lack thereof could possibly have such an impact on a man twelve years my senior. I studied Pavlos as he swished wine samples for the sommelier. *Had I underestimated his feelings for me? Could this be the upside to today? The proverbial door that opens when one door closes?* Suddenly I felt as if I were the most desirable woman in the room even if, at the moment, there were only two of us.

"Sorry to hear about your job," announced Anthea, seated opposite me, her voice so loud that the waiters now stare at me as they search for water glasses to fill.

"Well yeah, it hasn't been a great day," I smiled queasily to Anthea and the wait staff. "But don't worry about me," I said as if untroubled, "It wasn't my dream job or anything. It was just ideal for pursuing acting. The hours were flexible for auditions."

"Oh do you audition a lot?" asked Anthea, the waiters, themselves, curious.

"Um… *sporadically*," I overstated. "I'm in a play right now," I explained, as if that were any reason to not be auditioning.

Despite my vow to remain mute on my unemployment, Anthea beckoned to hear more, sounding sincerely interested in the *fate du jour* of Eve so the story soon became our appetizer.

"I lost my job because of the baseball strike," I explained to her, wrongly suspecting that this would bring finality to the conversation. What with the sports tie-in, the men have abandoned all side conversations and now have their full attention on me.

"What did you say you did?" asked Red.

"I was working for two interior decorators in Marina Del Rey for the last two months until this morning when, not a second after I arrived for work, they told me that they had to let me go. It turns out their client, the Dodgers' shortstop, had decided to postpone all work on his house due to the unforeseeable end of the Baseball Strike. Given that he was their primary client and primary source of income, they said they could no longer afford me."

"So, you lost your job because of a baseball strike?" said Red, shaking his head.

"How's that for trickle-down economics?" I said, feigning amusement.

"She's better off, the woman was crazy," said Pavlos irritably, begging the question.

"Of course she's better off," said Anthea. "What woman?"

"The woman Eve worked for," Pavlos answered.

"Veronique," I offered, clearing my throat with a Herculean swig of Merlot.

"Veron…?" inquired Fabrizio, just joining us, his bartending shift finished.

"Veronica with a 'Q'" said Anthea, translating for fresh-from-gondola Fabrizio. "Veronique."

"Ah, Veronique with a 'Q'," repeated Fabrizio, pouring himself some red wine. "Who is Veronique? Is she coming?"

"Veronique is Eve's boss," explained Anthea. "*Was*. Eve lost her job today."

"Ahhh. Sadness. Then we drink," said Fabrizio, raising his glass. "And smoke," he added, patting his breast pocket of his white linen shirt for a cigarette, reminding me that the only tolerable smoker is a sun-drenched European who looks like he stepped off the pages of *Uomo Collezione*.

"Tell them about the cult," Pavlos nudged me.

I smiled feebly. *Had I not realized what a crazy woman I was working for?* Here I'd been bemoaning the loss of a job spent working for a nutcase! And I'd only just managed to acquire the sympathies of the entire table. Now they'll just think I attract bad people and want to disassociate from me. I put down my goblet.

"Two weeks after I had started working for Veronique," I began, "she confided to me over lunch at Café Del Rey that she was in fear for her life, that she'd just escaped from a Beverly Hills cult after belonging to it for twenty years."

"Beverly Hills?" inquired Fabrizio. "Aaron Spelling's Beverly Hills? 90210?"

"Actually 90077," I said. "In a commune on Beverly Glen, just below Sunset Boulevard."

"Hey, isn't that just down from the Playboy Mansion?" inquired Chuck.

"Yes," I answered.

"You sure it isn't the Playboy Mansion?" asked Red, drawing laughter from the table.

"Yes, I'm sure," I smiled. "It's a two-story townhouse just a few blocks below. Anyway, you'd never know it was a cult from the outside. Veronique told me that forty of them live there and eat together, sleep together, and work at legit companies owned and operated by them and then give 90% of their profits to the cult leader."

"So other than the fact that they all eat and sleep together and give 90% of their money to the guru, they're just like you and me," Pavlos summed up.

"So what made her finally leave?" asked Anthea.

"She said she got tired of giving 90% of her money away."

"But she didn't mind the group sex part," noted Red.

"Anyway, as she told me this, she was so nervous, her eyes darting back and forth across the restaurant, fearing that she'd be gunned down in a hail of fire *a la Bonnie and Clyde*. I tried to make her feel better. I told her, "I'm sure people leave every day.""

"Exactly," echoed Anthea.

""Yes,' she replied, 'but not the mistress of the cult leader and primary breadwinner.'"

"Oh," cringed the table, fully comprehending.

"And then she said, 'but it's ok. My lawyer knows everything,' and that seemed to bring a measure of comfort to her," I added.

"Yeah, well we all know what a source of comfort lawyers are," said Pavlos, raising his glass in honor of comfort-bringing lawyers.

"Well, it sounds to me as if you're better off," said Anthea, her eyes twinkling with reassurance.

"She doesn't have to worry about anything. I'll take care of her," said Pavlos, pulling me in by my neck to kiss my forehead.

THE HEADY herbal aromas and Mediterranean languages of Greek and Italian spilled into each other to create an intoxicating elixir. I was grinning wider than my muscles were accustomed, wider than I had in some time, certainly wider than I had all day. And then, Pavlos made a discovery. He spotted an actual prima donna seated with a man at a table for two in the corner. And so, after some lively debate as to which was the better champagne – *Veuve Cliquot, Dom Perignon,* or *Cristal* – Pavlos commissioned the *maître d'* to deliver a bottle of *Cristal* (my choice) to *prima* effectively bribing her to perform. As *prima* belted out an aria, and our table's bravura grew in decibels and as I considered how fortunate it was for us that the *prima donna* traveled with sheet music and dined with piano players, Pavlos pulled my face towards his, and then, noses nuzzling, eyes soulfully locked with mine, said, "I love you."

"What?" I asked, not positive I heard him correctly (and it's something one wants to be positive of).

He leaned in closer, "I love you."

I savored the words like wine on the tongue, and then with sober certainty, responded, "I love you too." With that, Pavlos thrust his sopping wet tongue into my mouth, his nose slaloming mine as the table chatter faded into obscurity. I was sliding off my chair dipping into euphoria, forgetting for a millisecond any troubles, wondering subconsciously what it was that had prevented complete bliss in the first place. So even as my chair began to tip backwards, and even as Pavlos continued to suck the air right out of me (threatening me with asphyxiation by way of tongue propulsion), I was much too enamored with *amoré* to bother with ... *caution*. Only when the soprano reached climax and Pavlos released me to whistle, did my chair regain its footing and me my memory. For it was then, in the reflection of our own *Cristal,* that I recalled the severance check handed to me that morning. It wasn't so amazing that I remembered it. It was amazing that for a split second I had forgotten. The company I was keeping had become my panacea, my cure-all.

"*Tout á bella!*" said Fabrizio signaling us to raise our glasses and join in on what had become our party-of-seven's trademark toast, imported by Fabrizio. "*Tout á bella,*" we joined, in our best Roberto Benigni accents. "Everything is bee-ahhh-yoo-tee-full, and shiny... with a kiss." And then the party of seven, topped off the toast by blowing a kiss to the heavens.

"WE'RE JUST GOING to take him for a fifteen, twenty-minute ride. We'll bring him right back to you. We promise," said Red, as he and George pulled Pavlos off his chair.

"They got me a limo for my birthday," whispered Pavlos into my ear. "I won't be long."

Pavlos brushed his finger gently over the bridge of my nose, kissed my lips, and deposited me at the bar five feet from the rattling door in front of a bottle of Perrier. After the door shut behind them and a quiet calm filled the restaurant, I sat there peacefully, so happy to be among people who cared, that my unemployment now seemed a *bagatelle*, a minor nuisance to contend with tomorrow in the manner befitting a person not so desperate – in a manner befitting the beach bourgeois.

"So the boys left you here?" asked Anthea, pulling up a barstool beside me, the thigh-high slit in her python-print floor-length dress revealing one tan and taut petite leg thrown over another, my red-painted toenails hardly titillating in comparison.

"They said they'd just be gone twenty minutes...taking the limo for a joyride. I don't mind. I'm not ready to drive yet anyway," I said as my mind wistfully recalled the events of the evening: of Pavlos declaring his love for me, of that deep, penetrating (if not too wet) kiss and what it would mean for my future, our future, the prospects of which suddenly seemed so much brighter than they had this morning.

"Well you know what they're doing in the limo don't you?" Anthea asked, puncturing her ice cubes with a swizzle stick.

I eyed her curiously, my eyebrow cocked as my mind swirled with the possibilities of what secret Anthea was daring to disclose: *Dare I consider that Pavlos is going to propose to me? Tonight? Is that why they got the limo? Is that why I couldn't go in the limo with them? Is his departure with the boys simply a ruse?* That certainly would explain why he was so depressed at the thought I wouldn't show! Even George, his very best friend, had shown great relief that I showed. And that would explain why Pavlos has his best friend here since before tonight he hadn't seen him in a few years! I know it's sudden but, after all, Pavlos is thirty-eight years old, and doesn't have much time to wait. And he did choose tonight to tell me he loved me, and a thirty-eight-year-old man doesn't extend those words lightly. *And isn't a limo a bit much for a man's 38th birthday?*

"Cocaine," said Anthea, placing a fractured, wrung lime on a cocktail napkin. I waited for Anthea to deliver the punchline. And waited some more. But nothing.

"Well," I said, eyeing the lime, "I guess that ends that." I pushed the water away; the announcement had the effect of smelling salts.

"So you don't do drugs?" asked Anthea, her position on the subject undetectable.

"No. Drugs are non-negotiable," I said flatly, my sunny side flipping, my eyes refusing to look into hers lest I find them complicit, instead fixated on the upside-down stemware on suspended glass shelves above the bar as my adoration for the party of seven plummeted.

"Well maybe Pavlos isn't doing anything," she said. "I don't know. Really, I don't. I just know that even the limo driver is. I think he's the one who brought it."

THE DOORKNOB of the Beau Rivage front door was like a Hitchcockian detail, the biggest object in the room, the suspense killing me. Because as soon as it turned, before the whites of Pavlos' eyes could be seen, I planned to say goodbye to him forever. But it was not to be. Pavlos came in from behind me, effectively throwing me off plan for which I had no back-up.

"Come on, let's go," said Pavlos, agitated, pulling me off the barstool by my arm – manifestations of cocaine I presumed.

"Wait, I need my jacket," I said, prying his hand from mine and shooting him a "look" to let my transformed feelings known, but he doesn't notice.

"Well where is it?" he demanded, just as the *maître d'* arrived with an armload of coats. Before my arm was through the sleeve, Pavlos escorted me out the back door into the parking lot where others had already reconvened like some scene from *The Outsiders* - standing around ready to rumble or drag race. Pavlos pushed me towards the driver's side, and waited at the passenger door, motioning for me to get in and drive.

"Take the limo!" insisted Chuck.

"No," said Pavlos.

"Come on, take it! It's a gift!" Red pleaded as if resuming a prior argument.

"Come on! Let's go," Pavlos said to me, his temper flaring.

"But they gave you the limo!" I said, never one to be ungracious for a gift (despite its double duty as an emissary of contraband).

"I said I don't want it!" yelled Pavlos, his voice drowned out by the screeching tires of a car exiting the parking lot. "Shit," said Pavlos. "That's George. Get in. We have to go after him."

I was still pulling on my seatbelt when the nose of my car reached the edge of the parking lot, ready to merge into the northbound lane of PCH. "Which way?" I asked.

"That way," Pavlos said, pointing southbound.

I cut across two lanes of northbound traffic and merged into the inside southbound lane. Seconds later, unable to see any car ahead let alone George's unless he was the red dot in the distance, I ventured to ask, "And so exactly why am I going after George?"

"Because he's in no state to be driving. And because when – *if* – he makes it home alive, his wife will kill him and blame me."

"Why would she blame you?" I asked, innocently, as if I didn't already know.

"Because George and I haven't seen each other in a long time, and she'll think it was because he was with me, that he's *this way*. She's a doctor. And Japanese," he said, as if the combination were deadly.

"So there were drugs in the limo?" I asked, already consigned to the relationship's demise.

"Cocaine," Pavlos answered unapologetically, staring straight ahead.

I nodded and refocused, steely eyed on the highway.

"Is that why you're mad at me? You think I did some?" he asked with the compelling indignance of a man falsely accused.

"Listen, Eve, I don't do drugs. Why do you think I didn't want to take the limo? For Christ's sake, the chauffeur was doing some!"

A silence ensued and I lost the red dot *(George?)* altogether.

"Look, I don't even see George, and I'm not going to get a speeding ticket," I said, expecting an argument. But Pavlos said nothing. He was slumped in his seat, arms interlocked, head drooping forward, eyes closed, and if he hadn't finally gurgled or whatever that sound was, I would have thought he was dead from a cocaine overdose he so vehemently denied. But he gurgled, so I suspected he was alive.

And, maybe, even innocent. *I mean whom but an innocent person, would reject a free limo?* As I moved into the slower, coastal lane, my mind merged to a new place as well because I believed Pavlos. And with that revelation came relief that at least one part of my life – my love life – was salvaged today. I was happy to resume thinking about the best part of the evening, the pivotal part of the evening, the first I love you... *Tout á bella...* Everything is beautiful ...and shiny…and…

Red?

I had not a second to assimilate the red sports car into the coastal Malibu landscape before it plowed into my car's passenger side, sending me and Pavlos careening across the highway towards the white headlights of oncoming traffic and/or the palisades – difficult to tell. It was if the driver had been lying-in-wait, opting to merge at the exact moment we were due to pass. The sound of metal grinding metal was deafeningly shrill. Dizzying blackness occasioned with lights. My right knee felt impounded and my ears throbbed. But, even as my mind accepted its inevitable death, my body resisted. My palms burned from the death grip as they wrestled to subdue the epileptic steering wheel, which was taking its direction from possessed tires. I had no doubt I would die upon impact.

Impact.

Only when I realized that no one would hit us – an assumption predicated on a certain amount of nothing happening – did I realize that I had survived. But then the pain took over, pain I was sure meant some major part of my body was in jeopardy. I turned my neck towards Pavlos, afraid to see how he was. His head was slumping even more than when he was sleeping.

"Pavlos, are you O.K.?" I asked. He turned to me with a blood-drenched face, only the whites of his eyes making a face, a face. He said not a word, got out of the car and walked away, leaving the door open, which for some reason struck me as thoughtless.

I weakly pushed open my door and collapsed into a fetal heap onto the pavement, my nose touching gravel. "Call 911," I screamed, only to hear a whisper. "I think I'm going deaf!" I touched my pulsating ears expecting blood to fill my palms, but nothing. Despite the absence of blood anywhere, I was positive one couldn't have this much pain and survive. Even after seconds of survival elapsed, I still imagined them – the seconds – to be finite. Only when I managed to stand did I begin to believe that I'd survived, as if the sole difference between life and death were the ability to stand.

A crowd of twentysomethings, the beach bourgeois I'd seen earlier, poured forth from their condos. Guys were sporting beers and girls were sporting looks of worry, their hands veiling their noses and mouths as if to avoid contagion. As more and more condo doors flung open, and ambulances and police cars pulled into the impact site, it began to sound like an accompanying wild track: a cacophonous mix of sirens, chatter, and battle of the bands, with the voluble tirade of an angry young man heard over everything.

"God dammit, who's the fucking prick who hit my jeep?" screamed a guy in a UCLA tank top as he inspected (my) white Nissan Sentra (with the USC license plate frame) that impacted the passenger door of his midnight-blue jeep, the door to which him, the partygoers in condo #5 owe gratitude for having saved their fighting Bruin lives. Had his jeep door not taken the brunt of the impact, my death ride would have led me straight through the front door of condo #5, making the party a surprise party and me a party crasher with no survivors.

I wobbled past the jeep-mourner towards Pavlos who was seated on a concrete step in front of condo #5. He lifted his shirttail to wipe the blood off of his face, exposing his own tan and taut abs. He looked up at me with a blank stare, touching his finger to his forehead and then pulling it back to see his blood, which, amazingly, was the same exact color of my Exactly Red Estee Lauder lipstick.

"Oh my God. Pavlos! Are you O.K.?"

Pavlos said nothing, just continued stretching his blood-soaked white shirt to his eyebrow to dab his blood glistening in the moonlight.

"I'm so scared. What if I wasn't O.K. to drive? I mean I feel totally fine, but what if...?" I trailed off, dripping as many tears as Pavlos is blood, anguished that Pavlos doesn't attempt to console me.

"Excuse me, Miss? Were you involved in this accident?" asked a handsome, buff, sandy-blonde haired paramedic.

"Yes, and so was he," I said, pointing to a shirt-bludgeoned Pavlos.

"Yeah, I can see that," he said, as two other paramedics crowded Pavlos, helping him stand. "And, how are you?"

"I've been better," I said.

The paramedic and a policeman escorted me away from Pavlos towards the highway, the scene of the crime. We took baby steps as I took in the phantasmagoric scene: cars in *tête-à-têtes*, people converging upon the scene like Hitchcock's birds to Bodega Bay, just before they wrought bloodshed on the town. The policeman queried me along the way, taking copious notes like the detective-friend of L.B. Jeffries in *Rear Window* yet giving me the feeling he wasn't getting it all.

"It was as if the driver had been lying-in-wait the whole time," I told the cop, "as if he said, 'here comes this car, and...*now*' opting to merge into my lane at the exact moment of my passing."

"So there was no time to react?" he asked.

"None," I answered emphatically but softly, my lungs petering out.

"Sandy" the paramedic hoisted me up on the rear bumper of the ambulance and assumed a stance between my parted, dangling legs. As the inside of my thighs rested listlessly against his meaty quads, Sandy proceeded to unbutton my white cotton blouse, pressing a cold stethoscope against my left breast as the crowd looked on shamelessly. Under the professional guise of listening to my heartbeat, Sandy unbuttoned another button, my fourth shirt button, exposing my black demi-cup push-up bra which caused me more embarrassment for my fashion faux pas (black under white is a no-no but I thought might be a nice surprise for Pavlos) than for my teetering cleavage threatening to spill overboard (for they too had followed the direction of the tires).

"Does it hurt here?" asked Sandy repeatedly as he pressed his hands lower and lower on my torso towards my pelvis, towards my underwear, finally pulling the infinitely long shirttail totally out of my (sister's) jumpsuit.

"No," I lied, afraid to complain of any pain, lest he strip me in front of everyone.

"Has she been drinking?" asked an approaching policeman with a stern face. I looked up to see his face, the "Sergeant," only to realize that my eyes up until then had been transfixed upon Sandy's crotch for the entirety of the exam. (It was the most soothing sight I could find.) *But did the Sergeant notice? Is that why he looked at me with condemnation? Or was his look of condemnation for something else? He couldn't possibly think I had anything to do with this?*

"She has a faint trace of alcohol on her breath," offered Sandy, implicating me.

After an accounting of my dinner (*tagliolini al samone, carpaccio malatesta*, and bread - some nutty some sour) and drinks (two glasses half full of red wine of which I only drank half, and Perrier) and timeline (dinner and drinks were consumed over the course of three hours), and weight (123 on my driver's license, 125 on the scale at home, 129 at doctor's = an answer of 120), another officer administered a breathalyzer.

As I puffed shallow breaths into the contraption, I became scared to death for *hmmm…* the millionth time of the evening. *I knew I had been fine to drive, but would my feeling of sobriety match their scientific calibrations? I mean who really knows the exact measurement of permissive alcohol consumption when relying on a potentially under-the-influence mind to gauge it? And what would happen should they discover I let my insurance coverage lapse (like some three years ago, a month after I bought the car)?* What with my unemployment, my bodily pain, my totaled car, and my potentially catastrophic finances (which were already a natural disaster before the accident), I was ready to go back to the white line – the highway meridian – although any white line would do. The only comfort remaining was Pavlos, but he was incommunicado with a blood-soaked face.

"She is as drunk as a skunk!" shouted a policeman from several feet away.

She? Did he say "she?" I couldn't possibly be the one he's referring to. *Could I? Maybe he's referring to a 'she' who has nothing to do with the accident? Maybe he found an underage girl from one of the condo parties?* I waited and watched for the "she-perpetrator" to be accosted but nothing. Maybe he said 'he.' *But then again, why was he looking at me when he said it?* He couldn't possibly be talking about me!

I stood still, frozen, so as to not appear guilty, as if the only guilty people moved about. As time passed and paranoid cells were attacking my already low-count healthy ones, I had to know.

"Who's as drunk as a skunk?" I asked Sandy, ready to contest any speculation that I could be the "skunk".

"What?" asked Sandy.

"The cop over there said someone was as drunk as a skunk."

"Hey Jack?" Sandy hails the cop over. "Who'd you say was as drunk as a skunk?"

Jack looks at me squarely. "The girl who hit you," he says.

"A… *girl*… hit me?" I was shocked. I had just assumed it was some big nasty man with nasty hair and a big smelly smell and beer gut. "Where is she?" I demanded, ready for a catfight.

"There," the Sergeant said, pointing to tan, skinny, Flex-haired girl dressed in jeans, stiletto pumps and a pink tank top, her posture unchanged, her tank intact. "After the accident, she ran back into her condo. Her husband, who's twice her age, turned her in. He's pissed. It's his car. Jaguar. Nice car. Was. She blew a 2.0, twice the legal limit."

"What was mine?" I asked, wanting my innocence confirmed once and for all out loud for everyone (the cops, the paramedics, the jeep-bellyacher-mourner, and Pavlos) to hear.

"You blew a .02" said the officer.

"What?!" I screeched, alarmed to hear I'd blown anything.

"It's under the legal limit," said the officer, reassuringly. Until then, I hadn't realized that any measurable amount of alcohol was legally permissible.

"Here," says the breathalyzer-administering cop, handing me the girl's confiscated driver's license. Serena Yack. Born April 11, 1984.

"Are you Eve?" asked yet another approaching officer.

"Yes."

"We have spoken to the drivers and passenger of the two cars that were following behind you and they have corroborated your account of the accident, confirming that you were going no more than 40 miles per hour – "

"I told you – "

"...and they have signed affidavits attesting to the fact that you had no time to react."

"They saw the accident?" I asked, suddenly choked up with emotion that others had a perfect view of my near demise, and touched by their solidarity with me.

"Yes. You've been cleared of any responsibility except, of course, for the jeep your car struck."

"But that wasn't my fault!"

"I know, but technically you hit it. But don't worry," he said, rubbing my shoulder, "Your insurance will cover it."

"Right. My insurance," I said, pretending to be comforted by his rub so as not to reveal I have no insurance. "So what will happen to her?"

"The State is pressing criminal charges. She'll probably spend at least a night in jail unless her husband can post bail. But I don't think that's likely, since he's the one who turned her in. He said they'd been arguing, and she had run out of the house and into the car to take off."

I eyed her. I waited for her to turn in my direction. I waited for her to approach me. I waited for her to tell me how sorry she was. But she never turned her head, not out of remorse, not even out of curiosity.

"On the count of three, lean back," instructed one of two paramedics. "One... two..." and on an unspoken *"three"* I leaned back into an upright gurney and was lowered into the back of an ambulance where I was surprised to find Pavlos already lying flat on his back. As the paramedics situated me beside Pavlos, I expected Pavlos to say something, ask if I was "O.K," extend his hand to me as a gesture of tenderness as men are supposed to. But he only looked once in my direction, his vacant eyes saying it all. He blamed me. Not an hour after exchanging our first "I love you's," here we were, lying side by side in the back of an ambulance incommunicado. I looked up at the bright cabin light trying to be thankful that it's ultraviolet.

"Why don't I hear sirens?" I asked Sandy, once the ambulance was on the highway.

"We only sound the sirens if it's a life-threatening situation. It's illegal otherwise." Sandy said.

"What if the patient is dead?" I asked.

"Well we don't sound them then either," said the other paramedic.

"So then, which ones are we?" I asked, jokingly but no one answered me.

As I waited in my room at the Santa Monica Hospital for the influx of doctors and the battery of tests, I wondered if Pavlos' best friend George wasn't nearby in some other room being tended to by his angry Dr. Japanese Wife, having caught some similar fate as if there were some communicable disease transmitted along Pacific Coast Highway.

"You're fine, just some contusions – thighs, knees, ribs – that will heal over time," said Dr. Sallie Melkin, underwhelmed, her civilian clothes showing through her open white jacket.

I was stunned by the diagnosis. *How could I be in this much pain and not have more proof of it?* I mean, if I was to get any sympathy from my family, they would want visible proof!

"What about my ears?" I asked.

"What's wrong with them?" she asked.

"Well they're pounding in pain and burning hot. I've mentioned it three times, but no one's looked at them." I whined.

Reluctantly, Dr. Melkin examined my ears with a cold, protuberant instrument, aggressively tugging and stretching my ears as she navigated the non-pliable appliance with more force than *Johnson & Johnson* would advise for Q-tips.

"Your ears are fine," she announced, letting go of my ears so abruptly that they snapped back into place.

"Well then why do they hurt so badly?" I asked, disbelieving.

"Your ears hurt because the decibels of an automobile crash are tremendous. No one realizes this," she said as if she is so tired of telling patients this over and over again. "The nurse will be in to see if you want a splint or a brace."

"For what?" I asked, alarmed.

"The nurse didn't tell you?" Dr. Melkin asked, exasperated.

"Tell me what?" I asked, bracing myself for the worst: that my pelvic pain means I will be adopting children, that the pain inside my torso means that I have internal hemorrhaging and will therefore have to eat frozen yogurt through a feeding tube.

"You've fractured your fourth metacarpal," she answered, poker-faced.

"My fourth metacarpal?" I asked, feeling faint. I scanned my lower extremities, guessing my fourth metacarpal to be my right leg which took the brunt of the dashboard, or maybe it was my pelvis or rib cage bone which took significant pressure from I think the steering wheel...yes, I bet it's inside my torso.

"There. That's your fourth metacarpal," she said, pointing to the fourth finger on my left hand, otherwise known as my wedding ring finger.

"GEEZ, THEY SAID she was fine" said Pavlos upon seeing me wheeled into the lobby where the party of four awaits, my forearm and hand wrapped to be casted at a later date. Other than the black eye patch over Pavlos eye that makes him look like a pirate, he looks unscathed.

"Are you ok?" Chuck, Red, and Anthea asked.

"I broke my fourth metacarpal," I answered, holding up my finger. "I'm sorry to have dragged you out here. I didn't know who else to have them call. My sister is in Oregon."

"Don't worry at all. You'll come home with us," says Anthea. We got inside Red's Mercedes and headed back to Malibu once again along PCH - Northbound.

"So did anyone hear from George? Is he O.K.?" I asked.

"Oh yeah, he's fine. Back at home. Sleeping I would imagine" said Red, eyeing me in the rear-view mirror when his eyes should be on the road.

"He came back to the restaurant seconds after you guys left," explained Anthea.

2. POINT DUME

Pavlos and I returned to the Point Dume compound of Red and Anthea's just a few miles north of the crime scene, to convalesce. As Pavlos continued to pluck imaginary windshield from his eyebrow, I maneuvered with a clicking pelvis and a fractured fourth metacarpal and pondered the fate of my missing cell phone. But, more disturbing than my injuries, totaled car, unemployment, and absent wireless lifeline, was how cold and distant Pavlos was to me, and how surprisingly inconsolable the view of the Pacific Ocean from the terrace was (yet, how enticing the drop).

It seemed like yesterday – in fact it was only the weekend before – that our party of seven was sun-whipped, lounging around the deck without a care in the world. The single drama of the house was that Anthea suspected her neighbor Pamela Anderson (yes, that Pam) had stolen her dog Betty (a dog she'd had 12 years!), and she was bound and determined to confront Pam who continued to deny the abduction even as she had the nerve to walk Betty around the neighborhood. And, the single drama of my life was that I hadn't met my deadline to become a famous actress – a deadline I had so graciously extended to the beginning of summer. Dinnertime coincided with sundown and was followed by a romantic, clandestine romp just below the terrace to the exotic *Bambolea's* and *Escucha Me's* of the Gipsy Kings.

Perhaps inspired by the romantic recollection, I left the terrace to find Pavlos. He was lying down in a spare bedroom, ours for the duration of our convalescence. I stood at the foot of the bed and touched Pavlos' sole, lifting his eyes to mine. But he was not there behind them. He was expressionless, his feelings for me dead. I felt a dreadful chill as if a ghost had entered the room, the same kind I'd felt in the back of the ambulance.

"What's wrong? Are you tired?" I asked Pavlos, hoping I was overreacting, wanting terribly to be shown how wrong I was in my psychoanalysis.

"My head is killing me. Does my eye have glass in it?" he said.

I got close to his eye, pupil to pupil, thinking how insensitive I'd become. Of course he's distant, he's aching. He has glass in his eye. "No, I don't see glass," I said, hoping my diagnosis would assuage his fears and compel him to invite me to lie down next to him. But, he doesn't. So, desperate for some reassurance that if I have nothing else – no job, no car – I still had his loving affection, I took the initiative and boldly climbed over him. But, with only one good hand steadying me, I lost my balance and fell onto his chest.

Pavlos shrieked.

"Oh, sorry. I'm so sorry," I said. "Your chest hurts too? I thought it was just your head."

"No. My whole body hurts," he said flatly, pushing the last of my body off of him.

"Sorry. It was an accident," I said, regretful that I couldn't find a word other than "accident."

Finally, after some careful body contortioning, I found a comfortable position beside him: my right leg resting over his right leg, the left side of my head buried into the crook of his armpit. I attempted to cuddle, even overlooked his underarm odor, but he was not in the mood, complaining only of how the impact of my weight next to him caused him great pain. Dejected once more, I flipped over like a fish in a skillet burned on one side, and laid as still as a cadaver, this time, making sure, nothing of mine touched anything of his. *Now if only I had a pillow…*

"Can you please lie still?" Pavlos asked irritably.

"Pavlos is there something you want to say," I demanded brazenly, suddenly free of fear of the relationship's end.

"No, it's just that every time you shake the bed, my head aches."

"Is that really it? Or is it something else? Because the accident is not my fault you know. You know that don't you?"

"I know," he said, reluctantly.

"Do you? Because it doesn't seem to me that you're separating our relationship from the accident. Because if it weren't for the accident, we wouldn't be having these problems. I mean an hour before the accident you told me you loved me in case you've forgotten."

"This is just difficult for me," he said.

"Well it's difficult for me too," I said, my voice cracking as I turned back toward the closet, allowing tears to free-fall, that is until my nose started running and I began to worry that the nose dribbling and the tear-dropping thuds on the mattress would make Pavlos' head pound.

But I had bigger problems. I had stopped breathing. I was trying so hard to muffle my heavy breathing (so as to not disturb Pavlos) that I had been unwittingly holding my breath. And the worse part was that I wasn't concerned with how blue I was but how loud my exhale might be. Perhaps if I could somehow emit small emissions of air, I might be rid of the surplus air in 3 minutes or so…

"Pebbles?" Pavlos inquired, using his pet name for me for the first time since the accident and in the tone of a man about to beg forgiveness.

"Yes?" I asked with measured anticipation, expecting a big fat apology.

"Can you get me two Tylenol?" he asked. "Extra strength."

Despite the fact that my body had only just made peace with the bedding, I forced my body up from the bed, feeling that the

Tylenol and my willingness to get them were directly proportional to the fate of our relationship. "Um, sure," I answered.

One step out of the bedroom and into the hallway onto the cold linoleum of '70s tile, a surge of emotion overcame me and stopped me dead in my tracks. I suddenly had the feeling, however irrational, that I was unwelcome in the house, not only by Pavlos, but by everyone. I looked into the living room where Red, Chuck and now Fabrizio were still watching golf on TV, and in the dining room beyond them where Anthea was sweeping up sand off the floor from her mixed media endeavor, suddenly aware of how parasitic my existence had become, completely dependent on the kindness of others. I had acquired the aura of a leper. I had become the dreaded party-killer. I wanted desperately to reclaim my dignity, say "good-bye," get into my car and go home, and relieve everyone of their Samaritan duties that they in good conscience could not escape. But I had no choice but to stay. I had no car, no house keys (they were buried inside my car at whatever junkyard it'd been towed to) and my sister, the only other person who could provide these rescue items, was not due back from Oregon until Sunday. I had no choice but to accept the generosity of others and accept that my usual Emersonian self-reliance was but a pipedream.

"Hi, I just came to get Pavlos some Tylenol," I said to Red who was in the kitchen, cleaning. I tried to avoid eye contact so he wouldn't see my red, blotchy, teary face, the mark of a *persona non grata*. But, with only one operable arm, I needed Red's help just to reach a glass. I prefaced each request with an apology: "I'm sorry Red, but could you please get me a glass... I'm sorry but could you please pour the water... I'm sorry but can you please open the Tylenol... sorry I can't be of more help... " *I'm sorry I bring a black cloud over Malibu. I'm sorry for Betty's abduction...* "Thanks."

"Sure," said Red.

I returned to the bedroom with water and Advanced Medicine for Pain to find Pavlos studying his reflection in the mirror of my compact bronzer (an Estee Lauder promotional gift with purchase) that he must have taken from my purse on the dresser.

"Do you think my eyebrow will fill in?" he asked, stroking his brow with his forefinger.

"Of course. It's hair," I said, handing him his medicaments. Pavlos drank and then as if I were his bedside nurse rather than a co-invalid, handed me his empty glass. I put the glass on the bedside table, which I notice is a far shorter reach for him than me when Pavlos began dabbing the bronzer onto his brow. "That's bronzer," I exclaimed, sure he'd mistaken the compressed brown powder for something else.

"I know," he said. "I'm filling in the bald spots."

"Bald spots? "Where?"

"Here," he said, parting his brow to reveal a total of three empty hair follicles. "In fact, if it doesn't grow back, I might have to get plastic surgery."

3. HOME SWEET HOME

"So we were heading down PCH…" I began to tell Olive about the accident and how I've spent its aftermath now that she's returned from Oregon a few days behind schedule. (No reason to rush, just because your only sister is at death's door.) It's a story I'm sure my whole family will want to hear firsthand if only to put their minds at ease.

"But did you break anything?" Olive interrupted, showing her trademark impatience, which only allows two minutes for life and death stories. Three minutes if they're funny.

"My fourth metacarpal. Otherwise known as my wedding ring finger," I said, getting to the punchline.

"Your *finger*," she said, under-whelmed, preoccupied with her cell phone.

"Yes. Look, I have no knuckle there anymore." It was true, my knuckle had disintegrated.

"But you're O.K.," she insisted, willing it.

"Well I've broken my hand –"

"Your *finger…* "

"My *finger*… my entire body aches, my pelvic bone clicks and I can't stand straight, but otherwise I'm fine," I said, losing Olive to the hall bathroom.

"So, listen," Olive yelled from the bathroom as if I'm not standing right outside it, "not to change the subject but I'm going for Chinese food with Nathan tonight. Do you want me to bring some back?"

I couldn't even begin to answer. Olive going out and pursuing a life independent of dependent mine felt a lot like child abandonment.

"Hell Low?" she called out impatiently from the toilet seat, waiting for an answer, then flushing and hiking up her drawstring sweats upon re-entering the living room. "Do you want me to bring you something back?" she asked, staring at her cell phone with consternation. "I can't believe he didn't call."

"Well, actually, I'm kind of starving now," I said stressing the word "starving" and "now" –

Olive holds up her forefinger, signaling me to "hold that thought." She plays a message on her cell. "Hey mamachita, listen…." goes the message…

"Oh that's old. Sorry, what?" she asks.

"Well, I'm kind of starving now and quite frankly I have no money and no transportation."

"Well isn't there anything to eat here?" she asked, popping open the refrigerator door and the cupboards.

"No. There isn't anything here."

"There's Top Ramen," she said, holding up a beef and pork noodle package to me like a model from "The Price is Right," but with bitten, flimsy nails.

I rolled my eyes contemptuously, ready to swallow a lot of pills for some goddamn sympathy.

"Well I'm just getting noodles myself," she responded defensively. "Fine, I'll just get Chinese for us. Actually, I don't feel like going out anyway."

With the promise of food forthcoming and fatigued by expending what little strength I had on negotiating for it, I returned to my bedroom. *The before picture.* The way it was hours before the accident when I had not known there would be one. My clothes (and Olive's! Great, I forgot to put them back!) are still strewn on the bed. That's right, I hadn't been able to decide what (of Olive's) to wear to the Beau Rivage, let alone whether to go. The answering machine still blinks with messages. The employment agencies have returned my calls and request that I come in with my latest resumé. Four producers of independent films (low budget, no pay, possible SAG agreement, tape and meals, possible nudity) have responded to my new headshot within two days of my sending. Considering I'd only sent out ten, they are a success. And there they are, all two-hundred and forty of them in a box on my desk, a $450 waste considering I couldn't even drive to an audition should I even get one. And there is the *Backstage* I'd bought during my short-lived optimism, the sixteen hours between losing my job and getting hit by a drunk driver. And there's my costume: my full-length fox coyote fur coat, Cuban cigar, red-framed glasses and black beret – all for my debut in The Casting Company at the Playhouse of the Foothills as the lead: Rhonda Riordan, lesbian casting director. I had been originally cast as the "naive receptionist" who meets the "various low-lifes" that come through the equally "low-life casting agency" door and then two weeks into rehearsals I was asked to play both parts – receptionist and lesbian – and then a week later asked to play only the lesbian. Now all I have to do is incorporate my injuries into the play and play a "convalescing lesbian."

I sit on the edge of my bed, contemplative, waiting for that seminal moment that will make sense of everything. The *raison d'etre.* Perhaps it is as Hamlet said: *The play's the thing.* Perhaps all this – the job loss, the car accident is divine intervention intended to lay the foundation for my true destiny: that I am about to be discovered! Perhaps there will be an agent or an equally powerful Hollywood executive who will see me in the play and greenlight my acting career. *If everything happens for a reason, then what other reason could explain all this?* Perhaps I needed to be stripped of everything in my life to make way for that long sought after something. It would make truth of the adage: the worse things are, the better things are.

And considering things couldn't get any worse, I must be but a moment away from the "better."

⟲⟳

AFTER CHINESE (chicken and broccoli with extra duck sauce) and a fortune cookie (mine was empty), and Olive's dinnertime diatribe on the rediscovered merits of Oregon: the crisp clean air, the crisp green trees, the crisp fresh water, how fun and hip and culturally dynamic and the performing arts of downtown Portland is, as if she were more of an Oregon Trail pioneer than Lewis and Clark, Olive returned from her bedroom with an announcement.

"Well, I've made a decision," she declared, clearing her throat.

I waited with bated breath, seated on the couch, magazine in my lap, for the pronouncement that she has a hangnail, or that she is "seriously" not spending any more money on things she doesn't need, or that she's "seriously" going on a diet.

"I'm moving back to Oregon," she said, her brows raised, her eyes popped open, her way of signaling me to just try and challenge the veracity of her pronouncement. "I'm going back to college and finish my degree. I've been thinking about it a long time and I'm going to do it."

"Wow. That's great," I replied and then returned to reading the alarming *US* magazine article *"The Waiting Game; when it comes to the movies' biggest roles, actors under thirty often find they need not apply."* I didn't mean to not take Olive seriously, but after all, it would be a year before she would start buying number two pencils and Pee-Chees by which time she will have changed her mind due to some equally inspiring or dispiriting vision. In any case, it was payback for her divided attention when I told her my harrowing, near-death story.

"I'm giving my two weeks tomorrow," she said, deadpan.

"Right," I laughed, touched that Olive was trying to make me laugh, humor being the best medicine, as I read yet another alarming sentence: *"No matter how hard-working or talented, actors in their 20s have become a generation in a holding pattern...."*

"I'm serious," Olive implored. "School starts in mid-September. I've already got my schedule. I'd like to be out of here in four weeks because I've got to start saving money."

Olive has worked at *Movie Beat* Magazine for seven years, had only just perfected impressions using authentic regional dialects of her Croatian employers, the company founders, and now with a moment's notice, with me in my condition, announces she's moving in four weeks. Given that I can't afford the rent on my own, and don't have the strength to put out a search for a new roommate, her four-week notice bears some personal consequence. Unable to find clarity in her gaze, I focused on the TV screen (an episode of "Fear Factor") and it came to me.

"So let me get this straight. I have NO job...NO car... and now NO place to live in four weeks?!!"

Olive nodded affirmatively, her lips parting open to an unrepentant disjointed smile, which admittedly some people do under terrible circumstances. I'm sure it has nothing to do with insensitivity.

"Wait a second," I said, "If school doesn't start for almost three months why do I need to vacate in four weeks?"

"Well I'm not going back to Oregon right away. School is going to be very tough, so I'm going to go backpacking in Europe with Clarissa first and I need to start saving a lot of money fast. I'm going to move in with Nathan for four weeks to save money on rent. And then, it's Europe!! You know how long I've wanted to do this! I can't wait! But it'll be hard when I get back. Think about it, I'm twenty-seven and moving in with mom! And going to school full time!"

"NOT TO BE A PEST, but have you found a place to stay?" Olive asked me a week later as I stared out the sliding glass doors at the ficus plant with rigor mortis while drafting a pro/con list. "It's just that I told Frank we'd be out by the end of the month."

Frank, our landlord, has seen Olive and me each occupy three apartments in his Buena Vista Complex each during the course of two years. He has seen every rent check come weeks late and by now knows to add a month onto any date we give him. But now in our last three weeks, Olive suddenly wants to make good on her word, show him more consideration than me.

"Don't worry, I'll be out," I said indignantly.

"Well do you mind telling me where you're moving to? I mean I would like to know you've got a place to go."

"New York City."

"Yeah right," she said, laughing in disbelief. "Seriously."

"I am serious," I insisted despite only having considered it for the last half hour, despite the fact that my pro/con list of Los Angeles vs. New York remained inconclusive.

"Don't be ridiculous. You can't afford it."

"It's no more unaffordable than it is for me to stay here."

"Do you have any idea what rents in New York are?"

"I've done the math," I said, not interested in dignifying her line of questioning with a response.

"You don't know the first thing about New York. It's not that just rents are higher. Everything is higher. You need more money just to keep the same standard of living."

"Look. I hardly think I need to justify my decision to you. It's not as if you've got a stellar track record in matters of finance and life decisions…." Olive was on a first-name basis with most credit representatives. One time I came home to a message on the answering machine from Erma. *"Olive? This is Erma. I'm still waiting for that check you've been sending for the past six months."*

Olive stomached my response and effortlessly changed tactics. "So have you told mom?" she asked, conspiring to undo this little idea of mine.

"You know, I can't really take this right now. I mean it's not as if anyone is jumping through hoops to help me make it here. I mean, my God, you announce you're moving in four weeks on the heels of me having my life stripped out from underneath me. So don't suddenly act all concerned, like you play a part in my survival." I slammed my bedroom door and battle-victory weary, threw myself onto my white eyelet duvet to cry, stopping midstream to check my math. As I recalculated the financial feasibility of moving to New York City, I suspected Olive was already on the phone to my mother to convince her of my idiocy by supplanting her with nefarious impressions of Manhattan.

I could see it now: my mother at home in Oregon, having returned from work, dressed in her business suit, nylons and peach slippers. She would be eating Grape-nuts, reading an old Danielle Steel book for the third time, picking the calluses on her feet. My stepfather would be using the poker on the firewood in the wood-burning stove, unconcerned about the flying embers that could ignite fire to Lulu, our longhaired calico cat. (He had a knack for burning things: Chili especially, and then covering up the smell with Lysol. No worse smell than burnt chili and Lysol.) He would slam the stove door shut to which my mother would look up from her book to admonish him with *"Geezus do you have to be so loud?"* to *which he would reply, "That too loud for you? Maybe I oughta turn the TV up?"* He took pleasure in their taunting ritual, indeed turning up the TV volume before picking up his $3.99 Fred Meyer bifocals and returning to his tattered Crossword Puzzle Dictionary and leftover Tater Tot Casserole. And then there would be the disruptive ring of the phone, and an even more disruptive, bellowing Olive, imploring (intimidating) my mother to do something. Two against one as it has always been.

I had apparently considered this scenario in my sleep because a tap on my door awakened me. "What?" I asked recalcitrantly, ready for a fight. If Olive so much as attempted to resume the conversation heads would roll. *Hers.*

"I'm going to get some frozen yogurt. Do you want to come?" Olive asked sweetly.

"O.K." I answered happily. Frozen yogurt was the proverbial olive branch.

AS I LICKED Espresso Mocha from my fifth pink plastic spoon, I had a *deja vu*. The last time I was at this Penguin's was two months ago when I met her – Jewel – the one who referred me Veronique, the cult mistress turned interior decorator. Jewel was the grandniece of Bing Crosby or so she said. We had stood here at the counter with tennis racquets in hand – hers was the newest Prince model, mine the obsolete. An impromptu discussion about tennis led to the revelation that we were both aspiring actresses, which led to the declaration that I was unemployed, which led to her announcement that she knew someone – Veronique – looking to hire. Jewel then invited me to lunch at her apartment, a cul de sac off of Abbott Kinney Road in Venice a few miles away. Even as I drove there, I thought, this is strange. No one in Los Angeles invites strangers for lunch. Maybe she's mistaking me for a lesbian. Maybe I've over-rehearsed.

After lunch and a tour of her apartment (pictures of her everywhere) and awards (tennis, ice skating, etc.) I left her apartment with three leads: the Marina Tennis League, Veronique the Interior Decorator, and the Penguin's Chocolate Macadamia.

As Olive and I exited Penguin's, I was lapping up overboard chocolate with my tongue, so I was woefully unprepared to see Jewel – as unbelievable as it was – coming towards us, her Prince tennis racquet still in hand, her ponytail bopping behind her.

"Hi. How are you?" Jewel asked suspiciously sincerely.

I nodded squeamishly.

"She was in a car accident," countered Olive, accusatorily.

"I heard," Jewel said.

"Really? How'd you hear about it?" I asked.

"Veronique told me. She also told me about having to let you go."

"Oh really?" I asked, annoyed that my situation was so freely discussed. "What'd she say?"

"Well, she just said that she didn't know what happened. That you were great in the beginning, but then," Jewel shrugs, "you weren't."

My mouth dropped like the screamer in Edvard Munch's painting, *The Scream,* as the duck sauce began to come back up.

"Excuse me?" Olive asked, threateningly, as I worked my way towards the car, desperate for cover, my chest feeling the pain of a bullet.

"I guess some guy is doing your work now?" Jewel called out to me before I could get inside the car, which in an ironic turn of events, now seems like the only safe place.

"Rex?" I asked in disbelief. He was the greasy-haired guy who was hired as a consultant but told me to my face that he can do my job too.

"Yeah, I think that's his name," Jewel said.

I couldn't believe my ears. The knife just kept turning and turning. *Was no place safe?* I closed the car door to put an end to my participation in the cell-splitting conversation. I used the napkins to wipe away the mascara floating in my eye, stinging. *Would it kill me to wear waterproof mascara??*

"Jewel? Is that your name?" I overheard Olive say through the cracked window on her side of the car. "Are you just totally stupid and insensitive? My sister's just been in a car accident. She's lucky to be alive. You can tell Veronica or whatever her name is that she's nuts, and she should go back to her little cult. And tell her that if I ever hear that she's bad-mouthing my sister I will personally see to it that she has a very difficult time working at all and believe me that's not an idle threat. Anyone who knows Eve knows she has the utmost integrity and work ethic. She's been honored statewide for her work experience and has more talent in her pinkie than Veronica has in her fucked-up head, so this little job is hardly going to hurt her. And it is a little job, and Veronica is a complete and utter nobody and please tell her I said so." Olive walks to the car, knocks on the car window for me to unlock the driver's door that, since March, can only open from the inside. I reached over and opened the door.

"That bitch," Olive announced, her husky voice suddenly comforting to me.

"Her name's Veronique," I said as Olive peeled out of the lot, rocking my body into a fresh orbit of pain.

"Here" said Olive, handing me a wad of fresh napkins. "You have chocolate in your nose."

"You mean *on* my nose?"

"No, I mean *in* your nose." Olive turned the rear-view mirror towards me as she exhaled the rest of her energy.

How did that happen? Oh maybe it happened when I lowered my nose to the napkins to wipe my snot from dripping into the chocolate.

AFTER WAKING from a cure-nothing nap, I decided to get it over with – turn the knife the full 360. I dialed my mother at dinnertime, when I knew her mouth would be full.

Chomp, chomp -

"The fact is that I have to start over somewhere," I tell her as she chomps on Grape Nuts.

Chomp, chomp, and chomp –

"…and given that the financials are the same whether I live in New York City or Los Angeles – "

Chomp, chomp –

"… it's really just a matter of where I prefer to live."

"Down Lulu." *Chomp, chomp –*

"…and given that Los Angeles has clearly made its intentions known to me over the past few weeks, let alone few years, New York is really the only other place I could live. I mean it's not like I have the whole country to choose from. There are only two cities I can pursue acting in." This last point made tears flow, for I realized that the land I'd so long considered my future Prince had turned into a Toad, the proverbial *Boulevard of Broken Dreams.*

To my surprise, my mother didn't disagree with me about my moving to New York. Ever since I told her a few months ago, what the psychic told me about her, that she was my mother in a previous life, and that "the one thing to know about your mother is that you're never gonna please her" she's kind of relaxed her criticisms. In other words, she says nothing at all.

4. GOODBYE PARTY

"Cheers," I said, raising my flute to my friends – what few I could gather on such short notice for my goodbye fete at Kate Mantilini's on Wilshire Boulevard, a place I have never desired to eat at, but where Olive suggested for our goodbye party. I threw back champagne to squelch my anxiety. I was hardly enjoying myself. I didn't think about how much I would miss my friends, how much I was looking forward to New York (if I was at all). I thought instead, of my one-way ticket and how very stupid I was to continue with my plans, which, as of two hours ago, don't take me beyond the Newark Airport.

Two hours ago I called Pavlos who was back at his home in New York City, to reconfirm the details of my arrival since I was going to be staying with him indefinitely.

"So, you're subletting the brownstone?" Pavlos asked, referring to a brownstone on West 108th street owned by a Columbia

University professor of landscape architecture whose advertisement I saw in the *Los Angeles Times* a few weeks earlier. I had nearly sent a deposit to the Professor a week ago, but Pavlos had balked at the idea. "Don't be ridiculous, stay with me" he'd said over hibachi entrees at Benihana's in Los Angeles, in full witness of my sister and Pavlos' friend, Malcolm – all of them imploring me to decline the sublet and accept Pavlos' erstwhile housing invitation. "The area is not safe. Nothing above *the hundreds* is. I myself wouldn't live above *the eighties*."

"I mean, really! Eve! It's the Bronx!" Olive cried out. "Harlem" she added, as if the name alone should put the fear of death in me if I had any sense at all. "Listen to Pavlos. He lives there. He knows!"

"Your sister's just being stubborn," Pavlos said to Olive, as I pretended to be absorbed with the sous chef's slicing and dicing, the twinkle of the blade mesmerizing.

I excused myself to the bathroom and when I returned, Olive, Malcolm and Pavlos announced that it was "decided." I was to stay with Pavlos and send my belongings to his apartment. *Fait accomplis.* No arguments. Pavlos insisted. And everyone nodded their heads with satisfaction.

But, two hours ago, when I expected Pavlos to be asking me when and where he could pick me up at the airport, he instead asked if I was "subletting the brownstone".

"You mean the brownstone you talked me out of taking?" I asked. "You mean the one that was too dangerous for a girl of twenty-four, because nothing past the Eighties is safe?" I asked him incredulously as the beef-flavored Top Ramen I'd ingested earlier, began to come up.

"Huh?" Pavlos asked with the attention span of a man feigning amnesia. "Here. Talk to my brother a sec," he said, handing off the phone as he initiated a conversation in Greek with someone else.

"Hey Eve," said Kristos, Pavlos' younger brother whom I'd never met.

I told Kristos how much Pavlos' sudden "memory lapse" impacted my situation, how it leaves me homeless.

"Yeah, he's been forgetting a lot of things since the accident," said Kristos.

The accident. Kristos said the word as if it were all that needed to be said to quiet me, as if it could rival the accident of the century, as if the drunk driver were my fault, like the iceberg was the Titanic night-watchman's fault. Frankly, it sounded more like Pavlos' memory was lapsing because he has decided not to be romantically involved with me anymore. Given my demotion, Pavlos was doing an about-face, and voila! It was now safe for me to roam the streets above Eightieth Street. The Bronx had gentrified in the last two weeks!

I ingested Pavlos' transformation and what it would mean to me logistically once I arrived, but I was too disconcerted by what it meant emotionally. It sounded to me like Pavlos was signaling the end of our relationship. I thought we had turned a corner when he bought a used Saab for me to drive and… *when he insisted I stay with him!* I hung up with Kristos. His family beckoned.

I used the silent moment and what few hours remained before takeoff to look freshly at my surroundings. I sat squarely in the center of a collapsed bed frame. My box spring and mattress long gone. My furnishings handed over, one by one, truckload by truckload to friends. Just empty closets and more than a dozen boxes packed and addressed to the Colossus, 394 East 38th Street, New York, NY, c/o Pavlos Polychronopolis which would soon read "return to sender."

I dialed Pavlos again. My last-ditch effort for clarity. I insisted that he take the call to a private area so his brother wouldn't beckon his attention away from me again, even though I knew the interruptions were calculated. Men always put themselves in the center of confusion when a girl is on the verge of becoming psychotic as he would most assuredly classify me. Men believe that the word "psychotic" applies to any person who can emote (read: female).

"So let me get this straight," I said to Pavlos, "on the eve of the night, FOURTEEN hours before I am due to fly to New York on a one-way ticket, you suddenly don't remember that I was going to be staying with you? Frankly, it sounds more like you're trying to end our relationship. So if that's it, I wish you'd just say it."

"No, Eve, that's not it," he said. "Look I can't really talk right now," said Pavlos. "I've got my mother here from Greece – my whole family is here. Besides I can barely hear you."

"So move to a place you can," I said.

"Now is not a good time," he said, losing patience.

"OK. Fine. So will you be meeting me at the airport tomorrow night?" I asked him, pushing the envelope.

"What time are you landing?"

"Around 8:30 p.m.. I'll get the information..."

"No, I don't think I'll be able to. I've got a business dinner. Let's talk later," he said and hung up.

Later? Later is me on a plane. Later is me arriving in New York City homeless.

I can't make sense of what has happened. Pavlos isn't rude so much as he is unmoved by my predicament, which invariably, is rude. And heartless. I tried to make excuses for him. He must have cold feet. He probably presumed, and feared, that I would be in a state of neediness (having no job, staying with him), asking himself, *"What's a twenty-four-year-old going to do in New York where she knows no one, but lean on the only person she knows?"* He must have thought I would be relying on him. Certain of this he bolted. *Victory goes to the man who runs away! - Napolean Bonaparte.*

But Pavlos was wrong and egocentric, and has underestimated me. Coastal hopping is easy for me. I have been taking cross-country flights since I was six weeks old beginning with a flight from Oregon to Rhode Island when my mother, sister and I flew to be with my father who got a job selling New York Life Insurance. And then again nine months later from Rhode Island to Oregon when my mother left my father. I'd flown cross-country from Oregon to Syracuse, New York for my freshman year of college, and again nine months later from Syracuse to Los Angeles to attend USC instead. In fact, I had never taken any kind of flight other than cross-country. *I was quite capable of flight and independence dammit!*

Still, even when faced with Pavlos' cold indifference (or selective amnesia), I just couldn't bring myself to sever my ties altogether. Too many things had been ending lately and I just couldn't bear the thought of another. Besides, I needed to keep my one New York contact, however strained, intact until I was on my own. I eyed my suitcases with reverence for I would be living out of them somewhere below Eightieth Street.

"To Olive and Eve." said Nathan, my sister's on-and-off-again boyfriend. I tuned Nathan's toast out. I couldn't even get top billing at my own goodbye party.

But then they sang. *Auld Lang Syne.* "Should old acquaintance be *forgotten* ...and never brought to mind...." My own personal funeral hymn.

———❧

"EVE!" Olive scolded me when she saw me paying the bill. "What are you doing?"

"Paying," I said, yanking out $400 from my insurance settlement stash.

"Hold on," she growled, cusping my wrist in an attempt to stop my money from reaching the eager hands of the waitress. "We're all going to pay."

But Olive's too late. A chorus of "thanks Eve" hit the airwaves as our friends shoved off. Olive tried to force some cash on me, but I refused, not wanting anyone to pay the price of admission to a hastily arranged wake.

As we stood outside the restaurant waiting for the valet to return with Olive's car, I prayed for just one sign, one sign telling me to stay. At that moment a spotlight converged upon me but then just as suddenly spirited away. I traced the spotlight to a crowd next door where Jim Carrey and a tall blonde woman in a red dress towered above the rest, as paparazzi, who were cordoned off by red swags, snapped photos. Maybe that was my sign, I thought. A wayward spotlight will find its way upon me and the paparazzi will rush over here. But just as the light's strobe came my way and the magic seemed inevitable, reality intruded. I heard the gurgle of Olive's embarrassingly flimsy Toyota Tercel spiraling up from the restaurant's garage. All I wanted to do at that moment was make a quick getaway before the spotlight found me in proximity with a crap car, but the valet was stuck inside the car, unable to open the door, pleading from within to let him out.

"Yeah, I have to get that fixed" said Olive, opening the door.

The valet emerged with relief as if he'd just been rescued from the human-eating plant in *The Little Shop of Horrors*, the one that only spoke two words, "feed me".

"Do you know what's going on over there?" we asked him as he rubbed his sweat onto his sleeve.

"A movie premiere," he answered, collecting his breath, visoring his eyes from the spotlight held upon him. "Jim Carrey's new film and some unknown."

We got in the car and left. The time for a sign had come and gone.

⸺⸻

"WHAT'S THIS?" I asked referring to the 13" Goldstar color television just inside our apartment doorway on the floor. The TV had blown up two months earlier. I had been napping on the couch during "I Love Lucy" (the episode where Lucy mistakenly thinks the neighbors are murderers when they are just rehearsing a play) when I was awakened by the noxious fumes and smoke erupting from the back. It has been unplugged in the doorway ever since waiting for someone to take it to the garbage. It used to say "dust me" in the dust layer, but now has one of my new headshots taped to the screen. It fits perfectly.

"Isn't that funny? Nathan did that," said Olive.

"Well that's one way of getting on TV."

"Can I dump it? Olive asked. "The TV I mean. It doesn't work right?"

"Yeah, you can dump it. And the headshot too."

Olive gave me a look of reproach and then gingerly placed my headshot on the couch and took the TV out the door down to the trash. I proceeded to my room where the collapsed frame of my bed looked like the outline of a dead body. Next to it was a face staring back up at me – my own – from my box of headshots on the floor, making me realize one thing: I had no where else to go but up.

EASTERN TIME

5. DESCENDING

"Ladies and Gentlemen, we are beginning our descent into Newark..."

"Miss, will you please put up your seat? Miss?"

"Huh? What?" I ask, my eyes still adjusting to the bright white cabin lights just enough to glean two, no three sets of eyes staring at me - the flight attendant, my seatmate, and the lady in a loud liberty print shirt across the aisle.

"Your seat" asks the flight attendant, her smile gone. The movie is over.

I begin to raise my seat when I feel blasts of turbulence from behind. I scream, surprised to hear only my voice without the accompaniment of other passengers.

"Basil, don't kick the lady's seat," says a woman from behind. "Tell the lady you're sorry."

I turn around to see a boy of three staring at me. She waits for Basil to speak. I wait for Basil to speak. We all wait for Basil to speak. But Basil doesn't speak. "Sorry about that," the woman says to me, sticking her head between me and my neighbor's seat, like a compliant Marie Antoinette.

"What'd ya think you were done for?" asks my seatmate, amused by my panic. "No one ever died from a little turbulence."

"Oh no?" I ask, as I oblige the flight attendant's request, forcing my chair to ascend even as we descend.

"Are you finished with that?" the flight attendant asks, pointing to my empty six-ounce bottle of my *vin rouge* tucked into the back pocket of the seat ahead of me. She takes it from my hands and drops it into an army green plastic trash bag, her last chore before strapping herself in, safely for descent. *Descent.* How apropos.

"We thank you for flying SunJet. Local time is 8:52 p.m. Eastern. Local temperature is 89 degrees with 100% humidity. For those of you making connections, please go to the Arrivals gate where connections are posted. We hope you've enjoyed flying with us as much as the crew has enjoyed flying with you."

"She's right you know," says the woman in the liberty print to my seatmate. "What she said before. Turbulence can kill. Didn't you hear about the man who was decapitated? Course he was 6 feet and sitting in bulkhead. Never sit in bulkhead unless you're under 5'5". Should be a rule."

The plane makes a particularly bumpy landing and until we come to a complete stop, I am not convinced that I will survive the ride. I used to think that being involved in one disaster spared you from another, that you had in effect, met your "personal disaster quota." But I don't think that anymore.

When the plane taxis to the terminal and stops, conventional wisdom would suggest that I am now safe. Seatbelts disengage before the plane's permissive bell has rung. As everyone collects their baggage from overhead compartments, I remain seated, staring out the window at fluorescent-vested employees unloading baggage. I'm in no hurry. I have no place to be. No one is expecting me.

I make my way through the terminal to a conveyor belt behind a lone, uniformed soldier. I notice his gold-fringed epaulettes, his shiny black shoes, his black attaché on the rubber platform beside him, and his trench coat draped over his arm with the neatness of a folded flag. Suddenly it feels like I am in a scene out of the 1940's and I'm the only woman whose soldier didn't make it out of the war alive. And this man ahead of me is the only soldier whose woman didn't show. Could it be that we are fated to meet - the only two still alone – the only unpaired animals descending SunJet's Ark? *Is this why I am in New York, at this airport, alone? Is this what will make sense of the last few weeks wherein nothing has made sense?* Perhaps I am meant to meet this man and live happily ever after. As the military man descends the platform, I quicken my step to close the gap between us, but just as I do, a blonde woman in a camel-colored ensemble cuts into frame and joins his side. The soldier moves his trench to his left arm and puts his free arm around her. I think perhaps they are just relatives, but he kisses her. And then I reach the end of the belt.

Once out of the terminal and into the baggage claim area, I see huddles of "loved ones," all pathetic with their homecoming tears and welcome signs for their *la famiglia*, lovers, kids. I walk past and realize how economical it is time-wise to not have anyone there to greet me. The only person I know in New York is Pavlos and given that he hasn't impeded my lone bolt to luggage, pretty much ends speculation of reconciliation, and of his humanity.

Amid the late-night frenzy of collecting my baggage and seeing east coast air accessible on the other side of the automatic doors, the reality that I am on foreign soil sets in as does the pain in my back, chest, fresh-from-cast hand, and the rickety-click-click of my left hip joint. My luggage comes immediately and all at once – if only the crowd would let me get it. With seconds to spare, I yank on my last piece, which strains my back, and work through the human perimeter to rejoin my other luggage rolling away on the dollar cart. With my luggage and me reunited, I have only one thought: *Now what?* I hadn't really thought past this moment, past Baggage Claim. I never wanted to believe that Pavlos wouldn't show. But now that he hasn't, I suppose I should find lodging.

I locate a wall of Manhattan-area hotel advertisements on the floor above. The advertisements are broken down by area and I recall Pavlos having mentioned Midtown. What he said was, "You don't want to live in Greenwich – it's artsy."

"But I *am* artsy," I told him.

"Yes, you're artsy, but you're not pink hair and nose rings artsy," he said, "you're more upper eastside."

"What are you?" I asked him.

"Well I live in Midtown. East side." he answered.

"I'm not Midtown?" I asked.

"No, you're Midtown too," he said, unenthusiastically.

I lift a wall-mounted phone that auto-dials a hotel reservation service. None of my first Midtown picks have vacancies, so the operator suggests the Ambassador West Hotel.

"Is it in Midtown?" I ask, as if that is my only requirement.

"Yes," says the operator as she calls them on another line to notify them of my arrival. I just have to taxi there.

6. AMBASSADOR WEST HOTEL

'A charming and intimate hotel in the heart of Broadway,' reads the Ambassador West Hotel brochure. I found it on the airport floor. It had missed the garbage. *'Step outside and find yourself surrounded by the excitement of Broadway theatre. And it's just a short walk to the city's most popular attractions such as Rockefeller Center, Radio City Music Hall, famous museums and Fifth Avenue Shopping.'* As if I was here for sightseeing.

"Excuse me, sir? Can you please go a little slower?" I ask the driver of taxi 1M24 as the ride threatens to undo six weeks of rehabilitation in one ride. "It's just that I'm recovering from a car accident," I explain as if the deadly ride would otherwise be fine. The taxi driver slows down but apparently just for the toll booth, resuming top speed into a full-tilt Manhattan, competing against yellow lights, yellow cabs, and pedestrians who are as equally indifferent to taxi 1M24 as 1M24 is to them.

The taxi driver stops alongside a parked car on a dark, desolate street (save for the bumper-to-bumper parked cars), jumps out of the taxi, pops the trunk and powers my luggage onto the curb and wants my money.

"Um, where is the hotel?" I ask him when I fail to see any of the usual signage or neon lighting like the green signature script of the Holiday Inn or the graphic sun logo of the Comfort Inn, which would suggest there's a hotel in the vicinity. Just then a young man with a pencil moustache tosses a lit cigarette as he descends a stoop and takes off with my luggage without a word. The driver then points absent-mindedly to a nondescript building in front of me, where to my relief the same young man is taking my luggage.

Problem now is I can't find my wallet. My hand has made several revolutions inside my purse without success. As my heart prepares for its final lap before giving out, I find it inside my red plastic make-up bag (another Estee Lauder gift with purchase). I had purposefully put it in there – the color and heft of which was supposed to make it more visible than my small black wallet. I pay the driver $50 and get out of the car expecting change but he speeds off.

⌒৹

"HI. I HAVE A RESERVATION," I inform a petite Asian woman behind the counter as I keep a watchful eye on my luggage on a brass carousel by the elevator.

"Are you Eve?" she asks.

I am unnerved. *How does she know my name?* I never spoke to her. I spoke to a voice, a go-between operator over the phone, sight unseen. If she knows I'm here, does Pavlos? *Did he send someone to follow me from the airport, someone to inform him of my every movement?* "How do you know my name was Eve?"

She just smiles and I decide what harm could come from this merry petite Asian desk clerk knowing my name?

"How many nights you stay?" she asks.

"I'm not sure. Is it possible for me to just reserve a room for tonight and then if I need to stay longer, let you know tomorrow?" I'm sure Pavlos will insist on me staying with him once he learns I'm staying in a hotel. Even if he just wants to be friends, I'm sure he wouldn't want me in the city alone, paying for lodging day after infinite day.

"Sure, let me know tomorrow in the morning by checkout time, 11 a.m.," she says and hands me the key to Room 463.

52

THE BROCHURE described the room's decor as American Federal, which by the looks of it, seems to mean mahogany. Mahogany furniture and evergreen walls. Very statesman-like, aristocratic, Jeffersonian. A place where an American patriot might have contemplated strategy for his duel to the death. And there is an armoire that apparently doubles as doorstop, which so far prevents me from entering. Most importantly there is air conditioning! I drag my luggage inside, bolt the locks. I take a seat on the edge of the twin bed, with hospital thin orange blanket wondering what to do next. *Go to the window.*

The single window looks out to a fire escape harnessed to the facade of the building, comforting considering fire is about the only natural disaster I have left on my "to survive" list. I listen attentively to the streets sounds of active life – a band blaring, cars whooshing and honking – audio proof that I am not some belligerent ghost who refuses to cross over to the other side. As I continue to crane my neck further and further out the window to see what all the excitement is at the corner, I begin to envision myself falling. Surely, the fire escape is adequate safeguard from falling. *Or is it? Or is this exactly the same sort of optimism that got me here in the first place?*

I grab my camera for a better, safer view, and look for some indication as to where I am. Through my telephoto lens, I can make out a street sign that reads "Times Square." Oh my God. It's *the* Times Square. Another street sign reads… *Sunset Boulevard?* I laugh. I can't believe the irony of traveling over 3000 miles only to be once again, north of Sunset Boulevard. But why is the Sunset Blvd. street sign so much larger than the Times Square sign? I zoom in for a better look to read the fine print on the Sunset Blvd. street sign:

SUNSET BLVD.
ANDREW LLOYD WEBBER'S MUSICAL

It's not a street sign at all! It's a billboard in the form of a street sign! On the Minskoff Theatre. I take a picture of it, even though the flash probably won't reach that far. My first frame of New York is destined to be black.

Well what am I going to do now? I simply cannot tell people for years after this that on my first night in Manhattan, in the City that Never Sleeps, I went to sleep at 11:10 p.m. and saw nothing but Times Square from my window. Besides, I'm starving and couldn't sleep if I wanted to. My appetite and bed-readiness are still on Pacific Time.

THE BAND that I'd heard from my window gets louder as I near the end of the block. By the time I reach the corner, I see the entire band: a large, muscular black man, shirtless in denim overalls wearing black leather gloves with the fingers cut out. He is seated on a green bucket beating with drumsticks on rusted hubcaps, a garbage can and Rolling Rock beer bottles. He's actually very good. He finishes a set and reaches into a KFC bucket beside him and pulls out a wing. He washes it down with a bottle of Evian as he takes in the view – the hordes of people – dressed in dinner theatre to scanty beachwear attire, crossing the intersection as honking taxis try to weasel through them.

It's about this time that I discover I'm being followed by a voluble militant man wearing a dilapidated army green trench and black beret, saying something unintelligible about my vagina. I enter the first store I come to in order to lose him but it's an X-rated shop, aptly titled "X-Site-Ed". But it's not the sign that tells me, it's the rainbow assortment of dildos just inside the doorway. I exit immediately and move up the street just one step ahead of the nutcase as the shops grow in X's. It's an entire block of open-all-night, neon lit xxx-rated stores and souvenir shops with "Closing" signs.

Finally, just as the nutcase starts meowing at me (inviting the head turns of a raucous group of young men) I see a red, white and green awning with golden pink interior lighting on the corner. It looks warm and inviting and Italian. Sbarro Pizza. Just as I enter, the sounds the trashcan beats fade as Sinatra house music takes over with *"Some people get their kicks stopping on a dream...."*

I order two pieces of pizza; one mushroom and green pepper, and one tomato and basil, and take a seat at a barstool facing a side street where I can think and relax, maybe even plan a bit. Unfortunately, my quiet dinnertime is rudely interrupted by peeping passersby who watch me as if I'm as much a tourist attraction as the band. They stare shamelessly. Couples arm-in-arm stare at me. Parents point inside at my pizza as their kids stare in awe or hunger. I am so self-consciousness that I'm running out of napkins, searching for my reflection in the window to see if I have sauce on my face. And I am so not enjoying eating my pizza with a plastic fork and knife. *I'd much prefer to use my hands, but how would that look? To the kids?* Here I'd intentionally chosen a window facing the side street! *Who would have thought there'd be so many people walking on a side street? What? Is there a sign around the corner that says, "Psychic this way, girl eating pizza the other way"?* I am near tears. *What the hell am I doing? Is this a joke gone too far?* I have no job, no apartment, and know not a soul in New York other than Pavlos, the Greek who has left me for dead. Worse is that the militant man is now standing squarely in front of me from outside, staring at my pizza. I pretend not to notice. I slurp my diet coke but there is only slush left. I try to nibble the tasteless crust.

He starts to talk. At least I think that's why his tongue is moving. Finally he takes off, trailing after a family of four with a baby stroller.

And then I get up to leave. As I stuff hundreds of red-splattered napkins from my tray into the garbage by the entrance while the A/C unit above the door blows my hair and napkins, I hear, "Give her a reason to live...." For a moment, I think it's God, or an Angel sent by God, like Clarence in *It's a Wonderful Life*, speaking to me but then I realize it's not God, it's Sinatra. Singing. From his Greatest Hits Album. From the speakers overhead.

7. MANHATTAN HOTEL

*P*anic!

I have awakened two hours later than I intended and now have less than twenty... *nineteen* minutes to reserve this $85 room for another night or check out, which means I have to convince Pavlos in less than twenty minutes to let me stay with him. Which means I have to call him.

Dialing....

I feel as if I'm soliciting the forbidden Garden, so tempted but so doomed. But really, what decent human being could say "no" and leave a girl to stay in a hotel in a strange city so... *indefinitely?*

"Hello?"

It's a woman's voice. *A woman? Answering Pavlos' phone at 10:41 a.m. on a Saturday? It was nerve-racking enough preparing to hear Pavlos' voice, but a woman's?* "Hello. Is Pavlos there?" I inquire, undeterred. I can't feel my feet.

"Who's calling?" asks the woman in a now noticeable Greek accent, leading me to suspect she's not Pavlos' paramour but his mother, the woman who thinks I am the perpetrator of her son's brow problem. (Still, if he didn't lie about his mother visiting him from Greece, then maybe there's hope for us.)

"Eve," I admit nervously, certain that the very mention of my name will cause her to slam the phone down. There is silence. Then phone smothering. I blow hot air on my hands and rub them together to give them some warmth they can't otherwise seem to find in the sweltering hot room. I press the soles of my feet into the floor to dull the sensation of straight pins poking at them.

"Hello." It's Pavlos and he's speaking in a tone reminiscent of someone begrudgingly accepting a telemarketer call.

"Hi. How are you?" I ask him in a light, conciliatory tone to demonstrate what a *viva voce* I've managed since our last conversation. To show him my old self, pre-accident, remind him of sweet, charming, innocent me. I wait for his reply, knowing that it - the tone and content - will instantly convey our status. I hold my breath.

"Fine. Are you in New York?" he asks, paving the way for my question.

"Yep. At a hotel in Times Square," I answer, waiting for the gravity of my predicament to sink in.

"Listen, can I call you later?" he asks distractedly.

"Well...um... when?"

"Later, this afternoon."

"Oh, um... Well...actually – "

"It's just that I've got to go. My driver is waiting for me," he says.

"Right. OK. Sure," I say, letting the cold wind settle, forage into the hemisphere of my brain that will intuit the end. "So... do you want my phone number?"

"Uh, O.K.," he says perfunctorily. I tell him the phone number of the hotel room but have the distinct impression he isn't writing it down, unless of course he just happened to have a pencil and paper behind his ear. He hangs up without saying goodbye. Not even a *"ciao."*   I continue holding the phone against my ear even after the signal goes dead. Even when a voice comes on. *"...if you'd like to make a call, hang up..."* I hang on. Only when a loud and repetitive *bonk...bonk...bonk* comes on do I finally manage to hang up.

⌐———꙳

"Hi. I'd just like to book my room for another night," I inform the concierge rather forlornly, my cash on the counter, my mind preoccupied with the visual of Pavlos' "driver" idling in a sedan outside his condominium complex, wherever that is.

"What room are you in?" she asks.

"463."

"Sorry but that room's been booked," she says, her hands clasped, portrait-ready, on the counter.

"What?" I ask, looking over the counter, only now noticing that the woman behind it, in the pea green sweater, isn't the same one as yesterday. "How is that possible?"

"You only reserved the room for one night and a man just called to reserve it," she says.

"But the woman I spoke to last night told me I could tell her today by 11 a.m. if I needed it another night."

"Sorry. I don't know anything about that."

"Well can't you ask her?"

"She's not here. She's on the evening shift."

"Well can't you just give this man a different room?"

"No we total booked."

"Fine. Then I'll just take a different room," I say, pushing my cash towards her.

"No, you no understand. We total booked," she says, pushing the cash back at me.

"Well can't you call that man back and tell him you were mistaken – that you have nothing available?"

"No because he call from airport. He already on way here. Very sorry but we find you comparable hotel if want," she says, proud of the comprehensive service they provide even after you're no longer a guest.

⌐———꙳

I STAND OUTSIDE the hotel in a heatwave, my luggage on the sidewalk next to the hotel trash as I try to hail a taxi. As a taxi approaches from the Times Square corner, I wave my hand, but it passes me by. *Could it have mistaken my wave for "goodbye"?*

"The taxi has to have its light on, or it's not available," yells the bellboy from the stoop, explaining the phenomenon.

"Oh! Thanks," I say.

Seconds later, a taxi with its light on responds to my hail and begins to pull over for me, but when I turn to collect my luggage it speeds off. *What in the…?!*

"He doesn't want to go to the airport," says an old man walking by me with his dog on a leash, peeing on the bumper of a parked car.

"But I'm not going to the airport." I tell him.

"Then hide your luggage," says a bellboy.

"Oh this is unbelievable!" I mutter as I move my luggage onto the sidewalk out of sight of oncoming vacant taxis (but within perfect reach of the old man and the bellboy and other assorted passersby). I attempt to straddle my vision from my luggage to the street, worried that I may catch a taxi only to lose my luggage. Eight cars pass but no available taxi.

"There's one," yells the man and the bellboy.

I walk into the street, losing all sight of my luggage, and hail the cab with my recently un-casted arm now that my right one's fatigued. It sees me and starts to angle towards me, but just as it does, a young thin blonde woman with a red baguette purse jumps out from between two parked cars and commandeers it for her. That blonde bitch. *Doesn't she know I'm crippled?* I stand there as if my body has blown a fuse, short-circuiting like the lights of the Titanic.

"Look there's another one" yells the bellboy.

A white light. Taxi 9PMZ. The man, the boy, and I hail the taxi, and the taxi cuts so close to the idling one in front of it, that the blonde taxi-abductee narrowly escapes purse-amputation.

As the taxi pulls over for me, I motion for the driver to roll down his window.

"Look. I'm not going to the airport, but I've got some luggage." The driver nods but he has no choice. The bellboy and the old man have heaved my luggage into the backseat and are now holding the door open for me.

"Thank you. 273 West 38th Street please," I instruct the driver. As we speed off, I wave goodbye to the man and bellboy – the Good Samaritans – out the rear window.

TWO MINUTES and $5.40 later, the taxi stops in... *Japan? China?* All the signs are written in characters and the driver is urging me out of the car.

"Where is the hotel?" I ask him. He points across the street to a slim brownstone with the only English sign on the block: The Manhattan.

The Manhattan Hotel is *not*. Comparable that is. Just inside the lobby, swags of fluorescent orange caution tape (I thought it only came in yellow) hang high and low like streamers, and white dust hangs in the air like Malathion, leading me to suspect that I've entered biohazard or a crime scene. The only thing missing is a chalk outline of the body. And, as unbelievable as it is, the lobby is twenty degrees hotter than it is outside. Even though there is no one in sight – not a bellhop, desk clerk or guest – I put down my bags and ring the bell for service, giving me the feeling that I am at a deli counter and should ask for pastrami on rye. I ring the bell again, and just as I do, a large astronaut-suited man emerges from the dusty rubble behind me, in a gasmask. I lift my luggage to leave *ASAP*, dreading not what contamination I've been exposed to but worse: hailing another taxi.

"Miss?" says an Asian man from behind the deli counter, *err,* concierge. He motions for me for me to come back, to give up my attempt to escape. "Sorry for 'pearance. Hotel winoshun." He says, removing my clenched fist from my bag.

"Huh?" I ask, not understanding his English. He points to a freestanding sign that reads: We apologize for the appearance during our renovations.

"Rinoshun," he repeats.

"Oh, renovation," I nod, following him up to the counter.

As we wait for my Visa to clear, he tells me, just as an aside, that the A/C units aren't working, and that "no" there aren't any fans left for my use. "Thee *ah* only eight and they *ah* all taken," he says, his few strands of grey hair getting blown from two fans rotating behind him.

"Well could I borrow one of those?" I ask, pointing to the fan behind him.

"Oh, no, no. They stay," he says with a non-negotiable smile.

I seriously contemplate finding a hotel with air-conditioning when he hands me the charge card slip to sign. After I sign, he hands me a heavy blue credit card. "What's this?" I ask.

"Key to woom." The credit card key is such a technological advance it gives me hope that the room will be a vast improvement over the lobby.

Wishful thinking.

The key, as it turns out, is the only part of the renovation completed. The bed is as firm as Posturepedic cardboard and comes with a peach polyester bedspread circa 1970 that has been pilling since 1971, not to mention that its fishing wire thread is spiraling out of its repeating wavy topstitch. There is one foot area between the edge of the bed and the walls, no TV, and the room is hotter than the lobby, which is hotter than outside. All this for $13 more a day than the Ambassador West Hotel.

But worse than all that, is that it is now almost one o'clock and I am seriously behind my "early bird gets the apartment" schedule. My only plan was to get to the apartment that Pavlos told me about a few weeks ago. His secretary, Liza, lived in the building and she supplied me with the phone number to the management office but when I called, hoping to rent the apartment over the phone, sight unseen, the rental agent would have nothing to do with me until I got to New York saying only, "you have to be here."

I took down the address when I was in L.A., even had Liza fax the studio layout to me, but where is it!? I swear I put it right here in my wallet. I inspect it five more times, looking for hidden compartments I may have not discovered in my three years of ownership. I scatter the contents across the bed. Nothing. I remove my clothes from my luggage, and when they lose their shape, I pelt them violently across the room. I move to the bathroom and scour through all my toiletries until I throw everything, and my Goody brush breaks in half.

I take a seat on the edge of the bed. My heart is racing from the stress. I could have easily have a heart attack. An article in this month's *Cosmopolitan* lists twenty-five potential stresses in life, and that if you had three happen within the year you were considered primed for a heart attack. And if you did experience more than three stresses in one year, it warned against making major life decisions like moving, getting a new job "because your decisions won't be rational but emotional and inevitably flawed." I counted nine:

1. Fired twice: first by Mr. and Mrs. Director of Brentwood after my employment agent told them that I was looking for other work (and no it wasn't me who flooded their billiard room), and then the cult escapee/interior designer

2. Three personal injuries: two nose breaks at Third Street Theatre in my acting class, and one broken fourth metacarpal

3. One car "accident"

4. Two (un)natural disasters: the 6.8 Northridge earthquake and the L.A. riot

5. Two personal catastrophes *(as if all the others weren't personal?)*: a broken engagement, and that I was still undiscovered

My perspiration has become indistinguishable from my tears. I curl up on the bed, the 1970's peach bedspread and heat making me psychotic. I feel like Faye Dunaway in *Chinatown* trying to slap myself straight. *Where would I have put the paper?* My bag, my purse, my pocket, my purse. I unpack everything and can't find the one slip of paper where I have put the address. I am near tears as the temperature climbs.

Wait. *Did I leave the address in L.A.?* Oh, I can almost picture it on my desk next to my bed frame. *Maybe I can call Olive and ask her to look by my desk?* If only my desk was still there. Still, maybe it's on the floor. *Would Olive even be home?* No answer.

Wait, what about my memory? Yes, maybe I can recall the address. I have an excellent memory. Let's see, I know the prospective apartment is in "midtown" on the "East Side" near Pavlos. I remember looking up Pavlos' address in the back of my *New York City Travel Guide*. I think I even marked the location with an ink dot, in which case maybe I marked the prospective apartment as well. *Now where is my Guide?* Found it. There is an ink dot marking Pavlos home on 38th between First and Second Avenues but there is *not* an ink dot marking the apartment. However, I think the apartment was a few blocks north and on the same longitudinal line (near the same avenue). That would put the apartment at about 43rd street. *Hmmm.* Let's try process of elimination. I'm sure it wasn't on 42nd Street. I would've remembered if it was on 42nd Street. It was definitely not in the Fifties. *Any distinctive markings?* I also recall being told by Pavlos' secretary that the apartment building was originally an eighteen-story hotel.

With that, I collect the contents of my purse, grab my camera bag, inform the concierge that I will be staying "indefinitely" and hail a taxi feeling comparatively confident and light given the absence of luggage and a destination. But I know what I have to do. I will simply count the stories of every apartment building between First and Third avenues, between 43rd and 49th streets until I have my eighteen-story former hotel.

8. BELLE ARTS

The cab hasn't moved. In four, *correction,* five rounds of green lights, the cab hasn't moved, and the fare is approaching $8.

"Where are we?" I ask the driver, secretly blaming him for getting me into a jam since it was his idea to take me to the corner of Forty-fourth Street and First Avenue instead of Forty-third Street and First. He said it would save me a buck. He neglected to tell me that the dollar savings will cost me an additional ten minutes and approximately $4.00, correction, $4.30.

"First Avenue's right there," he says, pointing to the end of the block, just four car lengths away.

"Well then I'll just get out here because I'm not even sure where I'm going." He hits the meter. The receipt spits out. I pay the fare and push open my door, which taps against the side of a parked car. I am unconcerned until a man's head cranes out the driver's window to inspect the topcoat for scratches. "Sorry," I tell him. He says nothing, just readjusts his side view mirror as if his car has come undone from my light tap.

I step onto the sidewalk and take a step towards First Avenue, my intended start line, when the words "Belle Arts" in elegant black script that are printed on a gold-trimmed, scallop-hemmed cream awning, catch my eye. Given that I'm a Francophile and an *artiste*, the combination is compelling. I look up to the top of the building, wondering if it's eighteen stories.

"What are you looking for?" asks the taxi driver still stuck in traffic beside me.

"For an apartment building that used to be an eighteen-story hotel," I say, hopeful that he can help. But he just shrugs and speeds off, the traffic jam miraculously lifting the moment I get out of the cab.

Well I might as well start my counting here at Belle Arts even though my plan was to begin at the corner. I can't stick to a plan even if my life depends on it. In fact, I should really see a doctor about this rash of impulsiveness and my complete dedication to it.

But where should I start the count? Should I count the street-level Szechwan Restaurant at the base of the building as the first floor, le premiere etage? Or should I begin with the second tier of French windows, which is presumably the first floor of apartments (if they are apartments). And, should I assume each row of French windows constitutes a story?

At this point, I am dizzied by the diarrhea of my subconscious and consider just entering the building and inquiring directly as to whether Belle Arts is eighteen stories and whether it's commercial or residential, but decide that I am not up to withstanding the public humiliation should I be told that I am trespassing private property and/or laughed off the premises for thinking that I could possibly afford it given my Gap attire.

Finally, I just count. Each attempt, however, is somehow thwarted. First, I back into a passerby, then a dog weaves his leash around my legs, then a pinched nerve in my neck sidelines me, and then, just as I'm reaching the fourteenth floor, the sun peaks out from the top and I am momentarily blinded. So, that's when I decide to continue my count from across the street, where I won't have to strain my neck in order to count, where the sun won't get in my eyes so much, and where, it occurs to me, I can quicken the addition by counting only half the stories and then multiplying the number by two to see if it adds up to eighteen.

As I cross the street, I begin to recognize the obsessive-compulsiveness of my search. I should really get it out of my head that I can only inquire about renting an apartment in eighteen-story buildings! *If I like this building, and it turns out that it's residential and has a vacancy and is affordable, who cares if it's eighteen stories or not?* I count. Besides, the idea that I could possibly find the eighteen-story on my first try is a million-to-one shot. *Ohmygosh.* To my amazement, both calculations add up to eighteen stories. A chill runs up my spine.

I am ready to run right into the building and say "I'll take it" when I think to look at my surroundings to see if it's even a street I'd want to live on. A futuristic metallic-green skyscraper on the corner says U.N. Plaza. A plaque on the building beside me reads: Mission of Kuwait. Two black Town Cars parked beside me have red, white and blue license plates that read Diplomat. *Is this some exclusively governmental street that forbids civilians?* I look up at the street sign in front of me for some indication one way or another. It reads:

NO STANDING

I do a double take, hardly able to believe my standing here is forbidden. I read the sign again:

NO STANDING
EXCEPT FOR TRUCKS
SUNDAY THROUGH SATURDAY
FROM 8 A.M. TO 6 P.M.

If this is indeed a sign meant for cars, since when does a car "stand"? Is that an east coast thing? Standing cars? Or is the sign meant for pedestrians?

Just then, a man in a dark black suit carrying a black valise walks by me and casts a scornful look that I recognize from *North by Northwest* when a "Diplomat" accused Roger Thornhill of the murder of a dignitary. He looks up and I wonder if he isn't signaling some sniper to take me out for "Standing."

I hurry further up the street toward Second Avenue where I imagine cars and pedestrians can co-exist, when I encounter the Belle Arts awning again. But wait, I should have had to cross the street to run into the awning. I look across the street. There are two Belle Arts awnings directly across from each other. I duck inside Belle Arts #2 through two sets of glass double doors and follow a man with a dog down a small flight of stairs to a tan, bald man dressed in a white shirt, black tie and trousers standing beside a wall-mounted switchboard writing in a red hardbound book backwards in what looks like hieroglyphics.

"Excuse me, is this building commercial or residential? I ask, suddenly emboldened, with no care as to how I am escorted out.

His voice is soft. "It's an apartment building," he says with brown eyes that look like they belong on a jolly Saudi baby instead of a grown Saudi man.

"Do you have any apartments available?"

"I don't know but you can speak to the rental agent. She should be back in about five minutes. The couple over there is also waiting for her. You can wait with them," he says gesturing towards a woman and a man in dark sunglasses standing beside a navy baby stroller a few feet away.

"Great. Thank you, I say, as I take my place between the couple and the double doors. "Hi," I say to them with a smile.

"We've been waiting twenty minutes," the woman says huffily, her arms crossed, checkbook in hand, apparently mistaking my proximity to the door as taking cuts. I nod in acknowledgment of their priority, and we stand here, all three of us, facing the door, watching tenants return (with grocery bags, luggage, newspapers, and dogs), waiting for the identity of the rental agent to be revealed, the couple intermittently eyeing me with suspicion as if I would snatch their baby.

Finally, a fifty-something redheaded woman in a dress and pastel green cardigan enters alone, her hair in a bun, carrying a large round jailhouse style key ring, watching her step. I look to the doorman. He nods to acknowledge "that's her."

"Do you have any two-bedrooms?" the couple frantically belts out as if at an auction.

"No," the rental agent says, still walking, thumbing through her key ring.

"One bedroom?" they ask in unison, their eyes darting contemptuously at me and then back at her.

"No," she says still moving.

"Any studios?" I venture, taking the couple's sudden catatonia as my cue.

"Yes. One," she says, looking up for the first time, "but it's $950," she adds as if that were the end of it.

"I can do $950," I announce without hesitation.

"Well why didn't you make an appointment?" she asks accusatorily.

"Because I was just walking by," I respond, half shocked yet half amused by the absurdist overtones of this entire experience, amazed to be encountering such stereotypical, unprovoked New York brusqueness so soon into my arrival. First the couple, now her. *Shouldn't the rental agent be the nice one in this scenario?*

"Excuse us but we were here first," says the woman as her husband cordons me off from the agent with the stroller.

"By all means," I say, sweeping them ahead of me.

"How large is the studio?" they inquire.

"Oh no. It's hardly big enough for one person, let alone two with a baby" she says, before turning to me again.

"Well is there a waiting list?" the woman cuts in again as her husband lets go of the stroller to move in closer to the agent and block me more.

"Excuse me you've had your turn, I'm now talking to this girl who has been waiting patiently," the rental agent says.

"Well can we just put our names down on a waiting list?" the woman asks expecting the *de riguer* answer.

"No. No. I'm not accepting any more names. The list is too long as it is," the rental agent says, turning away from them with finality, her full attention on me.

"No?" the couple asks, lowering their sunglasses, exchanging looks as if to say, doesn't she know who we are? As they turn to leave, I can almost hear their jaws drop like an elevator plummeting to the ground, caught only by the flimsy catch of a safety break.

"Rude people. I don't want them in my building anyway. Now, where were we?"

As the rental agent proceeds with the description of the prospective studio and its amenities, "...425 square feet... door opens up to a small kitchen... the bathroom is just inside the doorway to the immediate left or right... management pays for heating, you pay for electricity..." it rings eerily familiar.

"Excuse me, but did this apartment building used to be a hotel?" I ask.

"Why yes, how did – "

"Eighteen stories?" I ask, my hand quivering.

"Yes, but – "

"Ohmygosh. Is your name... Dolores?"

She takes a step back from me, her face blanching as if she's seen a ghost or rediscovered her youth. "Yes. How did you know that?"

"Oh my... I'm Eve. I spoke to you from Los Angeles a few weeks ago and you said I had to be here to speak to you about an apartment," I said, prodding her memory, my mouth parched.

"Right. Of course," she says, her own voice quivering and her face taking on a rosy, even human form. "Did you just arrive?"

"I arrived just last night. And I planned on getting here first thing this morning like you told me to when we spoke, but I unexpectedly had to switch hotels because I hadn't reserved my room in advance, and they booked up and then I couldn't find the address to this apartment. In fact I just told the taxi driver to drop me off right out there because we were stuck in traffic and I wasn't even sure where I was going. I had no idea this was the building, I just liked the outside."

"Well. Isn't that something," she exclaims, looking like Maureen O'Hara in *Miracle on 34th Street,* who despite her politicking to the contrary has just come around to believe that

Santa Claus is indeed real. "But let me tell you something," Dolores says, her grave tone worrying me, "If you had been here at 9 a.m. I wouldn't have had anything available for you. I've got 600 units – because you know I've got the building across the street too. Each 300 units. And at 9 a.m. this morning I had nothing available. *Nothing.* You heard me with that couple. I didn't have a two-bedroom, not a one-bedroom, not even a single studio, UNTIL one hour ago, 11 a.m., when a couple up and left. Skipped out on their lease. Not a word, nothing. Just took off."

"Wow, that's terrible," I say wanting to sound sympathetic.

"Well, not so terrible for you," she says, smiling.

"BY THE WAY, it's illegal what your hotel did," says Dolores as we take the elevator to the seventh floor where the only vacant apartment out of 600 units is. "Once you are in a room, they can't kick you out for another guest. Legally, you had the right to stay."

"You're kidding!" I exclaim.

"No I'm not kidding. You think I don't know the law?" she remarks defensively. "It's my job to know all the housing laws of New York City. Even if you refused to pay, they couldn't just kick you out like that. Trust me, it's very hard to kick someone out of their home in New York City. I know, I've tried."

"Wow. Well I wish I'd known that sooner. My new room doesn't even have air conditioning and it's $13 more than the last one."

"Yeah, you've got to get A/C in New York. Can't live without A/C here in the summer. And this summer's the worst. But if you can survive today, you'll be fine. Today's the worst. I just heard on 1010 Wins radio that it's 103 degrees out there with the humidity factored in."

"OH YOU'RE LUCKY," says Dolores, "a previous tenant, not this last couple, this last couple was good for nothing, just shameful, disruptive young kids. But a tenant before them built shelving here and I believe in the closet too. Yep," she says, opening the door of a walk-in closet where shelves have been built. "And most of the other studios have their radiators exposed," she says referring to wooden slats built over the radiator, hiding it, and the bookcase built out from it and extending to the wall.

It is just like the floor plan Liza faxed to me: The door of #704 opens to a small kitchen just as she described. It has black and white checkered linoleum tiles, at the end of which is an arched door space, past which is the "studio" which extends to an exterior wall of French windows – one set of the eighteen that I had counted. And there's a view of the Kuwaiti Embassy and they into mine – something the floor plan didn't show. Windows to a view just like in *Rear Window.* A perfect place for me to convalesce and from which to position my camera.

I stand in the room while Dolores points out this and that, and I feel like a top, spinning.

"It's perfect, I'll take it," I say, not needing to see anything more, if there was anything more to see.

"You know," she says, searching my eyes for her thoughts, "I always tell people that if they have any hesitation, they should pass. If they're undecided, I tell 'em it's not for you." But this? This is meant to be."

She smiles. I smile. We have participated in a *Miracle.*

As I sit in Dolores' office filling out the multi-paged application, the phone rings no less than six times with calls from prospective studio-renters. And each time, Dolores tells them, "Nope, don't have anything available. Just had a studio open up an hour ago but have a young woman seated right in front of me now, filling out paperwork." Each time she hangs up, she smiles at me, looking nothing like the woman that came down those steps an hour ago. That woman, the one who first came in the doorway, would have told Mary there were no bedrooms (let alone studios) at the Inn.

I smile too, but mine is now an attempt to mask my nerves. For with all the thought of the Miracle, I had overlooked one thing: my credit sucks. *A month ago, I couldn't get a Gap card, what makes me think I can get an apartment?* Now I remember why I felt it so important for me to get this apartment where I have the advantage of having a reference of a tenant even if it is the secretary of my estranged boyfriend and someone I've never met in person. If I can't get #704, I certainly don't have a shot elsewhere.

"Generally we don't accept tenants whose rent accounts for more than 25% of their monthly take-home salary. Net I'm talking. There are some exceptions, but we find that most tenants run into trouble if their rent accounts for more than 25%," says Dolores.

I nod.

"And what is your annual salary? asks Dolores.

"Fifty-thousand plus bonus," I lie.

"And how much is your bonus?"

"Well I'm not sure yet. I'm just starting with this company, that's why I moved here, but no less than ten thousand," I lie.

"Sixty-thousand is about right. And what kind of business is... Decade in? she asks reading off the application.

"It's an import-export firm, I say, recalling how Pavlos described his business when we had lunch at Cafe Del Rey. God forbid she asks me what Decade imports and exports. Pavlos and I didn't get that far. But his was the only New York company I could think of writing in the space where it says "Employer".

"In order to complete the application, I'll need a few things from you." She writes them on a piece of paper, 1) first and last months' rent which comes to $1900, 2) a deposit equal to the amount of one month's rent $950 for a total of $2850 in a check drawn on a local bank, I can't accept out-of-state-checks, and 3) a paycheck stub in order to confirm your annual salary," she says, unsuspecting.

"Oh, I won't have a paystub for a few more weeks because I'm paid by the month," I lie, knowing a paystub would be near impossible to fake.

"Well can you get me a letter from your employer on their letterhead confirming your employment and annual salary?"

"Sure," I say, determined to make Pavlos fulfill his agreement to write me the letter. It's the least he can do.

"Well, try to get everything to me first thing Monday, at the latest Tuesday," she says. I can't begin processing your application until all the paperwork is in. And if someone were to get their paperwork in before you, I'd have no choice but to give them priority. You understand. But I'll at least get the credit check underway which will only take a business day, so that will be completed on Monday. Then, once I have the letter, if everything checks out OK, you can move in, in two weeks, say August 15th," she says, eyeing a desk calendar.

"Two weeks?" I ask nervously. "Is there anyway to move that up, because the hotel I'm staying at is $90 a night and if I had to stay at it another two weeks that's just a lot of money for me."

"Well they have to get the apartment cleaned up. The carpet's fine, but the walls need painted."

"They don't have to paint. Really, it's not necessary. Or, I can paint," I say, thinking that my overconfidence that I'm moving in might bode well, convince her that a credit check isn't necessary.

"Well they have to do a once-over," she says, "caulking nail holes, that sort of thing. It's for your own protection so that you aren't held responsible for any damage done by the previous tenant." She looks into my eyes again and must see the desperation in the corneas. "Let me see what they can do." She dials the phone and after a brief conversation with Sammy, the Maintenance Manager, she says that they can have it ready for me by this coming Wednesday. "Is that soon enough?"

"Yes. that's great," I say, relieved.

"So if all goes well with your paperwork, and I'm sure it will, you can move in Wednesday, August 5th. Eight days from now," she says, eyeing me with congratulatory eyes. So confident.

Suspecting no hitches, certainly not financial ones. To her, this is a mere formality. As far as she's concerned, the apartment is mine.

"That's great. Thank you so much. Really," I tell her, shaking her hand, as she places her freehand on top, sandwiching mine, like clergy do.

9. CENTRAL PARK

I walk out the double doors and stand under the Belle Arts awning, noticing the sun for the first time, how it reflects off of the windows and chrome of the cars, the heat now pleasurable, the scent of a miracle still in the air. I see a cab with its light on approaching and instinctively hail it. It screeches to a stop just like in the movies and I slide in.

"Where to?" asks the taxi driver, blazing down the street that only two hours ago was at a dead stop.

"Oh... Ummm," I have once again not thought past this moment, the moment of hailing a cab.

"Where to? I need to know," he asks nervously, approaching a green light.

"Take a right," I instruct him, trying to buy me some time to decide.

"I can't," he says, turning left into the direct path of oncoming sunlight. "It only goes one way."

"Oh, right" I say, thankful he didn't follow my directions.

"Look, I need to know where I'm going," he says again. Relentless.

"O.K. then. Central Park please." I will ease my mind and the fate of the apartment by relaxing – even basking if I'm so inclined – in pastoral tranquility. I will take a well-deserved breath, and I'll start now by looking out the window at the sights.

The scenery along First Avenue is eerily reminiscent of Los Angeles. For some reason I never expected New Yorkers to look so outdoorsy and nature-loving. I came here for the antithesis after all. But everyone is tan, wearing shorts and tanks, walking dogs. And I know I should be walking too, if only to save my cash which has to last until Monday when I can get to a bank and deposit my settlement check, but I feel too encumbered to walk aimlessly given my overall aimlessness.

Speaking of money, I will redo the math just one more time before I embark on basking. The big question: can I afford $950 a month? OK, assuming five more days at the luxurious hotel at $100 per day, plus first and last months rent, plus deposit, plus payment on all my monthly bills including old and new medical bills... *should I elect to pay them...* and assuming I can get a job within three weeks (four at the very latest) which pays no less than $45K per year... then YES, I CAN afford the apartment but I'll have to wait six months to buy a bed and can't even think about buying new clothes for job interviewing. I put away my makeshift abacus and look out the window just in time to see a woman scooping dog-poop in front of Tiffany's, which is where Capote wrote in *Breakfast at Tiffany's*, "nothing bad can happen." I think of Holly GoLightly, and how comparatively Holly GoHeavily I am.

"Which entrance do you want?" the taxi driver asks.

"Oh. I hadn't realized there was more than one. Umm… the main one."

"57th and Columbus?" he asks.

"Um, sure," I say, not having the faintest idea if that is the preferred entrance but confident the taxi driver knows, given the last one delivered me so well. Besides, I'm fairly sure it doesn't really matter which entrance. *Does it?*
"Is this OK? Columbus Circle?" the driver asks.

"But I wanted Central Park," I say, exasperated as to how he confused Columbus Circle with Central Park.

"This is," he says.

"Oh. Sorry. Thanks," I say, looking out the window and spotting the equipage, bicyclists, and pedestrians littering the corner. I suppose that even if I am at the wrong place, what harm could come among horses, bicyclists, and pedestrians save for occasional green briquettes of poop underfoot?

I begin taking pictures when I hear instrumental music coming from over the grassy knoll. I trudge up the hill and discover two men in loose Bermuda shorts, sweaty polo shirts, and knee-high socks, playing instruments – an accordion and a clarinet. They read sheet music set atop a tipsy aluminum easel. They are joyous. Their smiles are broad and not American. Russian, I think. I snap a few pictures as people cross into my line of vision and then duck for my camera. Such respect for photographers!

"Are you a professional photographer?" asks a sixty-something man dressed in a pink polo and khaki shorts, standing beside a fifty-something woman in a floral summer dress, each straddling a bike.

"Well, amateur" I answer. "Black and whites mainly, although I'm doing color right now."

"Would you mind taking a picture of us? We're on our first date," he says, smiling broadly.

"Sure," I say as they dismount their old-fashioned bikes and lean them against a hedge. I snap a photo, and then they learn it's my first day in New York and invite me to have lemonade with them.

—⁓

"YOU DON'T wear fur, do you?" Jeanne asks me as we take our seats at a table by a lake.

"Oh leave the girl alone," says Ray, handing me pink lemonade.

"Thanks so much," I tell him.

"Jeanne is a documentary filmmaker. She just did a piece for PETA," says Ray.

"It's in post-production now," she says. "You've heard of PETA?"

"Sure. Protection of animals...?

"People for the Ethical Treatment of Animals," she corrects me.

"In fact, a woman friend I used to work with just gave me a full-length fox coyote fur because she didn't want to wear it anymore, because she joined PETA," I tell her. "But I don't plan on wearing it."

"Keep it. You'll want it for the winters here," says Ray, smiling as Jeanne's face sours.

"So what brings you to New York?" asks Jeanne.

Again the question. I really should come up with a new version. Until then, I stick with the same plot. "A bad day. Lost job in morning, got hit by a drunk driver that night, then was told by my sister/roommate to find a place in two weeks...so I thought, "where do you move without a car?" New York!"

"That's terrible," says Jeanne, her brows forming concern. "Were you hurt?"

"I broke my wedding ring finger," I say.

"You should hit Ray up for a job," Jeanne says to me as Ray dumps our garbage. "He's very wealthy. He has his own advertising agency." When Ray returns, she tells him, "You should give her a job at your agency."

"What is your background?" he asks.

"Well, I'm an aspiring actor," I say.

"You know how many actors actually make more than $10K a year?" he asks us. "One percent."

"Anyway, that's my dream, but my paying job since college has been as an assistant to celebrities, managing their homes."

"Which celebrities?" he asks.

I mention the Mr. and Mrs. Multi-Millionaire of Bel Air and Mr. and Mrs. Director of Brentwood.

"And they couldn't help you out with the acting career?" he asks.

I smile feebly.

"What you should do is set up your own company, a personnel agency, placing people in those types of positions. You just call yourself an expert in that field, which is what everyone does anyway even if they aren't. But you do have the background. And you'll make a lot of money," Ray says emphatically, case dismissed.

"But that's not my passion," I say defensively, exasperated by an ambition that no one historically seems to relate to.

"So, you just do the personnel agency long enough and then train others and they'll make the money for you while you're acting or doing whatever it is you want to do," he says.

"I appreciate the advice, but I'm not the least interested in doing personnel, and I'm not the least motivated by money."

"Then what are you doing in New York?" he says, smiling gummily.

I shrug. "Does anyone have the time?" I ask, wanting to quickly return to the hotel to find out if Pavlos called me back. My not having a cell phone yet is making everything so much more complicated, annoying, and surreal.

"Oh, it's almost Five, I really should go home and shower if we're going to meet up for the movie later," says Jeanne, queuing us all to get up from the table. "So I'll see you tonight at 7 p.m.," Jeanne says to Ray, her foot poised on the bike pedal, ready to go. "Pleasure to meet you," she says to me. "And you must go see Shakespeare in the Park – *The Two Gentlemen of Verona* is playing now," she says with one final smile to Ray before she pedals away.

So that's where the gentlemen are! "Well, it was nice meeting you Ray," I say, attempting to depart.

"Where are you headed?" he asks.

"Oh I don't know, going to take more photos," I say.

"Well I'll just walk with you." he says.

I don't argue. It's hard to know when it's OK to break free from a man who's bought you lemonade and who may be in a position to employ you even though you really want to be left alone to daydream.

"So you're meeting up with Jeanne later?" I ask, a minute into the walk.

"Yeah. I don't like her," he says in a gruff alter ego.

"Why not?" I ask, shocked by his admission not a minute after agreeing to reunite with her later. And it was his idea that I take the picture of them!

"She's not attractive," he says.

"Oh I think she is."

"Besides, she's for PETA."

"PETA's a good thing," I say.

"Not the way she does it. She carries it too far. Plus she's a vegetarian. She won't eat meat or ice cream. And, she's fat. Did you see her arms flapping in the wind? I want a woman in shape," he says.

"Gosh, I don't think she's fat at all," I say, hardly believing that this man who himself has a stomach the size of two watermelons, a receding hairline, and jowls that ripple when he talks. He should consider himself lucky to have a date with a woman as attractive as she is. "You know you don't have to walk me through the park," I tell Ray, "I mean you've got your bike, please go on ahead. I don't want you to have to walk your bike."

"No, no I don't mind. I'm enjoying your company," he says, as if the choice to walk with me is entirely up to him. So I continued walking with him mainly because I had no excuse available. He already knew I had no place else to be, no one else to meet. And perhaps he could help me with a job as Jeanne had suggested. We take a windy path and come upon a man manipulating the strings of a flute-playing marionette that dances on top of tan and patched vintage leather-bound suitcase. Further down, is a brunette woman playing the violin. "A virtuoso," says Ray, pulling me over to listen, the pressure of his grip uncomfortable.

As we listen to her play, her hand in the feverish motion of someone sawing their own neck, I wonder why I can't just say goodbye to Ray. *Haven't I been tormented enough in the past twenty-four hours?* Finally she finishes. We applaud. I'm ready to say goodbye to both of them but Ray inquires about her schooling and other venues she performs in, of which he appears well versed. As she answers him, I begin to see she's as weary of his company as I am.

We have that same look, that false naiveté, just like Melanie had in *Birds* before the first bird attacked her and drew blood. I begin to feel as sorry for her as myself, both of us unwittingly detained by this man. Then again, it's every woman for herself. I make my move. I begin to take pictures of increasingly distant scenery: a couple staring up at a sign that says, "Look What's Going On," an abandoned TV set (with a broken screen) resting in the shade of a tree, a squirrel on a tree limb, the Essex House in the background of tree vines, and shadows of trees cast upon the grass. I'm hoping my artistic preoccupation will lead Ray and me to incompatible paces and eventual separation. But when Ray notices me slipping away, he abandons the virtuoso and catches up to me.

And he keeps talking. About what I'm not sure. I am zoning off, catching only portions of Central Park and New York history – something about the Dutch and the Indians, and how pigs and dogs used to roam the streets freely.

"So where are you staying?" Ray asks me.

"In a hotel in Times Square, just until I can move into an apartment on Wednesday."

"You know you're welcome to stay with me until you move into your place. I own an eight-story brownstone in Chelsea, and I live on the first two floors and rent out the rest. You'd have your own room, run of the first floor."

"That's really nice of you. Really. But I'm fine in a hotel," I tell him.

"Well here's my card, if you need a place to stay until you get the apartment, just give me a call. It wouldn't be free of course. You'd have to paint the deck. No free rides," he says with a gummy smile.

I RETURN to the hotel feeling faint at the realization that I have only had lemonade all day long, or perhaps feeling faint that I can only spare about $7 for dinner tonight so that I can eat tomorrow. Or perhaps I'm feeling faint because I have belatedly realized that if Pavlos called, there's no way to know. Pavlos has the number to the Ambassador Hotel and I am now at the Manhattan Hotel.

I call the Ambassador Hotel and ask if there are any messages from Pavlos.

"No messages," said the voice of the woman who kicked me out.

I hang up depressed and attempt to console myself with the possibility that Pavlos still might have called me. I mean, just because the Ambassador concierge has no messages for me, doesn't mean he didn't call. It just means that The Ambassador West Hotel formerly known as my hotel doesn't take messages for guests they no longer house. Of course it could also mean Pavlos didn't call, but the point is there's no way to know, and no way to hear from him unless I call him again. Deep breath. I dial. And get voicemail!! I leave my new hotel phone number, and fall asleep, expecting a phone call from Pavlos to awaken me.

10· COLOSSUS

I wake up hot and sweaty. I look at the clock. It's 9:01 p.m. and Pavlos hasn't called, which means it's been almost an entire day since I first spoke to him, on my first day in New York, and he blatantly lied about calling me back. I hate him. And what's worse I never saw this coming. I never prepared myself for this. I never prepared for the possibility that I would move to New York and he would not speak to me. *Who would be prepared for someone doing that?*

Maybe he doesn't have any idea how dire my emotional state and predicament is. I mean if he did, he would call. *Wouldn't he?* Maybe he's busy and has no idea I'm counting the seconds until he calls. And maybe I'm being a bit overly dire here, counting the seconds. Maybe I should be counting minutes. *How could I have been so wrong? Am I wrong? I mean what kind of person could just walk away?*

Wait! The phone's red light is lit! I guess the phone rang but I didn't hear it. It must be Pavlos. I call the lobby.

"Hi, it's Eve Foster in Room 463. My red light is on my phone. Is there a message for me?"

"Oh yes," says a woman's voice. "We want to know if you'll be reserving the room another night."

"Um...yes....I guess I will be," I answer. "No other messages?"

"No. Are you expecting one?"

"Kind of. Yes. Thanks anyway," I answer and hang up and heave over onto the bed, feeling kicked in the gut and cry myself to dehydration. I take out some paper and start to write. I'm going to write Pavlos a letter. Maybe after I get it all down on paper, I won't even feel the need to give it to him.

⌒〜⌒)

"394 East 38th Street," I instruct the taxi driver. I'm heading to Pavlos' apartment now. I simply must have closure. I want to know that the person I cared about is not some inhuman, thoughtless person who could end things by disappearing. It simply alters my whole way of thinking to allow for the possibility that someone I care about could treat me like this. I've been making myself crazy trying to figure out his motivation. *For if actions speak louder than words, what does inaction speak? His inaction?* I have been waiting around for him to make the move to provide closure. I've simply got to assume a more active role in my own life! Since he won't come to me, I'll go to him. If he isn't brave enough to make it official - I'm brave enough. The idea that he thinks he's in control. *Ha!* Wait till he sees me on his doorstop. I wonder if the tone of my letter to him is too... *strong?*

What in the world? I am sure the driver has mistaken my destination.

"Are you sure this is 394 E. 38th Street?" I ask, torn between paying the $7 or backing out.

"Yes," he says, pulling forward at the behest of the curbside, red-uniformed valet so that a black stretch limo can pull in behind us.

Who have I been dating? Maybe Pavlos *has* been busy importing and exporting.

You'd think I would have guessed as much, what with the name "The Colossus." The "apartment building" is a sable-colored Jetson-era skyscraper and everything in its dominion is key lit: the circular driveway and overhead rotunda, the waterfall in the epicenter, the four valets, the three revolving doors, and the surrounding garden. Just as I consider leaving, fearing Pavlos might be in the limo behind us, a white-gloved hand of the valet reaches into the car. As I take it, I feel like Cinderella right before her carriage turned into a pumpkin, her clothes turned to tatters, her prince into a frog.

"GOOD EVENING, can I help you?" asks the man at the Colossus concierge. He stands behind a limestone countertop running about thirty feet long.

"Hi. Yes. I'd like to leave this for Pavlos Polychronopolis," I say, handing him my letter. "Oh. Do you have an envelope?"

As he searches for an envelope, I feel nervous about being within such proximity of Pavlos without an invitation. I picture his car fetching him just this morning. It must have idled in that very circular, the red-coated doorman must have held the door for him.

"Here you are," says the desk clerk, sliding an envelope towards me. I seal the envelope, return it to the desk clerk and leave.

Hmmm. Dropping off the letter was supposed to make everything better, but I feel more depressed than when I entered. Pavlos resides like a King while I walk the city streets like a pauper, unemployed, alone and homeless.

A block away from The Colossus, I look up at Pavlos' home. *Was there ever an indication he was this wealthy?* Well, there was the time when he almost bought a Porsche on his American Express card at the Marina Del Rey lot but other than that, no.

I continue walking up Second Avenue – Pavlos' neighborhood – past the Lucky Convenience store, recalling the times Pavlos told me on the phone how he'd just ran out to pick up a paper or coffee or food, and how I tried to picture it. And now I was here seeing these places for myself, like a ghost casing tombstones.

As cars whiz pass, I half wonder if the passengers can see me. *If I don't exist in the minds of others, i.e. Pavlos, do I exist at all? If no one is aware of my existence here, do I exist at all?* I eye the people in the cars as they pass. They have places to go. They've left one place and are heading to another. They have point A and B. They have people to see. I'm just wandering. The city doesn't stop for wanderers.

In fact, I'm beginning to feel as if I'm not so much wandering as I am trespassing, not just a street now, but the entire city. I feel as if I have no business being in a city that doesn't want me, as if Pavlos were the Landlord of Manhattan, the Gatekeeper, the man at the red velvet rope who decides who gets in and who doesn't, waiting for the pronouncement that I am not on The List, waiting for the boot. Strange to think someone, anyone, would want me gone so badly. The fact is that I have no desire to stay where I'm not wanted. I would voluntarily exit any location where someone had prior rights. I would have left Manhattan to the Native Indians.

I taxi back to the hotel feeling defeated. But, with each passing avenue, particularly just after Fifth in the shadow of the Empire State Building, something happens in the taxi, within me, as conspicuous as the city lights. I am emboldened. So much so, that by the time we reach the hotel, whatever defeat I felt on Second Avenue has turned into fierce resolve on Ninth Avenue. Once in my room, I reach for my purse, take out Ray's business card and dial the number. It is time to take matters into my own hands. "Hello?" he answers.

"Ray?" I ask.

"Who's this?"

"It's Eve. Sorry did I wake you?"

"What time is it?"

"10 p.m.."

"Well, when do you sleep?" he asks, clearly irritated.

"Well I'm a night owl actually. But I'm terribly sorry for waking you. Do you want me to call back tomorrow?"

"Well I'm up now, what do you want?"

"Well, I wanted to know if it was still O.K for me to take you up on your offer and stay at your place for a few days?"

"Until when?"

"Well, I get the apartment this Wednesday,"

"Fine. You coming over now?" he grumbles.

"No. I thought tomorrow."

"What time?"

"Well I have to check out probably by 11 a.m., so 11:30 or so if that's OK?"

"Fine," he grumbles.

"O.K. Thanks so much Ray, I really appreciate it."

"Bye," he says and hangs up.

I hang up the phone more depressed. Ray's tone wasn't very nice at all. Maybe he's just tired.

11. CHELSEA BROWNSTONE

"You're late" are Ray's first words to me on the phone. "Yes, I'm on my way out the door now. Sorry," I say from my perch atop the windowsill of the Manhattan Hotel.

"First you said you'd be here at 11 a.m., which turned into noon and now it's almost 1 p.m." he says furiously.

I can't believe it. Here I am, in my condition, prepping once again to alter my existence for the unknown for the third time in less than twenty-four hours, getting harangued by a man I've known for less time. I haven't even moved in and he's already lording his landlord position over me. I really am not in the mood. I woke up late, thankfully got the hotel to agree to a late checkout at no extra charge, and I've diligently notified Ray of my two previous time changes.

"I'm very sorry Ray," I tell him in a calm, commanding tone. "I overslept and had an unexpected phone call (a lie). I didn't realize you were waiting on me or that I was holding you up. If you'd rather I not come..." *(que sera sera)*

"No, I just don't like lateness. When will you be here?" he asks.

"I'm leaving in ten minutes" I tell him. "So depending on how long it takes me to get a cab, I will be there as soon thereafter."

We hang up and I kvetch, kvetch, and kvetch. *Ehhhhhh!!!!!!!!!!!* I have such an urge to call him back and tell him that I won't be coming after all. But financial self-preservation dictates desperate measures. Besides, I actually welcome the opportunity for someone to pick a fight with me. Dredging up the hostility won't be difficult. I am looking for any excuse to vent. In fact, if it weren't for this antagonism, I wouldn't feel anything at all.

THE BROWNSTONE on West 20th Street, with its brick red facade and white trim looks innocent enough. Ray is outside hosing an empty garden when my taxi pulls up. He is wearing Bermuda shorts and sandals. His toenails are decayed. Hadn't noticed that before. Noticed the brown gums but missed the rotten toenails. He leads me into the house empty-handed as I manage four pieces of luggage and two shoulder bags, first through an office and then into a hallway past a kitchen where a large black woman in a fuchsia headdress "Hasana," his maid from Cote D'Ivoire, is slicing kiwi and strawberries into a bowl with an oversized butcher knife. He asks her the whereabouts of his slippers. She doesn't know and she's not looking for them. They squabble – him antagonistically, her indifferently.

"My room" is past the kitchen, and notably, the room furthest from the front door.

"Put your things down and follow me," says Ray.

I set my suitcases and bags down and follow Ray through a screen door that opens from my room to an enclosed deck.

"I had a Chilean guy who was supposed to paint this deck, but he just smoked cigarettes. Lazy son of a bitch," Look at that" he says, picking up an empty pack of Kool cigarettes and half-filled Corona bottle from a rusted iron table. "A paint tin and a paintbrush are already here," he says, pointing to it.

I am surprised Ray means business about my painting the patio deck. I hadn't exactly expected him to follow through on the deal. I expected it was just a pretense, his way of inducing me to stay by posing it as a trade/business arrangement so it, otherwise, wouldn't appear so intimate. It actually brings me some relief that he didn't extend his invitation under false pretenses. But then again, I have enough things to do without painting a deck.

He walks me through the rest of the apartment showing me his upstairs den and bedroom both of which are covered red wall to red wall with paintings and drawings – of erotic nudes, exposed vaginas. *Fine Art.* I wonder if there might be a Picasso among them, not readily aware of any less-distinguished vaginas, *err,* fine art, to own.

Ray wants to go on a bike ride which sounds like a repeat performance of the Park. I just want to relax and think in peace alone.

"But I don't have a bike," I say, thinking I would be spared.

"That's O.K. I've got an extra one," he says.

WE HAVE BIKED the lower half of Manhattan, from Chelsea to the East River down to the Ferry and now back to the lower west side. Resting on a sidewalk curb at the waterfront, our bikes parked beside us, Ray tells me the history of Battery Park, how it used to be a landfill, that downtown used to be part of a vast forest, a lush hunting ground for the Native Americans, inhabited by beavers and other animals, and then he asks if I am a virgin.

"Excuse me?"

"Are you a virgin. Have you had sex?" Ray asks.

"Thanks. I know what a virgin is."

"Well?"

I look away, not knowing how to answer or whether I should answer, trying to determine the ramifications of answering and not answering.

"It's a simple question. Or are you modest?"

"No, I'm not modest."

"Don't tell me you've never been asked? It isn't a come-on. It's a matter of course – adults talking." Ray persists.

I watch two gay men in tight spandex shorts rollerblading in front of me, a woman and a small boy passing by on rollerblades as she steadies her wobbly self by resting her hand on the boy's shoulder.

"No. I'm not a virgin." I answer.

"When did you lose your virginity?"

I stare ahead blankly.

"Did you like it? Because most women don't like it the first time."

"It was *fine*," I tell him flatly, wondering whether I'll take a kitchen knife into bed with me or set the phone on speed dial to 911. Or both.

Ray continues to ask me a few more raunchy personal questions and then chastises me as an immature, prissy girl because I beg off responding.

"Any woman of some sophistication or worldliness wouldn't have any trouble answering such questions," he says. "I think you'd better grow up a little if you plan on staying in New York," he says. This isn't Oregon," he says.

"No it isn't," I agree, prideful. I hardly need more sophistication to know that he can't stand that I'm not buying into his verbal pressure and intimidation. I know he has to keep the pressure on me to answer lest he feel ridiculous for having asked a question not suitable for our one-and-a-half-day relationship, not suitable for any relationship I would ever have with him. I secretly wonder if he isn't a pedophile.

"I'm a Rothschild" he announces, an interesting (non?)sequeter from pedophilia, "but don't tell anyone. I mean it. I don't need people knowing," he says in an irascible, threatening tone.

He must think his self-professed elite heritage will redeem him from my censure and unuttered speculation that he is simply a dirty old man. He moves on from discussing sex and into Rothschild lore, telling me how the ancestral connection came to be. "My mother's father's sister's husband... *blah blah*." He tells me the historical banking prowess of his Rothschild heritage, as if knowing the history proves his blood ties. It's public access information. I could get it on Google. I don't know whether I believe him or not, and I really don't care. I'm simply grateful that it's an improvement over the prior conversation.

"In fact, an uncle of mine, a few generations back, was disinherited, found to be into S&M," he says. "You know what S&M stands for don't you?"

"Yes," I answer.

"What?"

"Why don't you tell me," I say, calling his bluff, realizing how difficult it is to look at him. He started out unattractive and he's getting harder and harder to look at. Sunspots, jowling chin and cheeks, large teeth secured by brown trimmed gums, and a hairline and hair color reminiscent of George Washington. Just a few more days and I can move into the apartment if my credit clears. If I don't get the apartment I will go back to a hotel – any hotel.

BY THE TIME Ray and I returned to "Home Sweet Home" with leftover borscht (he insisted on stopping at his local Borscht haunt where he paraded me in front of old geezers and the proprietor) and the late edition of the Sunday *New York Times*, darkness arrived.

After circling six *Help Wanted* ads, the time had come to call Pavlos. I mean I presume that by now he has read my letter, the crux of which simply expresses my desire to clear the air, confirm once and for all if we can or can't reconcile if we've in fact been unreconciled as it seems. I am perhaps more anxious to hear his reaction when I tell him my whereabouts, that "I am at the home of a man I met in Central Park," which should show him how fearless and independent I am, what happens when I am left to my own devices, and convey how wrongly he suspected I'd be lost without him. (There's no way for him to know Ray is a pedophile.)

I sit on the edge of the bed facing the mirror opposite me, already giggling in anticipation of his reaction, yet preparing myself for either scenario: A) that Pavlos is going to come and save me from the Rothschild or B) continue his heartlessness.

I dial. Phone rings. I breathe. "Hi, is Pavlos there?"

"No, he's not. Who's this?" asks his mother.

"Eve. Do you know when he's due back?" I ask.

"No I don't. He's in Los Angeles," she says.

"Los Angeles?" I ask incredulously. "But I just spoke to him yesterday morning."

"He left yesterday afternoon," she says as my mind flashes back to my conversation with him. *My car is waiting for me. Can I call you later?* It was his car to take him to the airport! I want to tell Pavlos' mother exactly how dishonorable and indecent her thirty-eight-year-old son is but she would hardly find fault in her grown Greek.

"Do you know when he'll be back?" I ask evenly, unable to swallow.

"Just a moment," she says. I hear her speaking Greek and a male voice replying in Greek. "A few days. A week. I don't know. Any message?"

"Yes, would you please tell him Eve called. And could you tell him it's rather time-sensitive?" I ask her gently, to secure her compliance.

"Does he have your number?" she asks.

I give her my new phone number, with a warning to Pavlos to not call after 10 p.m. and we hang up. I stare at the phone as if it were a crystal ball. In it I picture Pavlos' mother hanging up her phone, returning to her leisurely tasks: fixing dinner, floating around Pavlos' house without a care in the world, maybe stopping for a magical view at the curved windowed wall to see the twinkle of the city, without any lingering consideration of the message she has just taken or the dire circumstances of the person who's left it.

I turn my attention towards the bed, suddenly concerned about the cleanliness of the sheets, concerned about undressing without a deadbolted door, concerned about sleeping under the same roof of a stranger. Just then the phone rings twice and stops mid-ring on the third – *abruptly*. I brace myself for the possibility that I may have to run for my life should Ray come into my room bearing pliers with which he's just severed the phone cord. The only way out would be out the door leading to the deck. I wonder if I can scale those walls. They're fortress-sized.

Thud, Thud.

I jump out of my skin and my head swells from the anxiety from the two loud knocks on my door, which attest to Ray's proximity.

"Eve!! Phone for you!" says Ray, perturbed.

Oh geez. It's Pavlos! A wave of relief overcomes me.

"And tell whoever's calling not to call so late," Ray yells.

I look at the clock. It's 10 p.m. His bedtime in the City that Never Sleeps.

I pick up the phone nervously. "Hello?" I ask, anticipating the long-awaited sound of Pavlos' voice, our truce about to start.

"Hiiiiiiiiiii sissy," says Olive, in her trademark husky man's voice. (I forgot I placed a call to her.) After the initial disappointment that it's not Pavlos subsides, I feel some relief that Ray probably thinks a man has just called – a vicious, powerful man from the lower east side for all he knows.

The last time I saw Olive was just two days ago, the morning of my departure. I'd overslept (Olive's fault – I had packed my alarm clock and she was supposed to wake me up). Consequently, we raced to LAX to catch my SunJet. Olive parked in a no-parking zone and we fell into a dismally long line with only a few minutes before the plane was to take off. Olive was sure we were in the wrong line. I was content to take my chances, but Olive just had to find out. She asked some uniformed personnel and returned with the verdict. "Wrong line. I told you," Olive said, rolling her eyes. "Give me your luggage. We have to run. It's clear on the other side." So then we ran through a tunnel to the correct terminal that looked like it was providing greyhound service. Olive cried. She would miss me, worry about me. I didn't cry. Could hardly give a convincing hug. I was too preoccupied with the arrival to give much thought to the departure.

"So who was that who answered the phone?" Olive asks.

"Ray," I answer.

"Who's Ray?" she asks, intrigued.

"Oh, a man I met in Central Park," I tell her in the same way I'd planned to tell Pavlos – dry, aloof, amused, evoking romance. I sit on the edge of the bed facing a mirror, cringing merrily as I await her alarmist response.

"What?!" she asks, incredulous, just as I predicted. But then she laughs instead of worries, and I realize she's actually bought into my charade and thinks Ray is some ravishing paramour I've caught the eye of instead of the local pedophile that he is.

"He says he's a Rothschild," I tell her, escalating the charade to build her up for a bigger fall, and me a bigger comedic payoff.

"Ohhh..K," she says, dragging up a big breath of air which she often does, with dramatic flair, what with her clinically diagnosed Mitral Valve Prolapse which she characterizes as a death sentence. (It's a slight heart murmur.)

As I tell her the events leading up to my demise in Chelsea, I am amazed she doesn't rail into me for my idiocy for accepting the invitation to live with a stranger, and wonder if the miles separating us aren't already working to my advantage, or in this case, disadvantage?

"But the real reason I called is that I have good news. I found an apartment. I call it my Miracle on 44th Street," I tell her.

"That's great," she says, her exhilaration leveling.

I explain my lucky twist of fate to have exited a cab exactly in front of Belle Arts, but she doesn't quite get the Miracle aspect. She does, however, sound relieved. But I soon discover it's not relief she feels for me. It's relief she feels for herself, of her own guilt for having contributed to my *coup de grace*, my homelessness that put me on a one-way ticket to NYC in the first place.

"Nathan won't let me stay with him," she interrupts.

I can hardly believe Nathan - my favorite of all her boyfriends - a guy who grows his own herbs and who hide chocolate eggs for Easter, has refused to let her stay with him, has pulled a Pavlos.

"Why? Did he say you could stay?" I ask, knowing my sister's propensity for assuming, yet on the other hand, amazed at how identical our situations are.

"Well I asked him if I could stay with him for a few weeks and he said no. My feelings are so hurt," she says.

I avoid pointing out the obvious: that Nathan said "no". (Olive thought he'd change his mind.) So I consoled Olive the best I could in spite of the fact that I thought it was her just due, her karma coming 'round.

"So who are you going to stay with?" I ask. The question of the day.

"Jennie. Do you know Jennie? She said I could stay with her as long as I wanted," she said, not sounding the least consoled.

"Well then what are you worried about? At least you have a place to stay!" I exclaim, perturbed she has the nerve to not know how relatively easy she has it, and has the nerve to express self-pity to me of all people, of all times.

"I know. I'm just really hurt by Nathan. Anyway, sissy! I can't believe you're in New York," she says excitedly. (I can already hear her planning her vacations here.) "So are you going to be at this number tomorrow?" she asks.

"For a few days until I can move into the apartment, but you can't call this late or Ray will hacksaw my head."

She laughs. And then I laugh. And then we can't stop laughing. The image of my head being hacksawed hard to dispel.

"Yeah, it was funny," says Olive, forcing her laughter into words, "because I just got this number on my cell phone and didn't know where I was calling you at. When are you getting a new cell phone?"

"When I have money – *Ehh!!! OHmyGod, ohmyGod, ohmyFRIGGINGawd,*" I scream, jumping onto the bed like a jumping bean.

"What? What?" she asks, demanding a response.

"Oh, God. I squeal.

"What?!!!!!!!" Eve!

"The biggest.... *FUCKINGGGG* rat I've ever seen. The size of a watermelon. With legs. It just ran past my bed out the door onto the deck I'm supposed to paint for my keep. And the door's still open."

"So close it," she implores.

"I don't want to touch the floor! O.K.... there ... *ohhhh.....* I did it, I did it, *ehhhh,* " I squealed, squirreling back from the floor to the bed, like I'd walked on molten rocks.

"God, you're going to give me a heart attack, she says, inhaling deeply. "Oh Sissy, I miss you already."

"Argh. Don't call me Sissy. I hate that. It's like we're in some Western... like we're from some hillbilly house on the prairie."

"Uh... hello? We are," she says.

"Oh yeah." We laugh.

We hang up and I remember the rat. *Ray.* I wonder why he didn't come running to help me when he heard me screaming. After all, it is past 10:30 p.m.! Because he was probably listening in on my phone call. *Yuk.*

Time for bed.

Gawd, I still have to turn the desk lamp off before I can go to bed and this will require me to walk on the floor in my bare feet. *Maybe I can straddle the floor to turn off the light?* For even though I've closed the door leading to the deck, I'm not really sure that the rat's on the outside of it. For all I know I've locked him into the room with me. I stand up on the edge of the bed, and stretch my right leg to the dresser, and aside from slight disorientation by my reflection in the mirror I manage to reach down and turn off the lamp. The unfortunate thing is that I didn't foresee that doing so would leave me straddling three feet off the floor in complete and utter Chelsea darkness.

Now, how do I get a good push off the dresser without rattling it so much the lamp falls, or the mirror breaks?

Gawd it's dark in here.

O.K. Here goes. I kick off the dresser but can't get my body weight to shift towards the bed. After a few gentle but futile attempts, I shove-off aggressively and make it to the bed. But then there's the sound of a soft crash. A crash I plan to ignore until morning. I pull up my sheets (too hot for anything else). And then, I hear a busy signal. The crash was the phone getting knocked off the receiver. I can't believe it. After all of that effort, I not only have to walk the floor with my bare feet, I have to do it in the dark. I get up off the bed, stomp my feet as if it will scare away any rat in proximity, and hang up the phone. Fortunately nothing touches my feet and I return to the bed, pull up the sheets and lie on my back (even though I sleep on my stomach), and wait a good half hour until I think it's safe to fall asleep. And then I wait another half hour just in case. And then an hour later, I flip on my stomach (my preferred position for sleeping) deciding that if it's my time to go via Rat/rat suffocation, lying on my back won't save me. In fact it might even be better to sleep on my stomach and not see the unpreventable coming.

12. CHELSEA MORNING

I have awakened to yellow sun coming through the patio door blinds, and a big "Uh-oh" in the pit of my stomach - the spot where fearlessness was the day before. Suddenly the strangeness of everything - the bed, the dresser, the unlockable door, the long path to the front door past his erotic art, and the biggest *fuuukking* rat I'd ever seen - worried me. And now I have to take a shower, far too intimate a task in a house I'm sharing with a man I've only known a day.

The thought, however, of the other tenants on the other floors comforts me. They all know Ray, rent from him. Ray can't be worth fearing if he is known by so many. (As if visibility or familiarity ever deterred a madman.) I am grasping here. But really, the other tenants would certainly hear my screams, wouldn't they? Then again, not a sole came running when I screamed last night. Sheer irritation at these menacing, paralyzing thoughts force me to reason; the sooner I get up, the sooner I get out. I throw open the sheet, and after a brief hesitation (concern for what lurks below) swing my legs over the side of the bed and press my feet to the floor, mouthing "courage" as if I were Jeanne D'Arc getting up to save France.

I open the bedroom door to find Ray in the hallway dressed in shorts and sandals and an armpit-drenched sorbet pink polo, putting soft food down for the dog (Chuck or Chester?). *What possibly could Ray have done this morning to exert himself so that he is sweating so? (Hacksawed anyone lately, hmmm?)* Seeing the front door open to the sunny outdoors beyond Ray is a reassuring sight. If Ray really wanted to do me harm, he wouldn't leave the door open for passersby to see, nor lead me to believe I could come and go at will. *Or would he?* Just to give me a false sense of security?

I head upstairs to take a shower in the master bathroom just off the master bedroom just off the masterpiece vaginas on the wall. (Ray said the floor-level bathroom is Hasana's and not for my use.)

"Make sure you leave the door open a crack for ventilation," Ray yells from the bottom of the stairs.

"O.K.," I answer, feeling suddenly that cleanliness is overrated.

Now naked and inside the shower behind a clear plastic curtain, I scrub my head and assorted appendages quickly, all the while picturing the reenactment of Hitchcock's *Psycho* montage. How does it go? Water splashing in face, curtain pulled open, and knife coming in at a 110-degree angle… I hurry as if the sooner I can turn off the showerhead, the sooner I can escape puncture, and the sooner this whole *mise en scène* will end. When the last soap suds are out of my hair, I turn off the water, step outside the shower, and wrap myself with a white towel, picturing each frame as my last. But, I am degrees more relieved to be clothed with a towel (as if it provides any more of a barrier to a knife-wielding Chelsea dweller!) I wipe away the steam off of the mirror, prepared to see Ray's face in the reflection and my towel turn into the Japanese flag. *Whew.* He's not there. But that only means that he could be waiting outside the door with the knife. I close the door to dress, and then open the door to exit.

"I thought I told you to keep the door open," Ray says, blocking my exit.

"I did while I was showering. I just closed it now for a minute."

I return to the bedroom to figure out my plan for the day, which ends up looking like a scavenger hunt to collect items to give to Dolores in order to get the apartment.

1) Open a bank account
2) Get "employment" letter from Pavlos'
3) Deliver letter and checks to Dolores at Belle Arts Properties
4) Buy a cell phone
5) Drop off my headshot and resumé to Juliet Taylor, Woody Allen's longtime casting director
6) Sign up with the four personnel agencies that listed jobs in the Sunday *New York Times* that I'm interested in.

Seems like a reasonable plan in a reasonable time frame. *If I make it out of the house alive...*

13. FIFTH AVENUE

I sit under a New Accounts sign facing a window of streets that look out onto Fifth Avenue, thinking how cool it will be to have "Fifth Avenue" printed on my checks. I present my cashier's check, and photo I.D. to Jackie, the New Accounts representative at Citibank. At last, I will have access to my money.

"I'll need New York I.D," says Jackie.

"I just moved here. I don't have any."

"I'm sorry but we can't open an account for you until you are a resident of the state," she says.

"But I'm in the process of getting an apartment on East 44th Street as we speak."

"Well, when you get the apartment, come back with the lease and we'll be happy to open an account," she says, starting to remove the paperwork from the desk.

"But I can't get the apartment until I can pay the landlord with a check drawn on a local bank," I tell her, as my hand presses down on the paperwork, "which I can't do unless you can open an account for me."

"Sorry" she shrugs. "That's our policy. It's the way every bank works." She starts to pull the paperwork again.

"No they don't," I say, leaning in further to immobilize the paperwork. "My mother is a bank executive," I tell her, "and I was a drive-through teller one summer."

She shrugs.

"Surely there's a way to make an exception? I can give you every other source of identification. My social security card, my birth certificate…" I mean, the federal government requires less to accept my money.

"We need a photo I.D."

"What could possibly be the risk with accepting a cashier's check with out-of-state photo I.D.?"

"People give fake I.D. all the time along with rubber checks and then we have no recourse if they don't live here."

"This is a cashier's check from a well-known national bank. It'd be very easy to verify. You could call them."

"I'm very sorry," she says.

"What's the point of a cashier's check then?"

She gestures for her manger to intervene. "Hello, I'm Mr. Luger, the Manager, what seems to be the trouble?"

I tell him what Jackie did, adding that I have had a credit card with their establishment for six years.

"Well have you got your picture on the back of it?" he asks.

"No…but I could get one taken right now."

He shakes his head. "Sorry. Jackie's right," he says with excessive supervisory pride, "We need photo identification and something with a local address on it."

Jackie smiles smugly. "Here's your I.D."

"And here's your credit card," I say, smacking it down on the paperwork as I get up to leave.

I WANT TO CLICK my heels three times and be anywhere but here. I stand outside the bank at the corner counting my money as people whiz by. I'm down to my last $70. I don't even have enough for another night at a hotel, yet I have over $9000 to deposit, most of which is meant for paying my medical bills, and towards the replacement car I will never buy. This money is supposed to float me in New York. A lot of floating it's doing.

Now what? It's almost 11 a.m.. I will have to worry about how to liquify this money later and get to work on the next thing on the scavenger/survival list: a letter from my employer confirming my employment and my salary. I must dial Pavlos. Although Pavlos is in Los Angeles – *or is he?* – I plan to speak to his secretary Liza, in his supposed absence.

I hope Pavlos will answer the phone so I can catch him in his lie. Then again, it's a few days later and Pavlos could actually be back from L.A. by now. The phone rings as I watch Jackie through the window. She is opening an account for a "resident."

"Decade" answers a male voice.

"Yes, is Liza there?" I ask, my voice cracking, wondering if it's Pavlos. *If it's Pavlos, he wouldn't pretend not to be, would he?*

"Who's calling?"

"Eve Foster," I say, waiting for the receiver to be hung up, presuming my reputation precedes me.

"Eve. Hi, It's Kristos"

"Kristos, Hi. How are you?" I ask, suspicious of his welcomeness.

"Good, good. How are you?

"Fine."

"Where are you?"

"At the corner of Fifth & 39th" I answer, wondering what he intends to do with the information.

"Oh you're in New York."

I cannot believe Kristos doesn't know I've been here. *Could I be so insignificant to Pavlos that he wouldn't even mention it to Kristos? Do I mean so little to Pavlos that I wouldn't come up in a conversation? Am I that far removed from Pavlos' stream of consciousness? Am I the only one thinking of me?* "Yes. I've been here since Saturday. Pavlos didn't tell you?"

"No he's in L.A.."

"Oh. Right. That's what your mother said. Do you know when he'll be back?"

"No, I don't. Maybe a few days. Maybe tomorrow."

"Oh." I said, my stomach dropping.

"Is there anything I can do for you?" he asks.

"Well, actually… yes, hopefully," I said, telling him of my need for a "proof of employment" letter.

"So come on up to the office, I'll get you whatever you need."

"Really? I ask, my heart venturing to open, unable to imagine such charity amid an otherwise uncharitable city, save for Dolores.

"Yeah, come up," he says, giving me an upper west side address between Fifth and Madison Avenues.

"Wow. Thanks so much. I really appreciate it. Would it be O.K. for me to come right now?"

"Sure. I'll be here. We have some construction going on so if you don't find me right away just ask someone to get me," he says.

"Great, thanks. I'll see you in about fifteen minutes," I say, hailing a cab while still connected to the phone.

As I taxi uptown along Madison Avenue towards Pavlos' office, the townhouses and stores look increasingly more expensive and colonial reminiscent of the *Age of Innocence* era when Rockefellers consorted with Carnegies, and the Rothschild's were no doubt the life of the party. My taxi would have been a hansom trotting along. But now, filling the streets, are women in dark sunglasses, carrying Prada totes, cell phones, and Evian bottles as their nannies push strollers. They have only to shop and get sunlight. They are the Beach Bourgeois of the East.

⌐‿⌐

THE TOWNHOUSE is buttercup yellow with vanilla moldings and pink geranium plants potted in front. It looks like a home. I had expected an office. I enter nervously – the only kind of entrance I've been making lately – anticipating an unwelcome reception when my presence is discovered, for even though I have an official appointment, these Greeks are known to renege, or as they call it "not remember".

I stand in the obelisk-shaped foyer on top of a white marble floor eyeing legs belonging to two men standing on a ladder as they install a chandelier in the ceiling above me. One steadies the ladder as the other, who appears headless, reaches into his tool belt, his head presumably in the ceiling.

"Hi, Excuse me, do you know where I can find Kristos Polychronopolis?" The lower workman looks upward at the headless workman who points his hammer to a plastic-wrapped circular staircase.

I walk up the staircase, admiring the exquisite detail of the balustrade when the steps recede unexpectedly to a dark narrow corridor. "Watch yourself," says a workman out of nowhere, passing me, the space so tight I have to suck up to the edge of the railing causing me to wonder if this is how they planned to dispose of me: force me over the balcony so that it looks like an accident, to which the chandelier workman will not doubt attest. "There's a lot of debris up there," the workman adds just before a plume of chalky air and paint fumes blast at me from the second floor. I cover my mouth and limit my inhalations. Finally at the top, I breathe. And cough. *Rinoshun!*

"Eve?" I hear a man's voice calling my name. "Eve? Is that you?"

I look out over the railing. There, in the foyer, from where I have just come, is a dark-haired olive-complexioned man, a heavier-set Pavlos. "Kristos?"

"Stay there. I'll come up." As he makes his way up the staircase, disappearing into the dark recesses, I gauge how far the banister to the foyer floor is should I be hurled. "I thought you were Sarah Jessica Parker," he says, kissing my cheeks.

"An easy mistake," I joke.

"Seriously. Her realtor called right after you to say she was coming over. She's considering leasing the fourth floor, the last of the unleased space we have, so I might have to abandon you for a little bit when she arrives."

"No problem," I say, holding back the instinct to point out that I've been abandoned before.

Kristos shows me through the building, pointing out the renovations they are making: the new French limestone floor, the 17th century rococo paneling shipped here from Italy "…and this is the office, and Liza," says Kristos, introducing me to Pavlos' secretary, a stout-bodied, cherubic faced, chipmunk-cheeked, long brown-haired young woman with a pug nose and cleft chin. It is safe to assume that Pavlos isn't leaving me for his secretary, a notion I'd briefly entertained upon hearing her unenthusiastic voice over the phone when I spoke to her from L.A..

"We've spoken over the phone, thanks so much for helping me with the apartment," I say, genuinely thankful.

"Sure," she says, cheerlessly. "Kristos, you need to sign these." She pushes a contract towards him on the desk.

"Kristos, there's someone downstairs for you," says a hard-hatted man wielding a buzz saw, as he pokes his head into the office.

"Just go ahead and dictate the letter to Liza and I'll sign it when I finish with Sarah," says Kristos and then he leaves.

Liza and I face each other. "I can type it if you'd like," I offer.

"I'll type it," she says.

I dictate the letter. She types, prints, and then hands it to me. "It's perfect, but I'm afraid I need it on the company's letterhead. Sorry."

"*Hmmm*. I wonder if we have any," she says glibly, thumbing through four sheets of loose paper on the desk. My distress grows with each second that she can't find one single sheet of letterhead.

She glances around the room. "Hmmm. I don't think we have any," she says again.

Finally, voila! she finds one, a needle in a haystack, buried under scattered paperwork. She reprints the letter with noticeable irritation. I keep quiet, feeling that the slightest change in my breathing pattern will dissuade Liza or Kristos from giving me the letter, my proverbial key to the City. Finally, Liza pulls the letter from the printer and lays it flat on the desk for Kristos to sign upon return. I stand beside it, reading and rereading it, afraid to let it out of my sight, ready to paper-nap it if need be.

Kristos returns. "Is the letter ready for me to sign?" Liza points to it for him to sign.

"Yes, but it's your last sheet of letterhead," I warn him so he's careful.

"Oh no, we have plenty. Liza has more in the closet," he says and then hands me the signed letter.

I read it again and get an eerie chill when I see that Kristos has signed not his name but his brother's: "Pavlos Polychronopolis". I'm grateful and relieved to have it but I'm saddened by the capital "P" and "P" and everything in between. I fold it delicately, put it into my purse, and thank Kristos and Liza profusely, wondering if purse-snatcher is on the agenda before I can safely deliver it to Dolores.

"So where are you off to now?" asks Kristos.

"I have to find a bank that will accept my out-of-state license to open a bank account. The one I went to before I came here refused to open one because I don't have a New York driver's license."

"Well my bank will. It's great."

"Really?"

"Sure. I'll take you there. It's Citibank. Do you know it?"

"Uh. Yeah. They're the ones that refused me."

Really? He asks in disbelief.

I nod.

"Listen, have you had lunch?"

"No, I – "

"Why don't you come have lunch with me? There's a nice little *al fresco* place on Madison."

"Oh. Sounds really nice, but I have so many things to do. In fact, do you have the time?"

"It's lunchtime. Come with me. You've got to eat. We'll have lunch and we'll work on sorting out your problem."

Problems. I have the urge to correct him.

"Well O.K. Sure. That sounds great," I say, planning to eat very little. I thank Liza for her help, smiling as warmly as possible, feeling bad that she has to stay and work while her boss and I go out to lunch. But she is unmoved. She doesn't care one way or another. And it dawns on me that no one seems to have any sensitivity here in New York City, so I need not expend the effort to spare their feelings. *Whew!* What a weight off of my shoulders!

14. MADISON AVENUE ALFRESCO

Kristos pulls on his chic dark sunglasses as we walk down Madison Avenue among the lunchtime sidewalk bustle. I visor my eyes with my hand, not wanting to use my Dakota Smith sunglasses, a gift from Pavlos. He had wanted us to match.

"So where are we going?" I ask, my eyes beginning to tear from the sun. "Egon's Ristorante," says Kristos.

"What kind of a name is Egon? I ask.

"Austrian, I think." says Kristos. It's only been open a few months. In fact, he's usually standing outside here," says Kristos as he presses his hand to my lower back to guide me toward a bistro table just one step removed from the flow of pedestrian traffic, just one car length removed from the flow of southbound auto traffic.

We are seated at a table under an umbrella with a perfect view of all traffic. "Is Egon here?" Kristos asks a waiter.

"No. Tonight, around 6:30 p.m.," he says, handing us menus which are French illustrated menus *a la* Raoul Dufy. Inside, is the menu, in Italian.

"Isn't' that funny?" I ask.

"What?" replies Kristos.

"We're at a restaurant that has a French illustrated menu but serves Italian and is named after an Austrian."

"That is funny. I guess there's not a big demand for Austrian food," says Kristos.

"Can I get you something to drink?" asks the waiter.

Kristos orders a half-carafe of merlot.

"And could I get some water too?" I ask.

"Spring or mineral?" the waiter asks.

"Oh, just tap," I answer.

"No, no you don't want tap," says Kristos.

The waiter shakes his head in agreement. "Mineral or spring?"

"Flat or sparkling?" offers Kristos.

"Flat," thanks.

The waiter returns with our wine, another with our water. "Would you like to know the specials?"

"I'll just have the Greek salad," says Kristos, handing his menu back to the waiter.

"The Greek salad for you too miss?" the waiter asks.

"No, no, no" I say, with perhaps too much protest. A Greek salad never looked so uninviting. I bury my head in the *menstre, paste, carni, pesci, insalate,* and *contorni* sections fearing Kristos might intuit my thoughts."

"Sorry, I should have given you more time. I've been coming here so often I already know what I want," says Kristos.

"No problem," I say, smiling. "I'll have the house salad please." The waiter removes our menus.

"Cheers," says Kristos, tapping my glass. "And welcome to New York."

"Thanks, cheers," I say. I sit back into my chair as the merlot swishes in my mouth and the sun beats down on my neck. This is the first peaceful moment I have had since arriving in Manhattan. The only thing I can do is wait to be served. Even though the natives swirl around me, Kristos' company makes me feel secure, like I can relax and let him do the thinking, the paying, the sorting out. Then again, perhaps the peace is simply due to the fact that I feel optimistic for the first time in weeks. Given Kristos' show of hospitality I feel strangely close to Pavlos, my faith renewed in men, in humanity. *I mean if Pavlos really wanted nothing to do with me, would his brother be sitting here with me? Leaving work for me? Dining with me? Offering to help me?* With each passing minute, it seems that I am that much closer to meeting up with Pavlos when the day draws to its inevitable close, when passing traffic has their headlights on, when these tables are set with votive candles, by which time, I will be inside the Colossus, inside Pavlos' apartment, the invited guest, discoursing with Pavlos' blood relatives who would be remarking on Pavlos' beautiful young girlfriend with innocent green eyes, peaches and cream complexion, distressed that such a girl could be all alone in the city. Kristos would vouch for my character, having spent the day with me, and they would all fall in love with me as Pavlos had, beseeching Pavlos to fall once more. *Dare I say everything is looking up?*

"So, let's get back to your problems," says Kristos.

"Right."

Kristos and I discuss my dilemmas – banking and apartment renting – with the zeal of an entrepreneurial undertaking. It was the same way with Pavlos – the spirit of deal-making effused with arrogance. I have the feeling, as I had with Pavlos, that I had nothing to worry about with Kristos at the helm. I began to tell Kristos about my banking catch-22 until the salads arrive.

"Fresh pepper?" asks the waiter.

"No thanks," I answer.

"So, you were saying," says Kristos, waving me to continue.

"Well, I have to get to the bank – "

"Oh don't look now, but here comes Pavlos' ex-girlfriend," interrupts Kristos, cryptically, wiping his mouth with the extra virgin olive-oil-splattered napkin. "Hello gorgeous," he says, rising to kiss her double-dipped bronzed cheeks as they exchange dutiful idolatries, once familial hellos.

I smile politely and wait to resume eating until after they're finished with their greeting.

She is much older than me; in her late '30s, soleil-weathered skin bared in a silk taupe skirt suit, her legs tan and bare in Prada or Choos. Her lips naked and glossy in Bobby Brown or MAC. Her sun-damaged brown hair is streaked blonde. Her nails are short and French-manicured, allowing the large diamond bauble on her fourth metacarpal to take center stage.

As she raptly discusses her "harried" life in her raspy smoker's voice, intermittently leveling her expressionless eyes at me, I meet them each time, smiling warmly, disarmingly – the proverbial white flag – until I realize how unmoved and unimpressed she is with me, as if my niceness and lack of pretension reveal that I am from the inferior stock, as if such virtues were symptomatic of the dreaded middle class and all that's wrong with America. Kristos finally introduces us by name. "Leslie this is Eve."

"Nice to meet you," I say, extending my hand. She shakes my fingertips primly managing no more than a forced, circumspect smile before returning her attention to Kristos, her tan elbow taking up residence directly in front of my nose, effectively blocking my reach to my merlot. After waiting very patiently for her to move her arm – a wait that is so long that I've now made out that her croc clutch is Louis Vuitton, and her silver bracelet is Cartier – I make my move. I reach for my wine and, as anticipated, inadvertently brush against her elbow, but she doesn't notice. At this point, I start to eat my salad knowing how rude and classless I am to do so ahead of Kristos.

As passersby watch me eating, as shamelessly as they had in Times Square, and I overhear Leslie speak of her "banking promotion" and "paramour, blah, blah, blah," it dawns on me that Leslie is Pavlos' infamous ex-girlfriend who threw knives at him. *Yes it's her!*

Pavlos had told me over lunch at Cafe del Rey (seems the place in L.A. to break news) that his last girlfriend threw knives at him. When I asked Pavlos what he had done to make her throw knives at him, he answered, "I don't know. All women are psycho." I had taken Pavlos at his word particularly since he said, "these were no butter knives" and also because he still appeared genuinely haunted by the memory of it.

I had imagined the then-faceless woman desperate and yes, "psychotic," but now, considering the way Pavlos has turned on me, I suspect that if Leslie did go psycho as Pavlos maintained, he undoubtedly provoked her. Now that she stands in front of me, I want to ask her in person what it was that Pavlos did. Instead, I imagine the *mise en scène*: Leslie in bed with Pavlos, both in their silky lingerie, and then – *insert provocation here* – she goes to the kitchen for a knife, clutching it to her side where her croc clutch is now, aiming it at little Pavlos who shields himself behind the stainless-steel kitchen island while trying to woo her out of her insanity that he no doubt drove her to. If only she had better aim.

So, here she is – a woman and aspiring manslayer – and I feel ridiculously childlike in her presence. She, in her *bon chic bon genre* tan and me in my *bon gap bon gap* and *démodé* paleness. Despite correcting my posture, pushing back my rounded shoulders, cupping and elevating the glass of merlot with more sophistication, all the self-contortioning does is call attention to my serrated thumbnail and unpolished nails. More humiliating is the idea that Kristos is having a good laugh over this serendipitous rendezvous of two dissimilar exes on Madison Avenue – a visual Kristos will undoubtedly share with Pavlos later. *Were we all pondering this at the same time? What could Pavlos have possibly seen in me, the antithesis of her?* No one would look at me and think for one second I'd draw anything more than a paring knife (which perhaps explains Pavlos' attraction to me.) And perhaps this explains Leslie's dismissive behavior towards me. It's not snobbery, it's poor sportsmanship. She can't bear the possibility that this "girl" captured the heart of a man she had wanted to marry (at least before the knife-provocation). Yes, for all her aloofness, she wants to place me. Still, I suspect she already knows that I had relations with Pavlos, as if all of his women bear some familiar marking (i.e. missing knuckles.)

Their conversation winds down and she eyes the face of her silver Cartier timepiece on the inside of her wrist – a subtle display of euro sensibility – *de rigueur* for anyone with European flair. First the European kissing, now the European watch-wearing and the un-American tan. Things I would have to replicate authentically if I am to be considered worldly and cultured with European panache. American dispositions simply aren't trending.

"Ciao," she says, putting on her sunglasses, dropping her clutch to her side and out of my face as she saunters south on Madison, her heels clicking, her tan calves pumping.

"Well, she eyeballed me oddly. Do you think she knows I dated Pavlos," I ask Kristos, wondering if he'll take note of the past tense I've applied to me and Pavlos' relationship, wondering if he'll correct me.

"Oh, I wouldn't worry about her. She couldn't care less about Pavlos. She's landed a much wealthier man," says Kristos, causing me to wonder if dating one wealthy man increased the chances of subsequently landing a much wealthier man. *Is a woman only as eligible as her last suitor? If true, do I now qualify for a much wealthier man too?* Perhaps there is light at the end of the tunnel. "So tell me what you have to do," says Kristos, reprising his role as my personal troubleshooter.

I tell him again about my banking issue, whereupon Kristos flips open his cell phone, dials, and waves away his plate to the waiter. "Marcus? Ben. Kristos Polychronopolis here," says Kristos, taking his call to the sidewalk and then returning a minute later to end the conversation with, "Yeah, tell Marcus I'm on my way to your office. I'll need fifteen minutes. Ciao."

Kristos throws down forty dollars on the table, refusing my hastily opened wallet (thank goodness) and walks towards the curb motioning for me to follow him. I'm still not sure whether he will hail a taxi or push me out in front of it, so I walk tentatively toward the curb just as a taxi swerves in dangerously close. Kristos opens the door for me and slides in behind.

"Empire State Building, please," he instructs the driver.

15. EMPIRE STATE BUILDING

I assumed I would eventually take a tour of the Empire State Building, I just hadn't expected to do it so soon into my arrival. In fact, I had never thought of the Empire State Building as anything more than a famous landmark, like the Statue of Liberty, constructed solely for tourism. So it is all the more surprising that on my first trip there, it will be to conduct business rather than sightsee.

As we drive through a tunnel cut out of the Helmsley Building which straddles Park Avenue, my body tenses. *If we don't drive under the legs of the Eiffel tower, why are we driving under this?*

As Kristos converses with someone on his cell phone, I wonder how long his run of knighthood will last. It's now 3:45 p.m., just two hours before all the banks will close and I lose another day towards completing my lease application with Belle Arts, not to mention getting access to my money. If my banking dilemma doesn't get resolved today, I have everything to fear: another day of dependency on the fickle Polychronopolis family.

Still, there is something attractive about this family. It's a constant flow of testosterone, red wine, sweltering sun and European intrigue. Amid this swirling city that is much too confrontational for one person alone and where any inattention can mean death, the Polychronopolis Brothers could be a sanctuary, which perhaps explains why I'm so attached to the idea of reuniting with Pavlos. The fact is that, before the accident, I had fallen in love with him, which was just after he fell in love with me. It would not have been before.

In any case, it's odd to be sitting here in a taxi getting acquainted with Pavlos' daily life in the city, vicariously through the escort of his brother, rather than Pavlos himself. I have now seen where Pavlos works, where he has his coffee. I've met his brother, his secretary, his knife-wielding ex-girlfriend, and scarcely a word outside of my loquacious subconscious has been mentioned of Pavlos. In fact, Pavlos' absence is made all the more inexplicable in light of his brother's presence. I can't imagine Kristos helping me if it weren't Pavlos' wishes. Perhaps Kristos is Pavlos' hireling. Perhaps Pavlos asked Kristos to play surrogate conservator. Perhaps Pavlos didn't leave me out in the cold or in this case sweltering summer, alone after all. I can almost hear Pavlos, in a Greek Godfather-esque manner discussing "the arrangement": that Eve would not know who was behind the mercenary action, and that all Polychronopolis family resources would be tapped but Eve would not know her true benefactor.

If, on the other hand, it is true that Pavlos and his family want me gone, which is in keeping with Pavlos' disappearing act, why blur the intention by helping me? Unless "keep your friends close, your enemy closer" is their family motto. I want desperately to ask Kristos about Pavlos' state of mind, and whether Pavlos plans to resume his affections for me or complete his withdrawal, but I fear initiating discussion or emoting will effectively sever my already tenuous lifeline.

I'D EXPECTED to come upon the tallest building in the world (circa 1932), as if by a slow unveiling, like a sensual disrobing, one block at a time. But the way the taxi weaves the street, or the street weaves the taxi, we are under its shadow before my eyes have a chance to accommodate the full-scale erection. When the taxi finally stops in front of it, all I can see of it out the window is a blue scaffolding with "Post No Bills" stenciled on it, and a throng of people attached to it.

I emerge from the taxi ambivalent. I want to look up as Deborah Kerr did in *An Affair to Remember* but fear doing so will cost me my legs. Or worse, appear to Kristos that I am engaging in the same kind of inattentiveness and inclination to sightsee that he and his family think led to the Accident. So my mind is made up. I won't look up. Kristos can report to his family that I was very attentive and hadn't even looked up. I'll look up the next time I visit the Empire State Building.

As if intended to serve as a barricade to wayward traffic, the kind of traffic that paralyzed Deborah Kerr, the curb is perhaps the tallest in the world. I step up and lead the way towards the entrance, past salesmen with boxed Seiko's, miniature monuments, shoes, belts, used books, cardboard sales signs, and incense. I push along with a crowd to get inside *The Building* when a revolving door sweeps me inside it at whiplash-inducing speed. Because I am at the back, the pivot point, the speed at which the door turns is, well, speedy, and the rate at which I can get to the front in time to leap into the building, is, well, rather slow, and the air that I can suck away from all the other suckers is well, rather negligible. All of which would be bad enough if it weren't for the fact that I am also mildly claustrophobic. By the time fifty of us pitter-patter like centipedes towards the exit, I am left a small window of opportunity to exit the current revolution and join Kristos on the inside where I see him waiting for me, smiling. I make a run for it and am ... *caught.* By my purse strap. As the revolving door now whips towards the back of me, I try to slip my shoulder out of the strap when I discover that my purse isn't a "shoulder bag" but a "neck bag," that is, I put the strap around my neck (to deter would-be muggers). By some miracle, and in the nick of neck-saving time, the strap pulls me inside the lobby of the Empire State Building. My purse was not caught on the door but on the bag of another person who has unwittingly managed to pull me inside with her, to safety. I am just about to rejoin Kristos, who thankfully has no idea of my near headless feat, when I trip – on lipstick?

"Are you O.K.?" asks Kristos.

"Yeah, someone's lipstick..." Crap, it's mine. It seems my purse is upside down. I scurry to collect my makeup rolling on the lobby floor of the Empire State Building. When I come up, I am momentarily blinded. Through the disco spots, I see an elderly Chinese man motioning for me. He's holding a camera. I am, as it turns out, standing in the middle of his photo. I try to apologize for my intrusion, but he doesn't speak English. He hands me his camera and points to a button. He wants me to take a picture of him and his family, presumably because he thinks it's the only way to keep me out of the photo.

"Say cheese… err noodle." Everyone smiles.

Kristos watches me take the Chinese Family Portrait. I hope he will be kind enough to report back to his family how the Chinese family chose me out of everyone in the foyer of the Empire State Building to photograph them. It would be proof that the outside world's view of me is one of approachability and trust with mechanical equipment. Perhaps I can call the Chinese family as character references should the Greek council convene for a character assassination attempt. I return their camera to them and discover I've lost Kristos. I finally find him eyeing a black marquee of a million miniature white letters spelling out the building's tenants and respective floors.

"I don't' know why but I never really envisioned anyone but tourists here," I tell Kristos, as I marvel at the marquee.

"This is the first time you've been here?" he asks.

"It's the first time I've ever been to Manhattan."

"What?" he asks, shocked, as he escorts me to an open elevator.

"You didn't know that?" I ask, encouraged that Kristos has assisted me without even knowing the severity of my predicament.

Unfortunately, that means that it's highly unlikely that Pavlos has had anything to do with Kristos helping me given Kristos' insufficient data.

We take the elevator up to the 45th floor where a surly suited man greets us.

"Eve, this is Marcus Riddell, Pavlos' lawyer. And Marcus this is Eve, Pavlos' girlfriend," Kristos says, a description that seems like a lie, or a code for "latest casualty."

"Oh right, you're the one who recommended the Sherman Oaks lawyer, Steve Levy to me and Pavlos," I say, a passive-aggressive remark given how unsatisfying the settlement was, and how inferior I found Mr. Levy to be.

"Right, um, how was he?" Marcus asked, fidgeting.

"I had hoped for a better settlement," I say, leaking bitterness.

"Oh. Well, I didn't really know him," Marcus says aloofly.

"You don't know him? I thought you referred him!"

"Well, um, he's the cousin of a colleague of mine. I'm not familiar with his work."

"Oh." I nod in disbelief that he recommended someone he didn't know, never understanding why he didn't represent us himself if he's Pavlos' lawyer.

"Follow me. We do actually have offices fairly intact," he says. "Sorry for the appearance. We're in the middle of renovations."

Rinoshun!

He removes papers from atop a dusty monitor unplugged in the hallway as he leads us further down the hall into his office that has a window with a Fifth Avenue exposure. Save for the view, it does not look like the office of a well-to-do New York lawyer, let alone like an office that would be inside the famed Empire State Building. In fact, Marcus doesn't look much more upstanding than the Steven Levy of Sherman Oaks. He seems skittish, as if we caught him right before the Feds are about to close in. Nonetheless, he seems willing to do his boss' bidding, and unless he is aware of the fact that I have fallen considerably out of favor with the boss, he is beholden to do my bidding as well.

I am instructed to take the only guest seat as Kristos stands behind me.

"So let's see the check," says Marcus.

Kristos explains to me that I should endorse my check to Marcus, and he will, in return, give me two checks from their bank account: one payable to Belle Arts, the other to open a bank account with.

I remove the checks out of my wallet and hand them to Marcus. It feels like this is a clandestine meeting and the checks are grade-A contraband. Marcus turns the checks over for me to endorse them. He hands me a pen.

As they wait for me to endorse the check over to Marcus, I suddenly have the strange feeling that this is a premeditated trap to take my money. What a coup for Pavlos it would be. Revenge for his severed eyebrow. For all I know, Marcus could have been a foreman in a hard-hat just twenty minutes ago, who at the urgent behest of Kristos changed into a suit and grabbed a few women to simulate a law office. Kristos' call from the taxi would have given them just enough time to pull a desk and chair together. But, then again, the Empire State Building property management, the grand dame of all buildings, would never allow squatters. *Still, how do I know that the checks they give me in return won't bounce?*

"Show her the books," Kristos instructs Marcus, seemingly sensing my mistrust or reading my mind.

Marcus produces a red bound ledger that shows a balance of at over four-hundred-thousand-dollars, actually less than I expected. Still, the ledger could be phony. I stare at the numbers. They're handwritten. Anyone can write figures in. Except there are plenty of completed "balance forward" pages before it. Then I notice Marcus' business cards on the desk – the first convincing paraphernalia I've seen that supports Marcus's legitimacy, because I don't believe they could have possibly printed these in the last fifteen minutes. *No one would go to that much trouble would they?* I look at Kristos behind me and see just beyond him on the '70s style paneled wall, certificates authenticating Marcus' passing the New York State Bar exam.

"O.K. Where do I sign?" I ask, proceeding with the exchange.

"There, by the "X", says Marcus, pointing to the red inked X as his and Kristos eyes watch me.

I thank Marcus, shake his sweaty palms and take his business card. Should I find myself sobbing in a police precinct over being swindled out of my money by a man who pretended to be a lawyer in the Empire State Building, I at least will be able to supply the police with his business card.

"SO DO YOU want to go up to the top?" asks Kristos when we reach the elevator in the hallway outside of Marcus' offices.

"Sure."

We step into the elevator and as the doors close, my stomach sinks. But it's not my stomach sinking. It's the elevator. "Why are we going down?" I ask, ready to press Emergency Stop, knowing that my worst fears have been confirmed. Kristos is planning on doing away with me.

"We have to buy tickets first on the ground floor," Kristos explains, amused by my fear.

"Tickets? Are you kidding? This is an elevator. Why can't we just go up?" I ask in utter disbelief that an elevator ride could possibly necessitate a ticket as if it were a carnival ride rather than an office elevator. "What if you work up there? Do you have to buy a ticket to go to work everyday?"

"No I think the employees of the building have building passes," says Kristos, fairly certain.

After a short wait in a line at what looks like a bank teller window or a window for placing off-track bets, I purchase my postage stamp-sized blue ticket #135840 to ride the elevator to the top.

Without lap or head restraints, the elevator thunders upward and my round face stretches oblong like it does when riding the Hammerhead at the Coos County Fair. The elevator stops and we exit only to fall into another line. "I think we're in the wrong line," I inform Kristos. This one is heading into another elevator."

"This is only the 81st floor. We have to take one more elevator to get to the top."

"Are you kidding? There isn't one elevator to the top?" I say, thinking it to be an architectural oversight.

"Well you have to remember what an architectural feat it was at the time, just to build a building this tall in the first place," Kristos says.

"Right. Good point," I concede.

As the second elevator makes its final ascent, and I contemplate the need for two elevators to take us to the top, I think of its parallels to life. Each is a pendulum of escalation and descent, and each carries the possibility of a quick, sudden death-drop.

SO THIS IS WHERE Cary Grant stood July 1st at 5 p.m. until midnight on a rainy day waiting for Deborah Kerr? Odd to be taking this romantic view with Kristos. Then again, what if Kristos brought me here just to occupy me long enough for Marcus to void the checks he gave me, and cash the check I signed over to him? *Why do such thoughts constantly interrupt what should be elation here at the top of the Empire State Building? Who needs the city when I am my own personal killjoy?*

I turn my eyes to the city that is now approaching its evening hours. As the whipping winds induce hair lashings and tears, I hold ever more tightly onto my blue ticket which has an illustration of *The Building* and reads "Souvenir of visit to the most famous building in the world."

I think of Cary Grant, and how unbeknownst to him, Deborah Kerr had been paralyzed, a catastrophe that resulted from his suggestion that they meet here if they found themselves in love six months later. Cary could have forgotten about her, could have ran away when he discovered her debility, but he came to find her, to be with her. Pavlos is no Cary Grant.

"SO WHERE ARE you staying?" Kristos asks as he hails two taxis simultaneously, each speeding in competitive tandem toward us.

"Oh with a sixty-year-old man I met in Central Park," I answer, the sound of it (not the reality of it), still amusing me.

"What?!!" Kristos belts out in that same "un-fucking-believable" look Pavlos had following the accident. "Are you fucking kidding me?"

I shake my head, unable to shirk my mischievous smile.

"Un-fucking-believable," Kristos says as he holds the taxi door open for me.

"He's harmless," I say, sliding in the back seat. "Except he is getting a little possessive, wanting me to accompany him everywhere. Yesterday he asked me if I was a virgin and last night a big rat the size of a watermelon ran through my bedroom."

"Come on. We're going to get your things. You're staying with me." he says, waving away the other taxi and then sliding into the taxi with me.

Kristos' chivalry makes me recall why I liked Pavlos so much. Pavlos had been chivalrous. He had been my attentive prince fulfilling his Greek heritage to protect his woman, that is of course until he decided to carry tradition too far and sacrificed me to the Greek Gods.

"You know what? Maybe I should call Ray and tell him, so he's not caught off guard. I don't want to piss him off," I say.

"Are you sure? How do you think he'll react?" asks Kristos.

"Oh, maybe you're right," I answer, suddenly envisioning all of my possessions aflame in the street.

RAY IS OUTSIDE his brownstone hosing off the sidewalk when we drive up.

"Slow down, slow down, here is fine," I tell the taxi driver nervously, half a block down the street, away from Ray.

"Do you want me to come with you?" asks Kristos.

"No, it's O.K. I'll be fine. Besides, it's probably better that he does not see you," I say.

No sooner do I open the door of the taxi when Ray's eyes settle upon mine. Ray shuts off the water as Kristos, presumably seeing the look of discontent in Ray's eyes, rejoins me on the street. We approach Ray like two undercover police officers on official duty.

"Hi Ray, this is a friend of mine Kristos," I say in a tone that animal trainers use to coax gentility into wild animals. Ray says nothing, just keeps hosing the sidewalk with a scowl on his face.

"Well, Kristos has invited me to stay at his place. So I just wanted to thank you. You've been so kind to put me up, but I'm sure you'll be glad to get me out of your hair. I'll just get my things." I say as I walk gingerly past him up the steps. Ray then drops the hose on the flowerbed and turns to follow behind me but Kristos restrains him by the shoulder.

"Get your hands off me," says Ray.

"Come on. Just let her get her things," I overhear Kristos say.

I hurry to the bedroom and collect my luggage as quickly as possible. I say goodbye to Hasana who is seated against the backboard of her bed, reading. She smiles. I don't know if she's happy I am escaping or happy to have the place to herself. As I descend the stoop, I suddenly have a tinge of guilt for running out on Ray so abruptly. After all, he really came to my rescue when I had no place to stay. He taught me how to save fifty cents by walking to the end of the block to catch a cab heading in your direction, as opposed to the way I was doing it, hailing it from my doorstep. He told me that Fifth Avenue divided Manhattan into East and West, with numbers increasing from the center to either side - an essential thing to remember when given an address.

"Thanks so much Ray," I say with my utmost sincerity.

"What about the deck? Ray asks, perturbed.

I can't believe Ray's audacity. "Sorry." I shrug and walk away towards the taxi.

"I think you'd just better stay here," I overhear Kristos, stopping Ray from following me with the hose.

"So get the hell out of here already," Ray bellows.

Kristos and I get inside the waiting taxi but cannot move. Ray is standing in the middle of the street. The driver waves for Ray to get out of the way. Ray doesn't move. The taxi driver honks. Ray doesn't move. The driver puts the ignition in park and opens his door. Ray moves out of the way, flipping me off as we pass.

"Well I'm glad we didn't call ahead of time," I say, relieved to be traveling away from Chelsea.

"Yeah, I don't think he took it too well," says Kristos, his eyes big. "But what'd he mean about the deck?"

"I was supposed to paint his deck for my keep and I didn't finish." You don't have a deck do you?" I ask.

"No, no deck," Kristos laughs. "But, there is one thing" Kristos says, his hand on my thigh.

"Sure," I say, tensed that my housing once again hangs on a condition, wondering what I have to paint or how many feet away from Pavlos I have to stay.

"I have a girlfriend," says Kristos, "Sydney."

"Right…"

"And we live together. And I'm sure she'll be fine with you staying, that's not it. It's my apartment. But just out of courtesy I need to call her and run it by her."

"Oh, sure. Of course," I say, relieved his "one thing" isn't something life-threatening, yet unnerved by the slim prospect that I will be homeless again. A fine time for Kristos to be telling me now after I've already moved out of Ray's house.

Sydney says it's fine. I can stay.

"But you have to promise me something," says Kristos.

"Sure, what?" I ask, certain it has to do with keeping a certain yardage away from Pavlos.

"You have to swear not to tell Liza I live with my girlfriend," Kristos says.

"Liza?"

"Pavlos' secretary. Well my secretary too," he says.

"Well I don't even know her. I don't imagine I'll be talking to her."

"Probably not, but you might, and I need you to make sure you don't let it slip."

"Fine. Of course. I won't say a word. But do you mind me asking why?" I ask.

"It's just that Liza has a crush on me, and she'd be upset if she knew I had a girlfriend."

"How long have you and Sydney been dating?" I ask.

"Two years," Kristos responds.

"Two years? I ask incredulously, "How have you managed to keep it a secret?"

"Well Liza knows Sydney. Knows I'm kind of dating her. She just doesn't know we're living together. And she would go ballistic if she found out. She's not stable. She has this idea that someday we'll be married."

"Why would she think that?" I ask.

"She's nuts. Really. There's really nothing else to say," he says. His "nuts" explanation sounds eerily familiar to Pavlos explanation for why his ex would throw knives at him. *If Liza is so nuts why employ her?*

"Why the delicacy? Shouldn't she just learn to deal with the truth? I mean that's crazy, having to hide your life from your secretary." I say.

"Well, Pavlos and I've been meaning to let her go for a long time but it's tricky. She has a lot, a lot, of our money in her accounts under her name - for tax reasons - so we don't want to piss her off. Or she'd take the money to some tropical island and we'd never see our money again. But don't get me wrong, we treat her very well. We give her big bonuses. Last year she went to St. Martin, this summer she's going to Cancun."

I wonder why I keep moving down the food chain.

"But I'm serious, if you end up talking to her, you can't even mention meeting Sydney. I know it sounds crazy, but you have to promise otherwise things could be very, very bad for me and for Pavlos," says Kristos.

I promised, and then before thinking asked, "So you're sure your girlfriend won't mind you bringing home a girl to stay with you?"

"Well it doesn't really matter what she thinks. It's my place. Besides, I've been thinking about breaking up with her," says Kristos, his eyes looking intently into mine, sweetly, as if I were next on his list.

16. COLOSSUS II

The taxi pulls into the circular driveway of the Colossus, my fourth temporary dwelling in four days. I can't believe I'm *thisclose* to Pavlos.

"Always get a receipt," says Kristos as the meter churns out his receipt.

"But I don't itemize."

"You should. You can write off company expenses that way," Kristos says, handing the driver a $10 bill, brushing my cash away.

"But I don't have a company," I tell him, flattered that he thinks I look like I could have my own company.

"So create one. Just think of a name. I'll show you what to do. Sydney does it too. Just collect the receipts," says Kristos, taking the receipt from the driver and stuffing it back into his wallet. He looks at me. "You have the most beautiful blue eyes."

"Wow. Well thank you. But they're green."

"Green?" he asks in disbelief, looking deeper into my eyes, turning my chin towards the sunlight coming through the rear window. "Well blue-green."

Kristos slides out and extends his hand to help me. I take his hand even though it makes sliding out of the car more difficult.

———◦

"CLAUDIA SCHIFFER lives here," Kristos announces, fanning his hand across the colossal lobby, suggesting that all of this — the chandeliers, taupe suede settees, and crack staff — is his.

"Is that so?" I ask, charting the curious double-takes from the concierge. I dodge their stares as I walk down a long taupe runner past three more minimalist seating configurations, fearful that the concierge will recognize me as the girl who delivered the (unrequited) love-letter to Pavlos last night. They certainly would be puzzled about how I fit in with the Polychronopolis family. Suddenly out of nowhere, I am at their doorstep for the second time in two days but with the brother that I didn't write the letter to, and luggage in tow. *Oh geez. What if they read the letter?* I feel as if I owe them an explanation of how I came to be moving in with Kristos when he's got a live-in girlfriend, lest they consider far more perverse explanations.

I follow Kristos into one of seven elevators. As the doors close and Kristos presses the 46th floor, just seven floors above Pavlos, I wonder if I am to intuit a hidden meaning in Kristos' mention of Claudia Schiffer living here. *Is Kristos trying to prepare me for the eventual news that Pavlos is dating Claudia?* My stomach turns sour at the thought until I realize how preposterous it is that Uber-model Claudia and I could have ever dated the same man. Then again, Pavlos dated me and Manslayer Leslie, which leaves a lot of leeway for what type of woman he dates. In fact, maybe this explains why Pavlos left me. And who could blame him? Claudia Schiffer!

The elevator zooms upward so fast I get lightheaded staring at the green digital numbers morphing from one to the next like a NASA launch, particularly when we pass right by Pavlos' 39th floor, not stopping. What a nice surprise it would have been if Kristos had planned to take me to Pavlos. The fact that he doesn't lends credence to the theory that Pavlos doesn't want to see me, as if the theory weren't already ironclad. I feel so nervous being in the building that houses the man who will potentially never speak or see me again, the possibility of which threatens the very core of my innate faith in human decency. *And yet, I still believe in Fate and Destiny and what other reason would I be here if not to reconcile with Pavlos?* Surely we will see each other again. Surely this is all just a temporary setback. Surely I have been overreacting to the events of the last twenty-four hours, or forty-eight. *What other explanation could there be for me to have been all but ejected from Los Angeles but to be with Pavlos?*

Kristos knocks on his apartment door. *On his own door? This must be Pavlos –*

"I just don't want to surprise her," says Kristos. Kristos unlocks his apartment door only to be greeted by a chain lock preventing the door from opening all the way. That's it. Kristos' girlfriend has thrown him out for bringing me here. The head of a black cat pokes through the opening in the door but is quickly yanked back in.

"Just a second," a woman's voice calls out. The door shuts, a chain slides, and the door opens again.

"Give me just a second," Kristos says to me as he enters his apartment and closes the door, leaving me outside in the hallway to wonder if this is my final curtain call. Not only will the checks they've given me bounce, I will have been taken all the way back here only to be stranded in the hallway.

A bell rings. It's the elevator. I hear a man's voice. *What if it's Pavlos?* I hear the rustling of paper and scuffling of feet coming near. Perhaps this was the plan all along – Kristos' plan – to leave me in the hallway for Pavlos to confront. A woman's voice. *What if it's Pavlos and he has no idea I'm here?* He will be furious! *What business do I have invading his home? On the other hand, how will I deal with seeing him with another woman?*

Whew. It's just a handsome young couple fresh from a workout in shorts and tank-tops with fresh produce and water bottles. They walk to the end of the hallway, enter their apartment and lock two bolts from inside. As their door closes, Kristos' opens.

"Hi, I'm Sydney, says Kristos' girlfriend extending a firm, masculine handshake as Kristos pulls in my luggage. She looks shockingly like me, albeit brighter: red hair to my strawberry blonde, piercing blue eyes to my green, and alabaster skin to my pinkish-pale. In fact, I look Technicolor in comparison. But I dress better. She is dressed badly in an ugly big-yarned royal blue sweater and black jeans. "This is Tom," she says, referring to a disheveled guy seated at a computer. "And that's Dimitri, the youngest brother," she says, pointing to a younger, fit version of Kristos, seated on a curved windowsill, his back to the city skyline. He stares blankly at me. Definitely Pavlos' brother.

"Make yourself comfortable," says Kristos. "I just have to finish some business with Sydney and Tom, if you don't mind."

"No, please," I say, waving them to continue.

I sit on the black leather couch with my back to a large Warhol-esque picture of Sydney. I notice a charcoal sketch of Sydney also on the wall opposite me - large and nude. On the side table are a mix of black and white and color photos of her ranging from baby to teenage years, mostly of her on horses. A bed sits along the same wall as the couch. Considering this is Kristos' apartment, she's certainly lent her own touches, in fact she's much more "moved in" than I anticipated, making me feel even more of an imposition.

I pet the two cats — Tyler and Taylor — as I eavesdrop on Sydney and Kristos discussing work. Something about a business dilemma involving the licensing of some music, options for a film deal, work done on the office building, leasing agreements. Kristos is angry about something and has words with Sydney as if she were his secretary. Sydney doesn't flinch. She responds as if she is his secretary. Then she sits down and begins typing very fast. Almost as fast as me and I begin to think the Polychronopolis brothers like smart, capable women like me and Sydney who can type fast.

"Ever seen someone type so fast?" asks Kristos.

"Yeah that's pretty fast," I say, holding back the desire to admit I type faster. How many words per minute is that?"

"About 95 wpm," says Sydney.

"Really?" I ask, sure that Sydney has overestimated her speed. I thought she was typing more like 80 wpm. I mean, I'm sure I type faster than her. At last recorded speed, I typed 85 wpm. If she types 95 wpm, then so must I, if not more.

"You two have a lot in common, Sydney's an actress too," Kristos says.

"Oh really?" I ask.

"I saw your headshot. It's gorgeous," she says, matter-of-factly.

"Thanks," I say, impressed by her ease in giving compliments. Women are usually too competitive and catty.

"Yeah. My whole family saw your picture," says Kristos, prompting me to recall how Pavlos told me he had my headshot propped on his dresser and how the whole family thought I was beautiful after seeing the picture.

"Oh you're the one in the picture?" asked Dimitri, his expression lifting. "On Pavlos' desk?"

"Yeah," I say, blushing, thinking the photo must still be there.

"Huh. It doesn't really look like you," says Dimitri flatly, as if he'd been gypped.

"Eve was in *Dracula Returns*," announces Kristos, compelling everyone to take a second look at me, with expressions of awe usually reserved for celebrities.

"*Bram Stoker's?*" asks Tom, excitably, as if it were his favorite all-time film.

"Francis Ford Coppola's?" asks Dimitri.

"Yeah. For a split second," I answer, "despite a three-day shoot."

"What part did you play?" asks Tom.

"Were you one of the three temptresses that seduced Keanu Reeves?" asks Dimitri, excited.

"No. I was in the party scene at the beginning, and then impaled and danced the waltz – in silhouette."

"Did you have any lines?" asks Dimitri.

"No." I answer.

"Oh. So you were an extra?" asks Dimitri.

"Well, yeah. A *featured* extra. The casting director told me I was hand-picked by Coppola himself," I say.

"I'm gonna go hang at Pavlos'," says Dimitri, unimpressed, heading for the door.

"Tell mom I'll be down later," Kristos calls out.

"It was nice meeting you," I call out after Dimitri, just before he slams the door shut.

"Don't worry about him," says Sydney. "He's just protective of Pavlos. Pavlos is more like a dad to him than a big brother because they're almost twenty years apart."

"So Dimitri is going to Pavlos' apartment?" I ask.

"Yeah. He lives with Pavlos until he finishes high school next year. It was the only way his parents would allow him to attend school here as opposed to Greece."

.   "So is Pavlos back from Los Angeles?" I ask.

"I don't know. Kristos? is Pavlos back?" asks Sydney.

"No, I think he's still in L.A," says Kristos.

"Do you know when's he coming back?" I ask

"No," Kristos says.

"Call and ask your mom," says Sydney.

As Kristos dials his mother, Sydney assumes Dimitri's former repose against the window, petting her grey cat as she focuses her blue eyes on me.

"Dimitri thinks you're a jinx," she announces nonchalantly.

"What?" I ask with disbelief.

"The whole family does, that's why I don't think Dimitri's comfortable seeing you."

"You're kidding right?"

Sydney shakes her head. She is dead serious. I can't form a response.

"What's wrong?" asks Kristos, seeing my mouth agape.

"So your family thinks I'm a jinx?" I inquire, expecting Kristos to diffuse the tense situation with the truth.

"Well, yeah," he says.

"Kristos?! Do you know why I was on the highway to begin with?" I ask indignantly. "Because your brother asked me to go after his friend George who was driving under the influence of cocaine provided by Pavlos' friends. I wouldn't have even been on the highway if it weren't for Pavlos insisting that I go find his friend George."

"Don't worry about it. It's just that Pavlos has had a string of… incidents… with the women he's dated," says Kristos, who clearly thinks the women in these "incidents" are 100% culpable.

"Did he tell you about the one who threw knives?" asks Sydney, laughing.

"I think I met her today didn't I?" I inquire, still perturbed.

"You saw Leslie today?" Sydney asks Kristos.

"Yeah. We ran into her at Egon's," explains Kristos.

"So I guess I'm the one who severed his eyebrow? is that it?" I ask.

"He'll get over it." says Kristos.

"He really liked you. He just needs some time," said Sydney.

"He needs time? I lost my job, my car and broke my hand, and he needs time?" I vent.

"So, my mother has made dinner and wants us to come down, but I thought we'd go out instead. You up for it?"

We nod.

"O.K., but I have to pop in and tell my mother. Why don't you come with me?" Kristos asks me.

"How would Pavlos feel about me being in his apartment?"

"He's not there."

"How would Pavlos feel about me being in his apartment?" I ask again.

"You're with me, my guest," Kristos said.

"O.K. I say, certain that once Pavlos' mother meets me, sees my angelic peaches and cream face, my good manners, my innocent aura, she will like me and banish the thought that I am a jinx.

17. MARKED WOMEN

Madame Polychronopolis. The Greek Matriarch. She has a nest of egg-grey hair swept up into a bun, olive skin, and bulging eyes that fill deep sockets rimmed in heavy brown eye-liner. She is barely five feet tall, and wears a loose, exotic maroon muumuu. She is barefoot and her toenail polish looks like dicings from an orange pepper.

They kiss. Son and mother. And then argue in Greek and laugh, and then turn their attention onto me still standing in the hallway. "Mom this is Eve," says Kristos.

"Hi," I say, extending my hand.

She wipes her palms against the dish towel in her hand.

I smile nervously, wondering how she could have a heartless son like Pavlos until I wonder if she can read my mind. Given the Polychronopolis' family's penchant for diagnosing jinxes, there's no telling what other black magic they're involved in.

Madame smiles weakly and reluctantly kisses my cheek - just one, and then walks into the kitchen and opens the oven door to show off a juicy, roasted turkey basting in a brown bath. She dips a baster into the aluminum tin and squeezes the thin murky brown liquid onto a silver spoon. "Here. Taste," she says, extending the spoon towards me, her hand cradling in case of spillage, steam rising, as her and Kristos eye me eagerly.

I take the spoon from her hand and blow repeatedly on the gravy even though Madame insists it's not hot enough to burn me. As the steam penetrates my nostrils, it all seems odd. *Why would Kristos drag me down here?* Enemy territory for me, and I'm their family's eyesore. Speaking of which, Kristos and his mother are eyeing me like the mother/son tag team in *Notorious* when they waited for Alicia (wife and daughter-in-law, respectively) to drink the tea they poisoned. This seems no different. Tea for Alicia, gravy for me, it doesn't matter. Poison is poison.

No fool, I wait for Kristos to taste the gravy first. Without so much as one blow he takes a whole ladle of gravy into his mouth, swallows, doesn't die, and I follow suit. The gravy is room temperature but spicy hot. As I flail my hands in a frantic flurry and my face and lips turn pepper red, Madame Polychronopolis and Kristos look at each other, pretending not to understand that I need an extinguisher: water. By the time Madame directs Kristos to get some water for me and loses time by asking if I mind it from the tap, I couldn't care less what the arsenic levels in tap water are. I douse my mouth with all of it.

"It's great, (cough), a little spicy," I say, wondering if the tap water wasn't the intended poison all along, the gravy the red herring intended to throw me off.

"Spicy? No," she protests, then looks at Kristos, speaks Greek, and then they appear to argue. (What to do with the body?) Or, perhaps she is blaspheming him for bringing me into their home. Now she'll have to exorcise the place.

"I'm just going to show Eve the apartment," Kristos says to his mother, and then whispers to me, "I had to tell her I'd have the turkey for leftovers. She was not happy to hear we were going out for dinner."

"So did she say when Pavlos would be back from L.A.?"

Kristos speaks to Madame again in Greek and she answers in Greek.

"She doesn't know. She says maybe tomorrow," says Kristos as he leads me into Pavlos' living room which is beautifully and expensively decorated in (crown) jewel tones of ruby and topaz (or is it merlot and cognac?) and Biedermeier furniture.

Kristos guides me in the U-shaped apartment, past a view of the downtown skyline, to Pavlos' office: a small room with a Biedermeier desk and a billiard style desk lamp. As Kristos fumbles to turn on the light, I soak up the images as quickly as I can so that I can complete an otherwise incomplete context of Pavlos' life: leather desk accessories, a few envelopes of mail placed neatly off to one side. This must have been exactly where Pavlos spoke to me on the eve of my one-way flight, where he found himself so conveniently distracted, where he passed the phone off to Kristos. And the place from where he told me he'd call me back, that his driver was waiting for him. Kristos flips on the light and I return my eyes to eye-level so he doesn't see that I've been inspecting Pavlos private desktop, trying to make out the mail as if it will impart the reason for his disappearance.

"What's back there?" I ask, referring to a dark room, the end of the line.

"Bathroom," Kristos says, flipping on it's light.

I glance inside the bathroom. White tiles. White porcelain. Ebony and ochre toiletry containers. Sparkling clean. Kristos cuts the light before I'm finished looking, leaving the afterimage of a tub in my mind, reminding me of the day Pavlos disappeared in my apartment without a word. Olive and I went from bedroom to kitchen to balcony, calling out for him before tracking him down to the hall bathroom. I figured he must have had diarrhea and, naturally, I left him alone. But after an hour passed I knocked and asked if he was O.K. "Yeah," he said, emerging in a towel wrapped around his hips. "I was just taking a bath," he said. Later he told me that he loved bubble baths, took them at least three times a week, and what a great deep tub I had but that I needed to clean it. With bleach.

Kristos and I say our goodbyes, promising to eat the turkey leftovers. Madame has put in extra gravy for me.

"I HAVE TO APOLOGIZE for the bed being in the living room," says Sydney upon Kristos and my return.

"Well where else would you put it?" I asked, knowing of no other place to put it.

"Uh, in the bedroom," Sydney says, sarcastically.

"There's a bedroom?"

Sydney nods.

"Where?" I ask, unable to believe I hadn't noticed there was another room to the apartment which was already much larger than the one I will hopefully be living in, not to mention at least fifty years more modern. Sydney shows me to the bedroom. It has a balcony with a dead stiff ficus tree and amazing, unobstructed view of downtown.

"We pulled the bed into the living room because I've been bedridden for two months recuperating from near-death colitis."

"Colitis?" I ask, cringing with sympathy and fright.

Sydney touches the tips of her forefinger and thumb to form a circle. "I have a hole this size in my colon. I'm better now, but for two months, everything I ate ran right through me. It was great dropping twenty pounds in two months, but I had no energy. Just couldn't get myself out of bed. I've only, just in the last week, been able to get up and work at the desk to do work for Kristos' – our company."

I have the unbelievable urge to take Sydney aside and inform her that we are marked women, that the Greek brothers have a plot to ruin us, have cast a hex from which there is no escape, and then grab her hand and run for our lives or search for the voodoo doll and pull out the straight pin through Sydney's colon, and the pins in my fourth metacarpal. I want to tell her this, but I realize she will think I'm nuts on top of being a jinx.

"Well that's great you're able to work from home then," I offer.

"Yeah but I really need to start looking for a job," she says. "I haven't worked for five months now. And the bills are enormous. I see like three doctors a week – nutritionist...."

"What were you doing for work before?" I ask, suddenly ashamed for my weeks-long pity party. It never occurred to me there were people worse off than me.

"I was a shoe model. But it's not steady work. And I don't get paid," she says.

"You don't get paid?" I ask incredulous, ready to call the labor union of shoe models.

"Well not in cash. I get paid with shoes and clothes," she says.

"So what do you do for money?" I ask, alarmed with concern for her well-being. "Have you thought about temping? You type fast. That's what I'll probably end up doing until I can find a job. You should come with me to the agencies."

"Oh I'm fine financially," says Sydney. "I mean, I have a trust fund and everything. It's just that I've had to live off of it more than I've wanted to."

I had begun to think of Sydney and me as two pears from the same tree. Just two struggling actresses in New York City. But I am wrong. She has a trust fund. Which is too bad. I was just beginning to feel sympathy for her. Still, there's something about near-death colitis that humanizes even a Trust Fund Girl. Almost. But clearly her trust fund isn't worth much or she wouldn't be dressed so unfashionably in a royal blue sweater that with her red hair makes her look like an American flag. Still, I recoil at the thought that I actually just suggested that she, a Trust Fund Girl, temp. It must have sounded comparable to suggesting she subsidize her income with food stamps. What's worse, is that there's no mystery left about me. I've now revealed my own inferior income and social standing, which she will no doubt find a way to use against me.

"DO YOU MIND if I take a shower first? You women will take longer than me," says Kristos, inserting a blade into his razor.

"No, no, go ahead," I tell him.

Even with the extra time Kristos' shotgun shower has afforded me, I can't decide what to wear. With few inspiring choices that aren't wrinkled, and not knowing exactly where we are going to eat dinner, I decide I can't go wrong wearing black in New York. I collect my basic black ensemble - cotton pants, sailor-necked button up shirt and Sabrina-heeled black suede shoes.

"If you want, you can wear something of mine," says Sydney, opening up a hall closet that is packed full of clothes in plastic bags, as if to offer poor Orphan Annie something presentable to wear.

"Thanks but I'm fine," I say, unable to fathom anything in her closet beyond basic royal blues. She clearly doesn't spend her trust fund on clothes.

"These are my headshots," says Sydney, bringing out a box. I've had two photo sessions in six years, and she's had three in the last year, each featuring a different hair color. Red, she tells me is not her natural hair color. She's naturally a blonde. "Have you ever read David Hare's, *Red-Haired Death*?"

"No. Sounds interesting."

"It's really amazing and I've been wanting to produce it. I'll get you a copy. Maybe it's something we can do together. I'm a huge David Hare fan."

Steam emerges from the bathroom, preceding Kristos in a towel around his waist. "Your turn," he says. "Just don't close the door all the way."

"No, so the cats can go in and out. Their food is in there," Sydney says.

"Right… and I noticed the litter box is in the kitchen? Shouldn't it be the other way around," I ask, amused.

"I know it's weird. It just worked out that way," she says.

Inside the bathroom there is hardly a hint of Kristos living here. It's filled with high-end hair and make-up products: Yves St. Laurent, Chanel, MAC, and Sheba food and water dishes on the floor for the cats. (I know it's Sheba because there are empty containers in the garbage along with Q-tips and other bathroom-related sundries.) The only obvious male product in the bathroom is the Gillette shaving cream canister and skin bracer inside the shower. But once I step inside the clean, modern shower, it is the most relaxing moment since I've been to New York, images of being impaled through the shower curtain long gone. Then, just as I begin to lift the razor to shave my legs, I hear the creak of the door opening. I wait nervously and then draw back the curtain to confront my intruder only to discover it's just the cat sitting on the sink in front of the mirror taking a bath. I resume my shower, finish, and dry off. And as I get dressed, the cat and I stare at our reflections in the mirror, both of us no doubt wondering if I am dressed too formally for the occasion.

"You look great," says Kristos, giving me a kiss on the cheek as I emerge from the bathroom, freshly made-up, toiletries in tow, shadowed by steam.

"Thanks," I say, the compliment reassuring me that I'm dressed appropriately. "So do you," I say, in deference to Kristos' maroon silk shirt and black trousers. As we stand there, cologned and perfumed, his body much too close to mine should a live-in girlfriend walk by, particularly since Kristos is giving me that look again. *What is he thinking?*

Fifteen minutes later Sydney emerges from the bathroom in a towel, and rummages through her hall closet before taking a plastic-wrapped something into the bedroom. Ten minutes later, she emerges – a vision in white.

"Wow! You look gorgeous! I say, amazed by Sydney's stunning, shocking transformation. She is wearing a provocatively plunging silk cream sleeveless dress with glimmering beading. Her skin is translucent, her eyes are searing bright blue, and her body lithe and petite, her cleavage ample, her fingers slender with sheer pink polish Her bright red hair is now upswept. Her mouth colored in deep mahogany matte lipstick looks peculiarly beguiling rather than simply peculiar. "What a beautiful dress."

"Thanks. It's Ev & El. Have you heard of them?

"No."

"I'm a diehard fan. They let me come for private viewings before their trunk shows. Can you cut the tag off?" she asks, her butch voice suddenly at odds with such a feminine presence. She hands me scissors and I cut a tag from the collar that reads $695, marked down from $1105.

To the very degree she looks translucent and amazing, I feel dumpy and dark. Suddenly my outfit, which I found acceptable just minutes before, makes me feel unsophisticated and cumbersome and opaque in comparison. It's just my luck to be with the only woman in New York who doesn't wear black. In fact, I feel like she bluffed me – dressing down initially to give me false confidence. I wonder why Kristos would ever consider breaking up with her, a Trust Fund chick with drop dead looks, and when not wearing royal blue, very fashionable. Then again, maybe he's rethinking it too. I try to focus on my strong points. My hair is a better red (and natural), although hers looks really amazing here upswept and a tendril hanging down. I still have better lips and teeth, and I'm SAG eligible. (While Sydney may have the money to get into the Screen Actors Guild, she doesn't qualify – a fact I noted after viewing her headshots.) I just need to pay the $2335 initiation fee which I'd planned to do with my settlement, so I need a new plan.

"ALWAYS GET a receipt," says Sydney as we leave Kristos alone to pay the taxi.

"Yeah, that's what Kristos said," I answer as we take steps to the goliath doors of Forty-Four, our destination for "drinks," having had our dinner at Asia de Cuba.

"I can't wait to show you the men's bathroom," says Sydney as Kristos rejoins us to walk down a royal blue runner past settees of chic, modern white chairs and tables and lighting with spindly legs, and oversized futuristic pesto chairs behind them, filled with chic people with chic drinks.

"Why is that?" I ask.

"The guys get to pee on the wall," says Sydney, envious.

"But why would they want to?" I ask.

"If you had a penis, wouldn't you want to?" she asks.

"No," I say.

"Well I have penis envy. Always have," says Sydney.

"Do you like the blue runway?" Kristos asks me – a segue from penis?

"Yes" I say.

"My design."

"I thought you said Philippe Stark designed it," I recalled him saying over dinner when he proposed the idea for drinks here.

"He did. I helped him."

"No way," I insist.

"Yes."

Kristos checks the bathroom to accommodate Sydney's wishes to show me the architectural, if not biological, feat. As a guy still zipping his pants exits, Kristos waves us in. Another guy in the bathroom is nonplussed seeing us in the reflection of the mirror as he washes his hands.

And then I see the wall where the guys get to pee. Sydney looks mesmerized as if it were the eighth wonder of the world. "So who cleans it off the wall?" I ask.

"It washes itself. Like a waterfall, an automatic flush."

"What kind of bathroom do the women have?

"Oh, it's just normal," Kristos answers as Sydney strokes the pewter fixtures.

"The rooms are made to look like cabins on an ocean liner," says Sydney. "Kristos, see if we can see one of the rooms."

Kristos holds the bathroom door open for Sydney and me to exit and I hold the door open for a man to enter. He looks confused and rereads the door's signage. "No, you're at the right place," I tell him. "Have fun."

As Kristos proceeds to the concierge to ask if we can see one of the rooms, I read the brochure about Philippe Stark, famous for "playing with weightlessness and appearances, defying both, creating illusions..." but there is no mention of Kristos designing the runner.

"The rooms are all occupied," says Kristos. I'll have to see the "ship" the next time.

Kristos leads us into a votive-filled room complete with its own wet bar and female bartender in a plunging backless Halston top, her armpits conspicuous as she mixes our drinks – Cosmopolitans for Sydney and Kristos, a Cape Cod for me. I fear how much the drinks will cost, for even if I forego a drink it still may be my turn to pick up the tab since Sydney paid for dinner – with her Platinum Amex.

We find seating and Kristos excuses himself to talk to someone he knows – a model.

"So how long have you and Kristos dated?" I ask.

"Almost two years," Sydney answers.

"So do you think you'll get married to him?" I ask, intending to gauge the level of devastation and shock she will feel when Kristos breaks up with her as he plans.

"No. In fact, I'm thinking of breaking off the relationship," she says, exhaling smoke rings.

"Why?" I ask, trying to contain my impulse to tell her how relieved I am because Kristos feels exactly the same way.

"I just don't know if I could marry him. His family is very old world – well *you* know," she says as if I were still under their influence, in harm's way, vulnerable to the family doctrine, as if I was still Pavlos' girlfriend. "Kristos wouldn't want me to work or have a career. And I'm not giving up acting."

"He'd make you give up acting?" I ask. That doesn't sound right. I certainly wouldn't have given it up, and Pavlos never alluded to it being a point of contention with his family, not that we got that far. "So you think you might move out?" I asked, suddenly hopeful that we could share an apartment (and, more importantly, share the cost of rent and utilities) which would certainly open up more possibilities should I not get #704.

"Oh, no. He'd be the one to leave," she says, reclining. "It's my apartment."

"It's your apartment? I thought it was Kristos'," I say, unnerved that Kristos invited me to stay at an apartment that he said was his, but isn't. It's one thing to impose on the brother of the boyfriend, another whole other thing to impose on the never-before-met-girlfriend of the brother of the boyfriend who really isn't a boyfriend anymore.

"No, it's mine. I had it before I met Kristos. Kristos was living with Pavlos until he moved in with me," she says. "I mean, he's paying right now, but it's my name on the lease."

"CLAUDIA SCHIFFER lives here," says Sydney as we descend the catwalk towards the elevator of the Colossus, Kristos trailing behind, collecting his receipt.

"Yeah, that's what Kristos said," I respond, figuring it's all but certain. I'm the last to know: Pavlos and Claudia are a couple. *Why else would Kristos and Sydney both separately in under twenty-four hours inform me that Claudia lives here?* Surely it isn't newsworthy otherwise. *Is it?*

Kristos jumps aboard the elevator and we ascend home to #4519.

"I HOPE the couch will be ok for you," says Sydney tenderly, fluffing her bed pillows − five of them: two standard, two euro, and one neckroll.

"Of course," I say, sincerely grateful, having vowed never again to take for granted, a roof over my head or a non-pedophilic host.

"Here's a pillow for you," she says, tossing me the neckroll.

I lie down on the couch, my back to the lovebirds-on-the-verge-of-breakup, facing the city of lights, amazed that I'm sleeping over with Pavlos' brother and girlfriend instead of with Pavlos himself. I wonder if Sydney or Kristos know how difficult this is for me, to be unable to see or speak to someone who I was (and still want to be) in love with. *Is it as Kristos and Sydney suggested, just a matter of time before Pavlos and me are together again? If Pavlos never wanted to see me again, his brother certainly wouldn't be putting a roof over my head − would he?*

Still, it's odd to think that only a few floors separate me and Pavlos. If he weren't in L.A. (if he's indeed in L.A.) we'd be looking up at the same skyline, he'd be thinking of me as I am of him, wondering why we should so senselessly be apart when only an elevator ride keeps our flesh from connecting. *Surely his libido would kick in and override any conflicting sensibility, like mine has, and he'd come knocking for me to return - wouldn't he?*

"Night," says Sydney and Kristos, turning off the light.

"Night." I lie in bed, the skyline even more mesmerizing, and recall the night I met him.

We met at the MTV Movie Awards. Olive knew the associate producer and had obtained coveted Talent Escort jobs for us. Olive begged to escort Kyle McLachlan and was told her wish would be granted. I was told I would not be escorting talent but signing them in at a desk. Instead, I was assigned Tom Arnold. As soon as Olive and I had finished escorting, we raced to Olive's car in the corner of the Sony studio parking lot and changed out of our escort T-shirts and volunteer tags into our black dresses and VIP tags, ducking talkative passersby as I duct-taped my breasts (no bra worked as well) and pulled on nylons. We then exited the car and headed toward the VIP post party in a tent on the lot, taking the red carpet – Olive boldly as if she belonged, me tentatively as if an alarm would sound.

I noticed Pavlos' drink before I noticed him. I remarked that we were both drinking Cape Cods. And then we must have introduced ourselves. And then Pavlos remarked that he had a girlfriend in high school named Olive which I took to mean he was interested in my sister or he would have had a girlfriend named Eve. I recused myself from competition by adopting a blasé loser pose but as instantly as I did, Pavlos' friend, Malcolm, engaged Olive in a private conversation and Pavlos turned to me.

At first I thought he looked Greek-Mafioso with his brown muddy pools for eyes, slicked back, dark brown hair, black euro-GQ mock turtleneck and slacks ensemble, prominent Athens-tan forehead, and devilish hairline. Just as I was deliberating over whether I could ever be attracted to someone with such a devilish hairline, he smiled and the corners of his lips turned up, displaying friendly teeth and the sweetest boyish grin, and I knew there was something there between us. And then came the defining moment. He escorted me to the Sanican section under a separate white tent.

After relieving myself with some difficulty due to my intoxicated state, I flung open the green fiberglass door where Pavlos was gallantly waiting to help me down. So when he additionally blocked the ricocheting door from hitting me in the face, I was smitten. Seven minutes later, Olive announced she was going home and Pavlos asked me to join him and his "party of five" (to be later known as the party of seven) to the Viper Room. And so, without a big-sisterly protest, Olive and I diverged paths.

Whoosh!

"Whaaa?" I exclaim, my heart palpitating from the unidentifiable whoosh! Sound slitting the otherwise silent air. I force my eyes open only to see complete, unnerving blackness.

"Sorry. I was just closing the blinds," says Kristos, his voice on the other side of the room near the window, explaining that the unleashing of metal was, not as I had thought, the falling blade of a guillotine. "Unless you want them open."

"No, no," I answer, too fatigued to respond further, as if there were more to say, *al a* "Rosebud".

"It's just that it will be light in a couple of hours and this room will be filled with light and keep us awake, and I don't know about you, but I want to sleep in," he says, his voice drawing near in the dark making me realize, perhaps belatedly, how easy it would be for a passerby to suffocate me with my own pillow. (Death by neckroll.) With all my might, I try to summon a defensive position in the event Kristos tries to do away with me. (People often do at night what they wouldn't do by day.) Even though I have no visibility, I force my eyes to stay open and tighten my body into a fist just until Kristos clears the couch, my bed. My brain, however, is preoccupied with how ridiculous Kristos would think me if he could tell through the bedcover how ramrod my body is. But, then again, Kristos will only know how tense I am if he touches me. And if he's touching me, my strength will have been summoned for good reason and not from misguided paranoia. Either due to difficulty navigating the darkness, or his uncertainty about how to come at me – pillow smothering, strangling, oh the many choices – Kristos' passing takes forever and I am losing the fight to stay awake. Then I hear laughter. Nonstop laughter muffled by bedcovers.

"What's so funny?" I ask, not opening my eyes, feeling overconfident for having survived this far into the night.

"Sorry Eve, we didn't mean to wake you," says Sydney, catching her breath.

"Sydney wants to have a threesome," announces Kristos, wide-awake.

"I do not," she protests mildly, muffling Kristos' mouth with her hand.

"Ever had a threesome Eve?" Kristos asks, breaking free of Sydney.

"No, can't say that I have." So that's why Kristos has invited me here. In Chelsea they want decks painted. In Midtown they want threesomes.

"Don't pay any attention to Kristos. He just has a fantasy of two women," says Sydney, reassuringly.

"And you don't?" Kristos asks Sydney who responds with what sounds like a sock to his gut.

"What about you Eve?" asks Kristos. "Ever fantasized about a threesome?"

"Nope. Can't say that I have. But if I did have a fantasy about a threesome... the other two would be men," I answer unequivocally.

"What if, hypothetically speaking, the other two were brothers?" asks Kristos.

"Actually, I just read in this month's *Cosmopolitan* that the top male fantasy is to sleep with two sisters."

"Well not me," says Kristos.

"Yeah, right," says Sydney, disbelieving.

"Listen. If I were lucky enough to sleep with two women, I couldn't care less if they were blood related or not," insists Kristos.

"Well, on that note, I think I'll say goodnight," I say, feigning mild amusement.

"Oh, by the way Eve. You have to be careful with Ty," says Sydney.

"Ty?"

"My cat. The calico one," she says.

"Why is that?" I ask.

"Because he likes to sleep on people's heads."

"Really? How does that work?" I ask.

"Not easily," says Sydney, matter-of-factly. "If he does jump on your head, just don't move abruptly or he'll scratch your face with his feet. In fact, it's better if you don't sleep on your back."

"O.K. Thanks," I say, pulling up the sheet over my head, feeling fortunate that I sleep on my stomach and therefore expose only one side of my face as if victory goes to the person who gets only one side of her face scratched. But when the image of just one side of my face scratched up persists and brings no consolation, I bury my head between the back of the couch and the armrest, under a neckroll pillow, in suffocating form.

"WHAAA?" I yelp, hours (and mid-REM) later. Oh. It's Ty. The calico one. On top of my head.

18. MIRACLE ON 44ᵀᴴ STREET

olores called. I got the apartment! It's my Miracle on 44th Street! Or a parting of the Red Sea – but that seems a bit over the top. This is the first time that I feel like Manhattan was fated. It seems that losing my job, getting struck by a drunk, being left homeless by my sister, and the couple skipping out on their #704 lease were not part of some random chain of events leading to an even more random destiny (which therefore wouldn't qualify as destiny at all), but part of a Master Plan to move me cross country. *But for what?*

———

As Kristos and Sydney help me load my suitcases into a cab, he looks at me in a way I understand but pretend not to. He has a girlfriend, but he would like to have me – at my new unfurnished apartment.

"I'll go with you. You'll need help," Kristos says, leaning his neck into the taxi, his face too close to mine.

"No really, I'll be fine. There's a doorman," I insist, closing the door after Kristos gives me an unwanted kiss on the lips.

"You sure you don't want to borrow a pillow?" asks Sydney, holding the neckroll.

"No, really, I'm fine," I say, my neck still sore from four nights with the neckroll.

"But what are you going to use for a pillow?" asks Kristos.

"I'll just use some clothes, really, I'm totally fine. Thanks again, really. I don't know what I would have done without your help." And I sincerely mean it.

With that, we exit out of the Colossus circular. I feel so relieved that my dependency upon others is officially *finis*. Even if Sydney had offered one of her other pillows (the euro, for example), I'd have refused. I don't want to be linked to Pavlos or indebted to any of his relations any longer, certainly not by a pillow, least of all by a neckroll.

"Where to?" the driver asks.

I want to say, "home James" but settle for "Forty-fourth Street between First and Second please." As we drive up First Avenue, approaching my new neighbors, the Diplomats, we are barricaded by police and Nuns. "What's going on?" I ask driver who's cussing under his breath and pounding on his steering wheel.

"The Pope is in town," he answers. "Messing up traffic."

Wow. And he's in my neighborhood! Well no wonder I got a Miracle.

"Sorry, you're going to have to keep moving," says a uniformed policeman to my driver when we try to stop at the corner of my street.

"But I live here."

"Well then consider it blessed. But you'll have to keep moving."

Eventually I arrive at my new home and pass through the double doors, down the steps, watching as some people stand in apartment-scouting position in the lobby just as I had only days earlier.

"Hello pretty lady," says a short man with large blue eyes and glasses, wearing a green custodial suit with a nametag that says Sammy. "Are you in 704?"

"Yes."

"Well just call if you need anything. My name's Sammy."

"Thanks Sammy, my name is Eve."

"Pleasure is all mine," he says as he presses the elevator button for me.

I arrive at my front door, unlock it, cross the threshold, drop my bags, and lock the door. I lie down in the center of my studio on the gray carpet, and stare at the white ceiling, thankful I have one. *Hmmmm. Now what?*

19. THE HAMPTONS

"Hi Pebbles, I'm walking down Fifth Avenue...."

That's what Pavlos had said when he'd call me at work from his cell phone, giving me an audio tour of Manhattan. It was the first time he'd used his pet name for me. Pebbles, as in *The Flintstones*.

"I've just passed St. Patrick's Cathedral..." he'd say as I stared out a window at cars in the parking lot of the Marina Del Rey interior designer office.

I'd tell him how much I loved cathedrals, that I was reading *The Cathedral Builders*, and he'd confess that he'd always loved cathedrals too – the architecture. And now, walking around Manhattan, I was seeing them for myself.

As I step into St. Patrick's, there appear to be as many tourists as there are worshippers, and the Cardinal's sermon is barely audible over the clicking of cameras. I push a dollar into an offering box which permits me to light a candle and say a little prayer (for me...) which I hope isn't drowned out by the Hallelujah chorus. I exit a side door and venture north on Madison and begin zooming in on architectural details when I hear a familiar refrain.

"Are you a professional photographer?" a man south of me bellows.

Oh no, not this again. The camera around my neck is like a garlic garland intended to ward off preying men, but attracting rather than repelling. I turn around to see a red-vested waiter on the sidewalk.

"No not really. More of a tourist I answer," I respond (as if downgrading my professional status will effect a different outcome than it did in Central Park).

"What's your name?" he asks.

"Eve," I call out as I continue walking away, viewing the details of Madison Avenue's skyline with my 210mm lens. *Hmmm.* Professional photographer. Maybe that's what I'm supposed to do since everyone is mistaking me for one.

"What?" he asks, calling after me, his hand cupping his ear, trying to hear.

"Eve," I repeat.

"What?" he asks again, motioning for me not to repeat but to come closer. I idle in the sidewalk, uncertain what to do. I consider the big picture. A waiter standing on the street under a green awning. It's broad daylight on Madison Avenue. There are plenty of passersby and traffic. *What could be the harm?*

I walk towards him. "Eve."

"I know, I heard you the first time," he says, smiling. "Marco. Nice to meet you. So where are you going Eve?"

"Just taking pictures," I answer.

"So, you're a tourist?" he asks.

"No, I live here," I say, however strange it sounds to me. "As of a week ago today."

"Have you been to the Hamptons yet?"

"No."

"You've heard of the Hamptons, right?" he asks.

"Yes, vaguely."

"You want to go tonight?" he asks. "There's a big event there tonight. My friend is going. He's driving out tonight. You should go with him. The city is no place for a beautiful woman in the summer. The city's just dead in the summer. Look at it." He gestures to four fast-paced traffic lanes.

"So why isn't he the one doing the asking?"

"He's too shy to ask. But he saw you walking by. We both did. Here come in and talk to him. Have a drink."

I take a seat at a table for two, my back to the sidewalk. As I wait alone, I feel ridiculous, wondering if this wasn't just a ploy to get me to order dinner. I contemplate leaving when a man, resembling a middle-aged Hemingway sits down opposite me.

"Hello."

"Hello."

"Would you like some wine?" he asks, his accent unidentifiable. "Compliments of the House" he says.

"Oh, that's very nice. A merlot would be great, thanks."

He has a few words with the garcon, and then bashfully eyes me, seemingly more ill at ease than me with the setup. I wonder if my company hasn't been forced upon him.

"I'm Eve by the way," I say, extending my hand. He shakes my hand listlessly. I wait for him to offer his name. But he doesn't. "And what is your name?" I finally ask.

"In Gone," he mumbles, then looks away, tapping his fingers nervously against the votive candle centerpiece.

"Sorry?" I ask, not hearing him.

"Egon," he mumbles again, as a waiter sets down cocktail napkins for us, and then two goblets of red wine.

He lifts his glass and we clink.

"Egon? Isn't that the name of the restaurant?" I ask, suspecting he's pulling my leg and I'm slow on the uptake.

"Yes," he answers, modestly.

He is the Egon of Egon's!

"Oh! I was here just a few days ago for lunch," I say, only now realizing this was where Kristos brought me for lunch, where the Ex showed up.

Egon perks up. "You were here?"

"Yes."

"For lunch or dinner?"

"Lunch – "

"What'd you have?"

"Oh, just a salad but it was very good," I answer.

He leans in. "Tell me. What are your favorite places to eat here in Manhattan?"

"I don't know. I've only been here for a week now. I just moved from L.A.."

He rubs his chin. "But you say you've been here twice now?"

"Yes, isn't that funny? I haven't been anywhere, seen anything, but I've been here twice. "What accent is that?" I ask.

"Austrian," he says.

"That's right. The person I had lunch with told me the owner was Austrian and I told him how funny it was that you have a French illustration on your menu but serve Italian food, and yet you're Austrian," I say.

"Yes, I never thought of that," he says, letting out a shy laugh. "Eve, what do you do?"

"I'm pursuing acting but otherwise looking for a job."

"Have you heard of the Naked Angels?" he asks.

"The naked what?" I ask.

"Naked Angels. It's a group of actors. They're having their annual fundraiser in Southampton tonight. If you're serious about acting you really should come with me, you could meet the right people."

"For some reason, all I can picture are actors on motorcycles," I say.

He looks confused, doesn't get my reference to the Hell's Angels, a more clothed angel.

"Have you heard of Mars Tomy?" He asks, confusing me.

"Who?"

"Mars Tomy?"

"No."

"You know she was in that Cousin movie…"

"Andi McDowell?"

"No Mars Tomy. *Cousin Vinny*."

"Oh, you mean Marisa Tomei?" I ask.

"Yes. She'll be there. She's one of the co-founders," he says, as if looking out for my professional interests.

"Hmmm," I answer, pondering the prospects of networking with other actors so soon into my arrival, feeling Destiny presenting itself. Like Cinderella's Ball. Maybe the Hampton's Naked Angels is where my Destiny begins. After all, I did pray in St. Patrick's less than an hour ago. *Could God work this fast? Maybe He's faster because the Pope is in town?* And it is called Naked Angels like it's a sign I'm not supposed to miss. *I want to go, feel that I must go, but why the hard sell on the Hamptons? Do Egon and Marco get kickbacks for sending people there?* "So why is Marco trying to set you up?"

"I…I don't know," he shakes his head. "You were walking by…."

"Ahh, so you guys just pull in women off the street?"

"No, no," he says, sounding somewhat insulted. "No, this is nice. You're nice," he says sincerely. "I like your company."

"Thank you. I like your company too," I say.

"So, what do you think of the Hamptons?" he asks again.

"I don't know…"

"It wouldn't be just you and me. Raffi is coming too. He's driving my car," he says, pointing to the curly haired, thin waiter/bartender who delivered my merlot. "We're staying at the summer home of a friend. She's the co-editor of the *Hamptons Magazine* and she's house-sitting for the Editor. It's a beautiful three-story house, just a walk from the Atlantic. You'd have your own room of course."

"Well, I've never seen the Atlantic Ocean…."

"How is everything?" asks Marco.

"Good, fine," I answer.

"You see my friend is not so bad. Are you going to go? To the Hamptons?" he asks.

The anticipation of my answer lingers in the air like the 100% humidity. Egon looks as if he's already resigned himself to my refusal and looks away aloofly or forlornly. I never noticed what a fine line it is between aloof and forlorn. "Well. O.K. Sure. I'd love to but I have to go home and change," I answer, surprising Egon.

His face lights up and his posture straightens. "How much time do I have?"

"We'll pick you up at 8 p.m. Give your address to Raffi," says Egon.

I give my address to Raffi. "You can just ring the doorman and I'll run down," I said, excited by the fact that I am a legit New Yorker, having just devirginized my address, like the breaking of champagne against a boat.

Marco hails me a cab with a loud whistle and I wave goodbye.

I know exactly what I am going to wear: the same dress I wore the night I met Pavlos. The black A.J. Bari dress (whoever that is) that I may have shortened too much. It's really the only outfit I own for such an occasion. Crap! I need sheer black nylons. Where will I find nylons at 6:30 p.m. and still shower, do my hair and makeup, and pack for an overnight stay in under one and half hours? Two blocks later, at a stoplight, I ask the driver if he knows of a drugstore nearby. He points across the street to a place called "Boyd's of Madison." I pay $3 and get out of the taxi. I cross the street and enter Boyd's. But they don't have nylons. They recommend Saks. I hail another taxi. I buy nylons and Estee Lauder bronzer at Saks. I take yet another taxi home, rush past the doorman, up the elevator, throw down my Saks bag, strip and jump into the shower with thirty-five minutes left in which to get ready.

It's a strange feeling I'm getting a little accustomed to. Men – older men – richer men – finding me desirable. Something makes me feel that New York is going to be a place that finds me much more attractive than L.A. had. Here, I must stand out. I wonder what the difference is. I feel that this is the start of a very good change for me. Perhaps I need to be in New York to meet a better-suited man, if not a better-suited dream. *What a great shower!*

I apply make-up to my face, Estee Lauder bronzer to my legs, duct-tape my breasts and string up my hair in heated rollers, feeling kittenish-in-the-city as I recline carefully on the floor when the most obnoxious *"buzzzzzzzzzz"* startles me. I trace the sound to the kitchen where, on the wall, is a silver panel with two black knobs and a speaker pad. I press one of the knobs. It's my doorman.

"Egon is here," he says.

I have an intercom! "O.K. I'll be right down." I say, wondering if it's proper etiquette not to invite Egon up. But I have no choice. I still don't know what to pack for tomorrow, and if I am to walk the beach barefooted, my toenails need painted. *Besides, is it safe to pull on nylons only seconds after applying my tan? Oh geez… what if the doorman gave Egon the go ahead to come up? Can he do that? Without my explicit permission?* I have no idea what the Intercom Protocol is. The door could buzz, ring, knock any minute, and I'm just wearing duct tape. *Ohmygod, they can see me and my duct tape through the French windows! The Kuwaitis!* I need to get a third set of blinds to cover up the third window and I need to remember to close my blinds when I'm running around naked in duct tape. Well too late tonight.

Finally, an entire fifteen minutes later, I force myself out my door, take the elevator down to the lobby, toting my bag complete with wrinkled overnight clothes, a non-travel-size iron, toenail clippers, polish and remover, and a bathing suit I am sure I won't wear in front of the naturally tan people I am certain to meet.

I wave goodbye to my doorman – my very own Mr. Yunioshi, prepared to take shelter behind him if I am reprimanded for being late.

"I'm soooo sorry to keep you waiting," I say as Raffi, the waiter/bartender/chauffeur holds the back door of a gold Range Rover open for me.

"It's no problem," he says.

I slide in the backseat only to discover no one else there. "Where's Egon?" I ask.

"He's at the restaurant. We're going to go get him now," he says, shutting my door.

I am relieved that I've only made the waiter-bartender-chauffeur wait. However, if I'd known it was just Raffi down here, I could have done the ironing so that I wouldn't have had to bring the iron along. It doesn't quite look right, perched atop my bag that's intended for a beach stay.

As Raffi and I chat and I learn he is Hungarian and has been a bartender for six years, I attempt to stretch my dress to cover my derriere, which I never noticed until now, hikes up to crotch level when I'm seated.

Once back at the restaurant and double-parked on Madison, Egon emerges from the restaurant dressed in a light blue pinstriped oxford shirt, white pants, and navy blazer.

"You look beautiful," says Egon, surprised, kissing my cheek.

"Thank you," I answer, understanding Egon's surprise. I am a long way from the Gap-jeaned attire from before. Lipstick, a duct-taped bosom, and a hiked black dress go a long way.

Egon sends Raffi back into the restaurant and a minute later, Raffi returns with a bottle of Cristal. He uncorks it on the sidewalk and fills the flutes.

"Cheers," we clink, as Raffi jumps in and pulls into traffic.

"What's that smell? Is it your perfume?" asks Egon.

"Oh, um, is it citrusy?" I ask.

He sniffs again. "Yes."

It's my tan. "It's lotion," I answer. "Is it too strong? Maybe we should crack the window."

"What kind is it?" he asks.

"Oh, I can't remember which one I used." Clarins self-tanning. "Gio, I think."

As we drove along, and the skies grew darker the further we got away from Manhattan, and the bottle got emptier, I learned how Egon's family got its financial advantage: a patent on a device now used exclusively by NASA. Egon then advised me to set up my own company and save my receipts so that I could get bigger tax breaks. He was a total gentleman, not even flirting, and I felt safe, ready to meet my destiny: Marisa Tomei.

AT CLOSE to 11 p.m., Raffi pulled into a dark lot where hundreds of cars are randomly self-parked on uneven dirt and mud which makes me think we've mistakenly arrived at a Monster Truck Pull.

"You need help?" Egon calls out to me when I drag behind them by several car lengths on our way to the tent entrance, the distant light.

"No, I'm fine," I answer. "Just sinking a little" I mutter to myself as I press against parked cars to keep my four-inch heels from sinking further. I would prefer to rest on the arm of a gentlemanly escort if there were any around.

"Here she is," says Egon when I reach the check-in point, a red table-clothed check-in table where two women sit and two others stuff *In Style* magazine logo'd shopping bags. Egon attaches a plastic red band to my wrist so that we all look Ken Kesey compliant and we enter the tent whereupon it is abundantly clear even in the dim votive and oil lantern lights, that I am the only one wearing black at a spring color theme. I would have thought the Sydney-white-attire a fluke, the exception to the otherwise world-renowned New York Black Rule. It's perhaps not the black I'm wearing that's so out of place, as is the formality of my attire. *Who would've thought A.J. Bari would be the most couture of the evening?* It seems the only fashion "must" is a tan and mine won't be ready for a few more hours. I notice that here on the East Coast, women put most of their effort into the things that I ignore: the details. Toenails, fingernails, and individual strands of hair − all of which has been color-treated and double-processed. And the skin-baring rule of thumb appears to be bare arms and cleavage, two things I've covered entirely by my dress.

We've arrived so late that the heat lamps and the citronella centerpieces are being loaded up by the crack wait staff. Meanwhile, a continuous stream of young women stop over to kiss Egon on both cheeks, making it clear: everyone knows Egon. Egon, however, seems disinterested in the women. He's starving. Fortunately, one of his admirers summons a plate for him and Egon tears into the BBQ chicken, never to be heard from again. I stand behind him with Raffi, starving, smiling a lot and trying to look at ease as we're virtually ignored. I get looks just like the Knife thrower had given me. Curious furtive glances. Passive-aggressive hellos. Pretentious chatter. Fortunately, I feel comfortable with Raffi, like Shirley MacLaine with the Rat Pack. I am the lone tag-along girl that could go anywhere, make no demands on her escorts, and find her own way. I keep my eye out for Marisa Tomei, to no avail.

At midnight, the party benefiting actors other than me is over and we are directed to collect our goodie bags on the way out. Exiting autos have pureed the ground and my heels swim all the way to the Range Rover.

As we inch along in the Range Rover while awaiting our turn to exit, I inspect my goodies: a *Hampton Magazine*, Kiehls lipgloss, and a $50 gift certificate towards a spa treatment.

"There's Marisa Tomei," says Egon.

"Where?" I look up just in time to the back of her black BMW.

"Oh you just missed her," says Raffi.

At nearly 2 a.m., we arrived at a white cottage mansion where the co-editor of *Hampton Magazine* is supposedly expecting us. Raffi and I wait in the Rover, training the headlights on Egon who has been standing in front of the door knocking for ten minutes. Just when he's about to give up, a dirty-blonde woman wearing a man's short plaid robe opens the door for us, using her hand to visor her eyes. After they talk for a minute, Egon signals us to come in.

"Cornelia" shows us inside, first to the kitchen where a table is filled with empty beer bottles, half-filled tonic water jugs, chips, and empty pizza cartons. She removes a tin of turkey from the oven and bread and pasta salad from the refrigerator, setting it out for us to eat as she excuses herself, apologizing for being so tired she can't stay up with us. Egon digs into the turkey and I eat some rippled potato chips (all the pizza is gone) before retiring to my cabana in a separate wing of the house.

I CAN HEAR Egon rustling outside. I dread getting up. Since the Point Dume lodging arrangement, I prefer home court advantage.

Egon taps at my door.

"Hello?"

"It's Egon. Am I waking you?"

"No, no, I was just getting up.

"There's breakfast in the kitchen when you're ready."

"Is everyone waiting?" I ask.

"No. Only me, you and Raffi are here. Everyone else has already headed up to the beach," he said. "I told them we'd join them later. Don't forget to put on your swimsuit."

"Oh I didn't bring a swimsuit," I lie.

"I'm sure Cornelia has a suit you can wear," he says.

"No really it's ok, I'm too fair to lay out anyway. I'll burn."

"We have suntan lotion," insists Egon, who leaves and returns seconds later with two bathing suits for me to choose from, which he hands through the crack of the door.

"Thanks," I say, finding his zealousness in getting me a swimsuit quite suspect. Then again, my only apprehension is my paleness, and the east coast can hardly be as tan as the west coast. For once my paleness might not be the palest.

I am wrong. I am the palest. The three of us are quite a sight: skinny pale man in shorts with high-top curly hair, a heavy thin-haired man in red floral Bermuda shorts, and a pale white girl in jeans and shirt with Cornelia's bathing suit underneath as I really did forget to pack mine. We walk over a sandbank approaching seven bodies on their back, sunglasses on their eyes, water bottles beside them, no doubt the same group who ate the pizza and drank beer the night before, now the vision of clean leaving. I am introduced to the four guys and three women, all clearly enveloped in their ritualistic weekend of tanning and beach companionship, all clearly not interested in pale newcomers. As Egon talks to them, I stand there, feeling all eyes registering my pale feet, the only part of my body fully exposed. Egon removes his shirt and with Raffi, runs into the ocean. Meanwhile, I notice that I have managed to embed sand into the topcoat of my toenail polish.

After a few hours at the ocean, and another couple of hours lollygagging around the house, and as Egon stroked a red Lamborghini in the garage, we loaded up the Range Rover to return to Manhattan. On the way, I received a message from a personnel agency: I have a job interview on Monday with a famous hotelier.

20. THE HOTELIER(S)

IT SEEMS a meaningful coincidence that my first job interview in Manhattan is with world-renowned hotelier, Ian Schrager, the man who owns the Royalton Hotel (one of several five-star hotels) where Kristos and Sydney took me in my very first week here. *What are the odds?* I'll be able to tell him that I've seen the men's bathroom, of course only if it comes up in conversation. And maybe my prior jobs spent managing the Five-Star estates of celebrities weren't so random after all, but apprenticeships. The psychic did say she saw me around a "lot of houses." Perhaps, the universe wants me to be a hotelier instead of an actor. And maybe I should be more open to what the universe has in store for me.

Unfortunately it's 90 degrees out and raining and it appears I have underestimated the time it takes to crawl westward in a taxi across town. *How could I have underestimated traffic? Why would rain slow everything down?* I might be fifteen minutes late. Only ten seems acceptable. I try and distract myself from the stress of time passing by focusing on the windshield wipers. My heart begins to beat with the rhythm of the blades. All of it somehow relaxes me. *Or am I hypnotized?* Just as the Indian Rock radio station breaks through my concentration, the taxi driver breaks free of the gridlock.

"SO ARE YOU familiar with my hotels?" asks Ian Schrager who is seated behind a heavy wood desk that is stacked with paint chips, wood blocks and fabric swatches. He looks barricaded, as if his only way out is from under the desk.

"Well, I've only been here a week, but I saw the Royalton," I answer, as I sit opposite him.

"Really?"

"Yes, in fact I went with the person who designed the blue runner," I answer.

"You know Philippe?" He asks me.

"Philippe?"

"Philippe Starck?"

"No, um, Kristos Polychronopolis," I answer.

Ian looks confused.

"He helped Philippe," I inform him.

Ian looks confused.

"And I loved the men's bathroom," I add.

"What'd you think of the women's?"

"Oh. I didn't see it."

Ian looks confused.

Ian spends five minutes with me, twirling a pencil, and then has me meet his entourage – the President, Director of Design, the Marketing Girl – all of whom question my ability to work for a temperamental person. After giving them a satisfactory answer (I have worked for very scary people, so he doesn't scare me) I am thanked and asked my possible start date. They tell me they have just one more person to see and will be in touch.

I share the elevator down to the lobby with a businessman and room service personnel. On my way out, I survey the landscape of where I anticipate I will be collecting a paycheck and mixed drinks. Suddenly, life is looking up.

Outside, however, is a veritable hurricane. But emerging from a hotel has its advantages. Instead of competing with the sidewalk pedestrians, a hotel valet whistle-stops a taxi for me. *Ahhh, the life of an ingénue!* I begin to imagine myself taking daily taxis here and get starry-eyed until I realize it's the same place a prostitute would work.

I am barely inside the taxi when the driver guns it to make a yellow light, only to abruptly break to observe the stoplight, such that the car bounces. As I watch others trudge through the flash flood, caught without umbrellas, I feel smugly cozy, so happy to be in from the rain while they brave a storm – until I hear loud banging. I figure it's the sound of envious pedestrians hitting the car but when the pedestrians clear the crosswalk, there is a short, blonde policewoman pounding on the hood of my taxi, her hands clenched around a wood baton, yelling something inaudible. She rounds to the driver's door, yanks it open, pulls the driver out of his seat.

"A cop's been shot, get out!" she yells at me.

My foot barely out of the taxi, I watch as she speeds through the red light and cuts across Broadway heading east. The taxi driver and I stand at the curb. I am shaken but swept up by pedestrian traffic. I search for my umbrella to no avail. I have left it in the backseat of the taxi.

"YOU'LL NEVER guess what just happened!" I exclaim as Egon and me exchange euro kisses. "I just came from an interview at the Paramount Hotel – "

"Here, come, come, sit. What do you want to drink?" Egon asks, guiding me from the doorway towards the bar.

"Oh I can't stay. Actually, I just need to get my iron," I say, embarrassed to admit I brought a full-sized iron to the beach. "I think I left it in the back of your car."

"Raffi will get the iron for you" he says. "You look nice. Why are you so wet?" I couldn't' get a cab. I just walked from Times Square."

"Here, have a seat with my friend, Dale Byle," Egon says, passing me off to a sixty-something old man, as they stand and pull a seat out for me, before Egon takes off towards the kitchen.

"Hi. Nice to meet you."

Dale is sixty-four years old. He is heir to a fortune made from his uncle and father creating pantyhose. He owns several four and five-star hotels in the U.S. and Mexico. Perhaps I would like to manage one, he asks. He tells me that he's divorcing his fourth wife who's just a few years older than me and who has hair the color of mine. He likes redheads. Do I have freckles, he asks? He likes freckles.

"So why are you so wet?" he asks.

"Well I just – "

Dale excuses himself from the table, he sees a friend walking by. He returns to tell me it was Joan Rivers. "She's a very good friend of mine," he says. "You know her husband shot himself."

"Yes I know."

Dale mentions he's staying at the Waldorf-Astoria. He *always* stays at the Waldorf. "Have you ever been there?" he asks me.

"No."

Raffi returns. He didn't see my iron. He said he'll have another look tomorrow, in the light.

"The Waldorf is where the Duke and Duchess of Windsor lived, lots of famous people. Every United States President since Herbert Hoover has stayed there. "Would you like to see it?" Dale asks.

"Now?"

"Well, why not? It's a famous landmark. It's where Princess Grace and Prince Rainier of Monaco had their engagement party. You should see it."

I wait outside the restaurant for Dale, who is supposed to let Egon know I'll be back. Dale rejoins me, toting a bottle of red wine.

"Did you tell Egon we'll be right back?" I ask.

"He's busy. We'll just go," he says.

As Dale escorts me out of the restaurant, I hope he grabbed the wine for his own medicinal purposes because the vision of me and him and a bottle of wine heading to the Waldorf is disgusting.

AFTER AN ASKANCE look at the Waldorf lobby clock (formerly of the Chicago World's Fair 1893), Dale and I take the elevator up to the 3rd floor. I don't know what I was thinking. It feels far too intimate a place to be visiting at 10 p.m.. Dale described it like it was a place to take a tour, but it's a *hotel.* Correction, hotel *room.*

And the room, which I expected to be large and grand – a suite – is no larger than any other hotel room I've been in. No larger than a Holiday Inn. I attempt to find the opening to the heavy drapery blocking this supposed "magnificent view" I just had to see.

"I'm just going to use the bathroom, make yourself comfortable," Dale says, after opening the wine bottle and filling two glasses, handing me one and setting the other on a cocktail table by the window.

The view is of nothing more than the side street I was just walking on. I sit in the chair, eye the wine and realize the danger immediately. I had looked at Dale as a grandfather figure, someone who had the intention only of broadening my knowledge of the "finer things in life" never dreaming he'd consider himself one of them. I stand up in bolting position, ready to leave the second he returns from the bathroom where I actually hear *sounds* – of a bowel kind.

Dale emerges from the bathroom, seemingly invigorated, places the wine glass back in my hand and grabs me at the waist, attempting to Waltz?

I push off his chest to extricate myself, and place the glass on the table in order to vacate, when he, in one unexpected motion, forcefully pulls me into his protruding mass of belly, aiming his face squarely at mine. As I fight with all my might to disengage and dodge his advancing lips, we stumble and fall onto the bed, his roly poly flesh on top of me. I could *kvetch.*

"Time for me to leave," I say, pushing his hands and legs away from their ensuing wrap around me.

"Fine," he relents. "I'm going to bed anyway. You can join me if you'd like," he says getting up from the bed, dropping his pants, exposing saggy white briefs, and saggier withered skin. He flops back onto the bed as I roll off towards the door. "Would you mind turning off the light on your way out. The switch is to your left."

I flip the switch and exit his room, the image of his of old saggy, droopy skin folds on his legs still with me even out into the well-lit hall. I press the button for the elevator, catching my reflection in a Georgian gilt-framed wall mirror, totally unable to see what it is these men see in me that would suggest I am compatible with them. Men my own age aren't the least forward with me so why should I have imagined the converse, that men more incompatible (i.e. into their sixties) would be.

I walk back to Egon's to retrieve my iron as the twin copper caps of the Waldorf and its less spectacular occupants recede behind me.

Egon meets me at the door with sad eyes. "Where did you go?

"I went with Dale to see the Waldorf."

"So where is he?"

"He's at the hotel."

"How could you leave with him? All this time, I've been such a gentleman with you."

"I just wanted to see the Waldorf," I respond innocently, feeling badly that Egon mistakes it for more. "That's all. I'm not interested in him at all." I shudder at the thought!

"So then come with us. We're going up the street to Frederick's. It's a club you should see," says Egon.

"Oh, I should really get home."

"Home? But it's only 10:30," he says.

"Only 10:30?"

"SO YOU DO know that it's not the original Waldorf don't you?" asks Egon as we walk up Madison Avenue.

"What do you mean?" I ask, my stomach sinking at the prospect that I have just risked my life to see a building that isn't the original but the equivalent of a xerox.

"The original one, the one that you're thinking of, was on 34th street where the Empire State Building is now."

Dale's skinfolds and pre(?)cancerous moles flash before me. I look straight into the headlights of oncoming traffic to shake the (hopefully short-term) memory.

Egon and Raffi escort me down some steep and dark stairs that lead to Frederick's where Egon is immediately hailed to a table of young attractive men and women. Egon asks my permission to excuse him for a minute, and then just as I get comfortable on a banquette opposite the bar, he hails me over. While Raffi begs off joining, the group squeezes together and chairs screech on the floor so I can join. Egon buys everyone a round of drinks and whispers to me that I should really get to know these people, that they are the "elite," young scions of famous clans, covering every industry, all of whom, as evidenced by Egon's introduction are one degree of separation from some part of the Hamptons. He'll introduce me.

He introduces me to a model turned interior decorator with a shop now in Southampton. We exchange a few words but when she hears I'm originally from Oregon, she appears to lose interest. He introduces me to a model turned investment banker with family in Bridgehampton. He loses interest when he hears I'm looking for a job. When all of their entrees arrive, we say our goodbyes.

Bye Egon, bye Egon, *mwah, mwah,* kiss kiss.

I'm ready to go home, but Egon has another stop in mind: Au Bar. We arrive minutes later but they are closed. I think that's the end of it, but Egon still wants to go in. Price of admission for an empty, closed bar: same rate as a filled and open bar. $20 each. Egon pays my admission.

The place is empty save for a couple dressed in black, dark shades, and powder-white faces. They look like they've emerged from a vampire party.

I heed the call of the music and empty dance floor in front of the deejay's booth, and dance. I wait for Egon to join me but instead spot him talking to the couple. The song ends and Egon announces we're leaving. He just wants to make one stop before he drops me off at home.

We park outside a hotel and take the elevator up to the sixth floor. Egon knocks on #610 and I am shocked to see the vampire woman answering it, her shades still on. Her boyfriend is in the back room, and "coming out shortly." She cleans off the table in front of the couch, removing filled ashtrays. The boyfriend comes out and plops down in the center of the couch, pulling out a bag of white powder. Vampire woman displays a broken mirror, lays it flat on the table. Boyfriend pours the white powder on the mirror.

"Want some?" Egon asks me.

"No thanks," I say, as Egon partakes.

Ten minutes later, we leave, and Raffi drops me off at my apartment. "Can I come up?" asks Egon, no longer the shy Austrian.

"No, sorry, I'm going to bed," I say.

"Well that would be fine. Seriously, I just want to see your apartment," says Egon.

"There's nothing to see. I don't even have a chair," I say. "Have a good night."

"Then can I get a good night kiss?" Egon asks.

I lean in to quickly peck his cheek but get a portion of his lip.

I enter my well-lit, doorman-guarded lobby, take the elevator up, relieved to have survived the night of taxi-commandeering cops, salacious pantyhose heirs, and vampirous cocaine dealers. But I still don't have my iron.

Before turning off my lights, I glance at my New York travel guide and discover Egon is right. The original Waldorf Hotel was built in 1893 on the site where the Empire State Building now stands. It says that a women's hospital was torn down to make way for the "new" Waldorf.

21. MRS. BYLE IV

"Eve, I made the reservation for 7 p.m. See you there," says Dale on my voicemail.

Sometime in between Dale suggesting that I could run his five-star hotel in Mexico and throwing me on his five-star hotel bed on Park Avenue, I had agreed to meet him for dinner to discuss running his hotel as opposed to running away from it. After baring his briefs and what lied beneath, he actually thinks I would still show up?! *Uck.* My stomach drops at the thought of going through with the dinner. My stomach drops at the thought of speaking to him even over the phone to give my regrets. I contemplate the ramifications of saying "no." I calculate karma damage and repair costs, consider the Golden Rule, and factor in Egon's friendship. I don't need someone new in my life to think badly about me. It's just dinner. I can be done with the whole thing in no time and make everyone (but me) happy. On the other hand, I can say I don't feel well. In fact, I am feeling a little nauseous.

Nervously, I dial Dale, ready to puke at the sound of his voice.

"Dinner's all set," says Dale before I can give my regrets. "And I've invited some friends to join us. The Zinnmans. A lovely couple."

"Well actually I was calling because I'm not feeling well. I've had a headache all day." *Headache is much more believable than gag reflex.*

"Well you're not thinking of canceling are you? I've made reservations," he says with appall. "And I've invited friends. It would be rude to cancel at the last minute. This kind of etiquette might fly in Los Angeles but it's unacceptable in New York."

"Well you could still meet them – "

"The reservation is for four. Besides, I've told them all about you. They want to meet you. You'll love them, they're a fabulous couple."

"O.K.," I say, dreading what lies ahead.

Five minutes later Dale calls back. "I wasn't able to get a reservation for four at the original restaurant, so we're going to have dinner at Egon's instead," he says, revealing that he lied about having a reservation for four.

"Fine," I say, practicing New York etiquette, relieved by the new, familiar venue. Two additional people, and Egon in proximity.

EGON GREETS me with outstretched arms. "Did you see the *Hampton's Magazine*?" he asks.

"No, why?"

"You're in it!" he exclaims. "On page two. There's a picture of you and me at the Naked Angels benefit. I'm going to put it up on the board," he says, referring to a wall of photos that cover the wall by the bar.

"I didn't realize anyone was taking pictures," I say, trying to recall the flash of lights.

"It was Patrick McMullan. He does photography for *The New York Post* and *Vanity Fair* too. Do you know some people live their whole lives in the Hamptons and never get their picture in the magazine, and you have it in your first week here?"

"Which reminds me. I found out why I got kicked out of a taxi by a cop yesterday."

"Oh?"

"It's on the cover of today's *New York Times*, in the Metro section. Did you see it? About the "Subway Cop Shooter?""

"No I didn't – "

"Well apparently a cop was shot in the subway on Lexington and other cops from the area raced to the scene, including the one that kicked me out of the cab."

"Oh. So, here sit, sit," Egon insists. He pulls out a chair for me, gestures for the waiter to greet me.

"Oh. I can't. I'd love to, really, but I'm actually here to meet, um, Dale for dinner. He invited me yesterday. Just as friends of course," I emphasize, not truly suspecting Egon would think anything more of me with this ugly old man. But, Egon's eyes lose their smile and he distractedly gestures to where Dale is seated – in a four top against the opposite wall – as he walks away.

"Eve." Dale motions for me. I walk over. He takes a tight hold on my hand and kisses my cheek. "What are these?" he asks critically, fingering the straps of my denim Gap overalls.

"Overalls."

"To dinner?" Dale asks.

"Yes." My plan is working. I purposefully wore my overalls to play up my youthful appearance to prove that I'm too young for a sixty-plus year-old man such as Dale and eliminate any idea Dale might have that this dinner would be romantic.

"I guess this is what they're wearing in Los Angeles?" he asks.

Mr. Zinnman stands and kisses my hand. Mrs. Zinnman looks up at me radiantly. They are approximately seventy-five years old. Conversation ensues as Dale attempts to touch my leg, place his hand on my hand. I withdraw contact every time, sometimes less subtly than others, and resist eye contact because of the lascivious look in his eyes.

"You know I have four children? asks Mrs. Zinnman.

"You do?" I ask.

"Yes, and they were all there to celebrate my husband and my 50th wedding anniversary last August. We've been married fifty years!" says Mrs. Zinnman.

"Wow. Fifty years. That's wonderful," I say.

"Yes and my sons and daughters, I have four, they all were there, and their children, my grandchildren. Yes we've been married fifty years. Last August we celebrated our 50th Wedding anniversary. Would you believe my husband and I have been married 50 years?"

"Yes, that's incredible." I tell her, turning away to take in the last part of a joke Mr. Zinnman is telling but I only hear the punch line.

Mrs. Zinnman laughs and grabs my hand. "Did you know, last August, my husband and I celebrated our 50th wedding anniversary with our four children?" she asks.

"That's wonderful," I say, smiling. "Did you have a good time?"

"She's going to be my fifth wife" Dale announces, taking my hand into his. I drag it away. "Isn't she lovely?"

"She's too young for you!" says Mr. Zinnman, the voice of reason.

"'She's a baby," Mrs. Zinnman says. "How old are you dear?"

"Twenty four," I answer.

"Age doesn't matter. My fourth wife was thirty," Dale insists, beaming at me, trying to seduce my hand atop the dinner table before I anxiously pull it away.

As Dale's other hand grips my leg under the table for the third time and I swat it away with a look of disapproval and disgust, Dale turns on me. Sharing eye contact only with Mr. and Mrs. Zinnman, he starts telling a joke – a joke that begins with Jews and Gentiles and has, by the end of it, the Jews and Gentiles and the Zinnmans and himself each able to make multiples of a million dollars if given the chance. And then he looks at me with a look usually associated with a bowel movement and says, "You give it to her? She'd piss it off in a second. At her age, she's got no intelligence for money, just for blowing it."

Apparently, Dale doesn't take rejection well.

"Well if I'm so stupid, why would you want to marry me?" I smile. *Wanna play rough old man?*

"Come to think of it, you're not exactly marriage material. I like my wives with sophistication, brains, a woman who doesn't wear coveralls to dinner," says Dale, waving me away.

"They're called overalls."

"Ready to order?" asks Raffi, looking around the table.

"You know? My husband and I have been married fifty years," says Mrs. Zinnman to Raffi.

"Really? That's wonderful," says Raffi.

"Last August, we had an anniversary party. All my family was there. It was beautiful. You know we've been married fifty years?"

"I'm sorry to interrupt. I'd love to stay for dinner, but I have to go," I say, removing my napkin from my lap.

"Oh, so soon?" asks Mrs. Zinnman.

"Yes she has to go. Has some other place to be," Dale says flatly, drinking his wine. "Shall we order?" He picks up his menu and begins reading.

"Yes, I'm sorry, I have to go. I told some friends I would meet them." I remove $20 from my wallet and, just as I place it on the table, Dale swipes it into his wallet and into his inside blazer pocket. "It was very nice meeting you," I say to the Zinnmans and disband from the table, instantly regretful that I left money. I should have thought more about my finances than my pride. I'm out twenty dollars just for coming. As my nerves rumble like bubbling lava, I make a beeline for Egon, the "gentleman" of the two, and my reality check.

I tap his shoulder, but he doesn't respond. I tap harder and he turns away from me even more. He must not know it's me. I try to come around his other side and put my face in his line of vision, but as I do, he rotates further, his back to me at every pivot. I am slow to realize that this is no coincidental rotation. Since he can't possibly know what just transpired between me and Dale, it can only be that he is mad at me for coming to his restaurant of all places to meet his friend, whom he must think I prefer or am interested in. Everything I tried to avoid by coming has occurred because I came. I push through a swarm at the door to get out, the air so thick I could choke.

As I walk a few steps down Madison, the fresh air and plentiful passersby nudge me back into reality and an undesired return to the depths of self-pity I thought were behind me. Only days into my fresh start, I can't understand how I've become so tainted in my new friend, Egon's mind. If only Egon knew how innocently I intended things to be. I feel like I'm floating in some alternate reality, on mean streets and need to reacquaint myself with the pre-Egon, pre-Pavlos reality. I need a reality check. I'll call Vicky. She's the perfect person to share this story with. She recently melted down four rings given to her from ex-boyfriends, and then put the stones into a new setting. Her loud obnoxious laugh is just the medicine I need to quell my nerves. I dial. The phone rings and rings. *Oh come on, answer.*

"Hello?"

"Vicki," I say relieved. "I'm in the middle of Madison Avenue and you won't believe what has just happened."

She laughs. "Let me get off the other line." She returns. "OK, guess who that was?"

"Who?" I ask, willing to give her ten seconds before I jump in.

"Bob. Remember the one that didn't want to see me because he liked me too much?" she laughs. "He wants to go out tonight. I told him I can't because I've just put on this facemask."

"So wash it off."

"No I can't. It's a prescriptive facemask. I'm on this regimen and I can't miss a day," she says.

"Wouldn't it be easier to just take pills?"

"Well I used to do that, but I don't want to do it anymore."

"Oh because of the side effects? You could have a disfigured child?"

"No, I don't care about that. I just never remember to take them."

"O.K. New subject. You won't believe this, I'm standing outside on Madison Avenue having just been blown off by two men – one who is 45 and one who is 65 in under two minutes." Vicki howls. It is kinda funny, my penchant for older men loving and snubbing in such quick succession. As I flesh out the story from beginning to end for Vicky, I realize how insensitive it must have seemed to Egon to arrive at his restaurant to have dinner with another man I have only just told Egon a day before I had no interest in. Egon clearly fancies me. And for the first time, it seems that I have been the insensitive one. And naïve for not recognizing that the age difference would be irrelevant to these old men.

As Vicki laughs and counters with her own messed up men stories I head home amused. But when I step into my apartment, I get the same sinking feeling I'd had the last six weeks of Los Angeles: *persona non grata.* I feel it all starting again. I've made three enemies plus Pavlos in less than two weeks in NYC. Then again, Egon does coke and Dale tried to rape me. I'm lucky they're out of my life. I'm lucky I escaped relatively unscathed. From here on out, things are going to change. I'm going to be more careful, more selective!

22. NANCY & DICK

If I were job searching in L.A. I would have had a job by now – and more than one offer. But in three weeks of hitting the sultry city pavement during a heatwave, working with six personnel agencies and seven smug counselors, completing eight typing tests (ranging from 60 - 95 wpm), fifteen applications (why doesn't a resumé suffice?), twelve interviews (one in publishing, two in advertising, two on Wall Street, three in private homes, one shoe company, one hotelier, one restaurateur), and spending $172 in taxis, and taking in seventy-six messages, I remain unemployed. Seems no one's in a hurry to hire anyone in New York City. Seems everyone here wants to think for a month or more as to whom they'll hire. Seems to me New York City takes hiring way too seriously.

And "the wives" take it too personally. When Mr. and Mrs. "F" interviewed me for a personal assistant position as we sat on a sofa in their gilded *pied-à-terre* on East 66th between Fifth & Park, and Mrs. F saw her husband smiling at me, she eyed my gams and then interrupted Mr. F mid-sentence to announce, "Well it was nice meeting you. Thanks, for coming." We all stood, Mr. F and me befuddled, and I was whisked out of the *salon*. I later learned that Mrs. F was the daughter of a movie studio tycoon and the one with the money, so it didn't really matter what Mr. F wanted.

Nancy, the 24-year-old recruiter from the Gage Agency, the self-proclaimed "corporate specialists" blames me.

"Why did you tell Morgan Stanley Smith Barney you wanted forty-five-thousand a year?" she demands to know over the phone. "There's no way you're going to get forty-five-thousand. You're twenty-four and the market just isn't paying it. I myself am not making over forty," she says sounding miffed that I could possibly think I could make more than she did, after only a week in NYC.

"Well if I can make forty in Los Angeles, I can certainly make forty-five in New York," I tell her. Even if Nancy was correct, the fact is that I simply can't survive on less than forty-five. I've done the math.

Nancy presents me with another address for an interview tomorrow morning. On Wall Street. Executive Assistant to the blah, blah, blah... of blah blah blah.

"But, Nancy, I told you. I don't want to work on Wall Street. I need to be in a creative environment."

"Well, that's the only way you're going to get forty-five. Now, remember, they're very conservative. You have to wear a black or navy suit."

"Fine," I tell her, wondering if she heard I wore ivory at the last financial district interview. I was sure that Nancy had overstated Human Resources predilection for navy or black. Even if she were right, I wasn't about to work for a company that would reject me on the basis of clothing color. Besides, really, I had no choice. My doorman had seen me in black the day before and I wasn't about to let him see me in the same outfit twice, particularly since it was saturated with sweat, not due to the interview but to the heatwave. So, when I arrived at the airport-terminal style lobby of the famous brokerage firm at the downtown offices, and took my seat, I recognized the other applicants. They were all dressed in navy or black. I didn't want the job anyway.

"By the way, how was Woodstock?" I ask Nancy. She'd invited me to the anniversary of Woodstock because one of their foursome had backed out of the road trip.

"It was great. You should have come. What'd you end up doing?" she asks.

"Oh, I went to the Hamptons actually. Have you heard of the Naked Angels?" I ask her, feeling smarmy. Hamptons trumps Woodstock.

DICK GRODEN, founder and co-owner of ASAP Personnel, sits across from me, buried under stacks of resumés. He's an attractive man with white hair, black eyebrows, a scratchy voice that is deep but squeaky, and looks to be too elegant for a desk from a Staples catalogue.

I elaborate on my work history. Perhaps too much. Because now I can't find a good way to backpedal from my Bel Air and Brentwood war stories of working as personal assistant/major domo for diabolical women in their multi-million-dollar homes. *I mean, how do I convince him that they were the crazy ones, and I am the normal, sweet one?*

"A few months into the job…" I confide to Dick, off the record, in an attempt to explain why I only managed four months with Mrs. X, "Mrs. X apologized profusely to me, saying that she was sorry, that her hormones were all out of whack because she had just had a baby six months earlier."

He nods. He believes me. But just to be certain, I go in for the kill. "In fact, I would get calls all the time from other personnel agents trying to recruit me away from her because they said, "anyone who could work for her, the "Infamous Wife of Famous Director" could work for the infamous wife of Famous Chef.""

It works. He has the perfect job for me.

"She's a famous fashion designer. Lovely woman, absolutely lovely," he says, "and you're just the type she likes.

23. QUEEN OF KNITWEAR

I am grateful that my interview with the reigning Queen of Knitwear has been scheduled for 6:30 p.m. so that I can wear my poly/crepe/wool blend black skirt and blazer, that by day would have appeared unseasonably heavy and dark, but by night can be mistaken for seasonably heavy and dark. Because, as any fashion victim knows, the only thing worse than looking unfashionable is looking unseasonable. Hopefully, the lighting in her office will be dim enough that she won't notice that the blacks don't match. Hopefully, she won't notice that the suit really isn't a suit but mismatched separates. Hopefully, she won't notice how severe the skirt hikes when I sit, so that it's almost flush with the blazer. Hopefully, the four bulbous gold buttons on the jacket aren't too gauche and passé. Hopefully, the threadbare second button won't detach until after the interview.

I had expected a grand, fashionable lobby, but this, the 21st floor of the fashion designer, looks like a loading dock, if not a dead-end of two opposing elevators. If it weren't for the designer's name – M I M I D E L A C O C O – in modernist silver block letters secured to the wall area between the elevators, I would have thought I came to the wrong place. I take a tentative step off the elevator, brushing past a tall man in his fifties, dressed in a navy-blue suit smelling of cigarettes. He's staring into my eyes.

"Are you here for an interview?" he asks, in an Italian-Brooklyn accent as he holds the elevator door for me or for him, I'm not sure.

"Yes," I answer, curiously. *How do they all know?* First the Ambassador West Hotel woman, now this man.

"Oh good. I hope you get it." He walks into the elevator and chuckles to himself.

"Thanks." *Hmmm.* I wonder who he is besides yet another man over fifty objectifying me. He must be affiliated with the Queen of Knitwear or would not have known to expect me. Maybe I just made a good impression on a powerful insider who might wield considerable influence over the decision to hire me. In any case, I am pleased for the well-timed support.

I turn 90 degrees whereupon I see the reception desk: a counter built into the wall, centered between two closed doors. I look over the counter. There's a switchboard, message wheel, but no receptionist.

"Hi, are you Eve?" asks a girl walking towards the switchboard just in time to catch me peeping.

"Hi, yes," I say, wondering why this job interview is the talk of the town.

"Great. Go ahead and have a seat. I'll let her know you're here," she says, pointing to two chairs opposite her in the short hallway of one of the doorways. She leaves her post and returns a moment later. "It'll just be a few minutes," she says. "She's going to like you."

"Oh good. Thanks. I hope so," I say, returning the smile.

I take a seat and watch the doors on both sides of the reception desk open and close as the receptionist buzzes in and out attractive, fashionable tan girls and gay men carrying assorted clothes, paper bags and Styrofoam boards, and steering overloaded, teetering clothes' racks. My feet and purse are in their way at every pass. None of them look very happy. All the women wear open-toed shoes, revealing tan legs and perfect pedicures. I have on sheer black hose and closed-toe pumps.

As I listen to the shrill buzzer and take in the scene, I recall what Parker Muller, a Sony Digital consultant told me just before I left Los Angeles. I met Parker at the home of the multi-millionaire of Bel Air when Mr. Multimillionaire was changing the Rose Tarlow-designed game room (of high backed, beige slipcovered French reproduction couches and various pointellistic Camille Pisarros) into a screening room (of beige mohair couches and prints from the Matisse Jazz Series). Parker was so knowledgeable that I brought him in to consult on the screening room my subsequent boss, Famous Director of Brentwood, was building. Anyway, when I told Parker I was moving to New York City, he told me I should try to get a job in the fashion industry, saying that I could learn a lot about how to dress very fashionably, "not that you don't dress nice enough already," he added, "but a job in fashion would give you some sophistication," not that I wasn't sophisticated he added, "besides, there are always sample sales where you can get designer clothing for next to nothing, not that you are a label whore."

I didn't give his words another thought given that I had absolutely no interest in a fashion career. If there was anything profound about the suggestion was that it was Parker, the antithesis of fashionable, who gave it. But now, in light of my belief that nothing is random or accidental, that everything happens for a reason, his words seem prophetic. Not necessarily prophesying that I would dress better, but that I am supposed to be in fashion for a reason I don't yet know. Of course if I don't get the job, and end up working on Wall Street, all of this is a moot, unprophetic, point.

"Eve?" inquires a deeply tanned, brown-haired young woman, dressed in an impeccably tailored navy suit with a crisp white undershirt, and polished black loafers, standing in the doorway.

"Yes, hi," I say, grabbing my purse to follow her down a narrow hallway past two racks of clothes and a bookcase where I catch the words Kilim, Textiles, Turkey, and Draping. We turn to the right where the hallway abruptly ends. All that is in the corner is a cheap white desk in front of two filing cabinets against a wall. But in the corner is a polished oak door that is so contrastingly elegant it's as if it led to the Wizard beyond the velvet curtain. She pushes through the oak door and I follow her in.

As Dick Groden predicted, I fall in love with Mimi de la Coco immediately. She is a beautiful woman. Streaked blonde hair, cat-green eyes with black eyeliner, skin that is tan but tenderized leather, a charming, feminine and Italian-accented giggle, gold rings, a gold Cartier watch. She greets me with a euro-kiss and a magical look as if I am the star in her presence rather than the other way around. It feels kismet.

"So Eve, tell me about you," she says, pressing her warm, maternal palm onto mine.

I want to tell her everything… especially how her eyes remind me of my grandmother's, but she might think I was aging her. But then I will tell her that my grandmother looks years younger than her age, taught dance at my high school for 20 years, and still waterskies to this day, preferring to start atop the dock so she doesn't get her hair wet till the end. I will tell her how my grandma is one of the most fashionable women in my hometown, how she was so fashion-conscious even in the Fifties that when her son wanted a Pendleton sweater and she couldn't afford it, she took the Pendleton label off of a second-hand sweater and sewed it onto a new non-Pendleton one. How her husband bought her a glamorous fox stole with the head and legs still attached in the '50s and how she made it au courant for the '70s by cutting off the heads and legs. Anyway, I won't tell Mimi that she reminds me of my grandmother, because she can't possibly be interested in all this.

Mimi asks why I have moved to New York. I tell her, breathlessly, about my "bad day".

"Oh that's terrible. Were you hurt?" she asks.

"I broke my wedding ring finger. Lost my knuckle." I say, showing her my knuckle-less fourth metacarpal.

"Ohhh," she says, softening, covering my hand with hers. "Eve, do you have family here?"

"No. They're in Oregon."

Mimi looks at me with sympathy and admiration. The poor girl, she must be saying. She's a knuckle-less orphan. My tragic tale was Dead-On-Arrival with Wall Street but has captured the compassion of the Garment District. *Fait accomplis.* I've managed to appear as pathetic and alone as I am and elicit the sympathy of Mimi, an empathetic woman with the ability to help me, to rescue me, to employ me.

"Well that's too bad. Family is very important to me. You know my business is run by my family," Mimi says.

"No I didn't know…"

"No of course you don't," she says, squeezing my hand. *Ouch.* She proceeds to tell me that her sister-in-law Maria is head of production, her sister-in-law Florence runs the boutique, and Luigi, her husband is the President of the privately-held company.

At that point, Luigi enters, sizes me up from under his glasses as he speaks to Mimi of "Don" and the "Le Fontaines" to which she replies "Luigi! I don't know! Can't you take care of this? Can't you see I'm in an interview?" She cries. Luigi says something in gentle Italian, chuckles and leaves.

"Eve, did Erin tell you about the position?" Mimi asks in her pre-Luigi, soft voice.

"Erin?," I ask.

"Erin, the woman who brought you in here," she says.

"Oh. No, she didn't."

"Well, that's just as well. I'll be honest with you. Erin has been my husband's assistant for six years and we love her to death, but you can't go by her. She has it very good here. My husband isn't as needy as I am but sometimes she takes advantage. Eve, dear, I need someone who can manage my life. As you can imagine it gets crazy. And I'm not so easy. I need someone to be on their toes. And often I need someone till 7 p.m. sometimes later. Is that a problem?" she asks.

"No, not at all. All my jobs have had long hours. Hours aren't an issue. As long as it's busy."

She reads my nod loud and clear. She seems inclined to hire me, but her eyes continue to scrutinize me as if to say she has one remaining reservation. "How is your handwriting?" she asks.

"Excellent."

She reaches over, presses something by her desk, and Erin walks in.

"Erin, darling, would you have Eve write a thank you note, and check it over?" She turns to me, "It's a test I ask all applicants to do. I get a lot of gifts and I believe very much in writing personal thank you's. I just received this pashmina scarf from Anna Wintour. I'd like you to write a thank you note to Anna as If you were me, and also write me a thank you for this interview, and also type them."

I take a seat at the desk outside her office, no doubt the seat I will have if hired, with only a view to a narrow hallway of clothes' racks and office doors. I write the thank you note to Anna, using the words "very much," and "exquisite" and then write the one to Mimi, and then type them.

"Are you finished yet?" asks Erin.

"Yes," I answer and hand Erin the handwritten and typed notes.

Erin takes them into Mimi as I wait outside the office. A minute later Erin opens the door and ushers me in. Mimi has read the note and loves my handwriting. "But," she says, "Erin tells me it took you ten minutes to finish. Most of the other girls finished in just a few minutes."

"Well, I…," I begin defensively, not knowing what to say. I had just kept improving it, waiting for Erin to come and fetch it. I didn't realize I was supposed to hunt down Erin and say I was done. *Dare I suggest Erin's a saboteur?*

"You're a perfectionist aren't you?" Mimi asks with a knowing smile.

I shrug in agreement.

Erin leaves.

Mimi places her hand over mine, studies my eyes. "Me too," she says. Tell me, Eve, do you think you can do the job?"

"Yes," I say, immodestly.

"Yes I think you can. And I like you."

"I like you too."

"Tell me. What salary are you looking for?"

"Forty-five-thousand," I say, flatly, non-negotiable.

"Forty-five? Oh. I think the most we've ever paid is Forty," she says, searching my eyes for some sort of acquiesce, negotiation, but I stare back poker-faced. "Well I'm not the one who makes the salary decisions, but I think that can be arranged," she says. "Can you start tomorrow? I'd like you to spend some time with the temp."

"Sure."

"Great. Well, Eve, I think this is going to be very nice."

"I think so too," I answer.

She cups my shoulders, kisses my cheeks. I love her already.

"Have a good evening," I tell her, lingering for a final warm smile from Mimi, but she only nods absentmindedly, and I find my way out to the loading dock. Her goodbye seemed a little cold in comparison to the rest of the interview. *Could it be the change associated when one crosses over to the other side, when one becomes the employed?* No, she's not that way. I'm sure I'm being overly sensitive. I mustn't let past experiences with tyrannical, abusive employers make me so cynical and paranoid. *Besides, what are the odds of me working for three tyrannical, abusive employers in a row?*

"Did you get it?" asks the same navy-suited man I'd seen at the elevator earlier, now milling about the reception area, holding a small black Barney's bag like a dainty purse, totally incongruous with his masculine presence. He presses the down button on the elevator for me.

"Yes, actually, I did," I say.

"Wonderful. Well then, I guess we'll be seeing a lot of each other. Better for me than for you," he says, smirking. "I'm Don, the de la Coco's driver," he says, extending his hand.

"Eve."

"Very nice to meet you Eve. So when do you start?" Don asks.

"Tomorrow actually."

"Wonderful," he says. "See you tomorrow."

"Don! Where have you been? We've been calling you," says Mimi, joining us at the elevator bank, bags in hand, husband by her side, Erin trailing behind.

"I've been right here," he says.

"We're going to be late for the ballet."

"Don't worry, you got plenty of time. I got the car downstairs," Don says.

"Eve which way are you going? Maybe we can drop you?" Mimi asks.

"East 44th Street."

"Oh. We're going on the Upper West Side, the opposite way," she says, looking disappointed that they can't drop me.

"That's OK. Don't worry, I'm just going to catch a cab, but thank you anyway."

The elevator bell rings, and Don steps aside to let everyone in, including Erin. "You should move to the Upper West Side," Don whispers to me. "Erin lives there and gets a ride home every night."

24. SAMPLE SALE

It's my first day at work. Should I ever get there. The traffic on 42nd Street at 8:45 a.m. is much worse than last night at 6:30 p.m.. Turns out, I should have allowed five minutes just to reach the lobby level of my apartment, two minutes to walk/run half a block up to Second Avenue and another eight minutes to fetch a southbound cab which apparently only picks up passengers on the side of the street I'm not on.

Twenty-nine minutes and $5.60 later I arrive in the Garment District, at my new company on Broadway. That's about $12 per day, $62/week, and $248/month. Maybe I could walk home. Maybe I could walk/run. Public transportation (i.e. subways) is not an option. I just can't bear the thought of being stuffed next to strangers. I'm partially claustrophobic and 100% west coast private transportation-bred. *There are just certain things I won't do!*

The lobby is quite a different scene from last night. Swarming with fashionable girls.

"Excuse me do you have the time?" I ask a woman wearing a skirt, nylons and tennis shoes by the first elevator bank.

"Eight fifty-nine."

"Thanks." A minute to spare.

The elevator, the only form of mass transportation I can't avoid, opens. Everyone moves in fast, sideswiping me with shopping bags and workout bags. Nearly everyone including me gets out on 21st floor and goes either way until I am the last standing in front of the receptionist.

"Hi, I'm Mimi's new assistant," I inform the receptionist, a different one than was here last night. She buzzes me in. I walk down the hallway, the florescent lighting buzzing and blinding, the white fiber walls buckling. I quickly drop my bag off at my desk, and head to the kitchen mid-hallway for some coffee, only to nearly collide with Mimi sweeping around the corner, in full stride spraying a large bottle of perfume on her neck, smiling solicitously. "Oh hi," I say, wide-smiled.

"Where were you? I called you at 8:50 and no one answered the phone," she cries, her face grimacing. Not quite a morning person I gather.

"Oh. I thought I was supposed to be here at 9 a.m."

"Well that's what time you start, but you should always come ten minutes earlier to a job," she says, the voice of perfect work ethic. "You have to be ready for *me*. *I* come in at 9 a.m.. Besides, I often call from the car and ask you to pick up cappuccinos. So please get me a decaf cappuccino and send Odette in." Mimi pushes through the oak door. It swings back and forth several times until it comes to a stop.

I dial Odette's extension listed above the phone on the wall.

The oak door swings open again. Mimi passes by me, heads down the hall peering into offices and returns. "Eve, would you call Givoudan Roure and get me more perfume like this, she says, handing me a big 24-ounce bottle of perfume with a courier type label that reads "citron and apple." Oh, and we're having a contest to name my perfume. So if you have any ideas, that can be your little side project, since you're creative. Oh, and by the way, I didn't see the need for the temp to continue. You can handle things can't you?"

"Sure – "

"I knew you could," says Mimi smiling, her mind elsewhere. "If you need anything, just call Erin. Oh, and make reservations at Barney's for 12:30 for two and call Anna Wintour's office with the details. I'm going to our home in Southampton after that."

"Oh, Mimi?" I ask as she trails off. "I tried calling Odette, but no one answered."

"I saw her. Never mind."

As she walks back into her office, her vote of confidence "I knew you could" brings me some comfort that she hasn't already lost faith. Given my most recent work history, I need all the encouragement I can get.

"Eve, did you remember to bring in the cappuccino to me?" says Mimi, her head poking through the partially opened oak door.

"Yes. They're on their way up," I smile proudly.

"On their way up?"

"Yes, from Sunset Deli" I answer.

"Eve, if I'm here already you should go down and get them. They won't be here for ten minutes now."

"Well I didn't think you'd want me to leave the phone," I say.

She stares at me as if looking for the words. "You're right," she says. "Good thinking." She smiles with her eyes. It's a warm smile.

"Hi. Nice to see you," Don says. "I've got Miss de la Coco's lunch. I'll just put it in the kitchen for you.

"Actually, she's going out to lunch."

"But she told me to go back home and get it," he says, shaking his head.

I shrug "sorry" and he shakes his head as he heads toward the kitchen.

At her word, Mimi is gone by, well, 11:45. I sit and become acquainted with my surroundings, thankful for a new exciting life, if not lacking a view. *What will I look at?* I look at the desk. The hallway. I look at the desktop calendar, upside down to me for the benefit of anyone coming by her desk.

"Eve, how long do you have to be here?" inquires Tiffany, one half of the Collection design team.

"Till 6 p.m. I guess."

"Didn't anyone tell you? Fridays are half-days in the summer."

"Oh, for me too?"

"Well Mimi's already left. And Bebe and I are leaving at 2 p.m. We're going across the street to Parson's. There's a DKNY sample sale. Want to come?"

We leave the office and walk across the street where a few others were already cashing out, showing off their finds. I only had $20 cash so there was only one thing I found that was affordable: a red DKNY hat for $13. One size fits all.

"What'd you get? I asked Tiffany.

"Four pairs of pants, two jackets, three bags...."

AFTER GETTING Mimi's approval to leave the office early, I walk home relieved. And happy. It's official! I have an apartment, and a job at my asking price with for a wonderful boss and in a warm, familial atmosphere. And in just the nick of time! I only have enough money for one and a half's month's rent. Everything has come together. It always does as they say. Just takes a little faith. It is the first time, since June 20th that I am not in need of anything, at least not items necessary for survival. My month and a half long scavenger hunt is *finis!* Hello Patience and Fortitude, I whisper to the lionesses guarding the New York Public Library. The taxi driver had pointed them out to me on my way to work. He said they were named "Patience and Fortitude" by former Mayor LaGuardia as qualities he deemed were needed to survive the Depression.

I arrive home to a call from my employment recruiter Nancy. "J.P. Morgan went with someone who wore black to the interview," she says, scolding me. "But forget about it. I have scheduled you for another interview next Tuesday with another firm on Wall Street, but you have got to wear black or navy."

"Nancy, thank you for all of your help but, actually, I just got a job," I tell her.

"Through whom?" she asks, accusatorily. "I thought you were working with us exclusively."

"Well, no. I don't know why you thought that. I mean I needed a job."

"Anyway, where are you working?" she asks benignly, as if she weren't scheming for more information to revoke my good fortune. "I know all of the jobs posted on Wall Street. I'll let you know what I know."

"It's not on Wall Street."

"Well can you at least tell me what industry?

"Fashion. I'm a Personal Assistant to a fashion designer."

"Why didn't you say you were interested in Fashion? I have a few fashion jobs I'm working on. I could have sent you – "

"I did."

"So, which fashion designer?" she asks.

"I'd rather not say, actually." I'm concerned she'll call up Mimi and tell her about her own exclusive applicant much better than me, someone who has a large navy and black wardrobe.

"Well do you mind telling me how much you'll be making?" she asks as if I owe her that much.

"Forty-five-thousand," I tell Nancy smugly, the exact amount she said I couldn't possibly get.

We hang up and I allow in a little giddiness. My luck has turned for the better. And then I remember the hat in my bag. I try it on. Although it said "one size fits all," it's too small. *All sales are final.* Oh well. I don't suppose this was the sophistication Parker was talking about anyway.

25. SPECIAL DELIVERY

I have managed to flesh out a new life in New York, forge a new existence exactly to the degree that I have no surviving memory of the old, exactly to the degree my studio remains empty, unfurnished, with no evidence of a prior life lived. So when the intercom buzzer rang thirty seconds ago and my doorman Ayman announced, "Delivery for you," I was half tempted to tell him "wrong apartment." But here it comes. Down the hall. On an upright dolly. My old life.

"You can just put it there," I instruct the delivery man, Joe, pointing broadly towards the empty studio.

"Signature here please."

I sign. And that is that. In a matter of seconds (and 3400 miles) my past has caught up with me. Its travels undoubtedly easier than my own, and completely paid for. A box's life. Treated more delicately upon its arrival in New York than me. Maybe I should have entrusted myself to Joe's care instead of to Pavlos'. Maybe someone should have had to sign for me. Maybe I should have been marked "fragile."

Joe closes the door and as soon as I lock the deadbolt, I flatten my back against the door, wishing the intruders and the boxes were on the other side of the door. I stare at the boxes. *Why does it feel as if my stalker has caught up with me?* I'd say for Professional Packers exceeding their delivery quote by $500, they should have had to deliver me a new life. Deliver me something I can use. But here they are, the things that bridge my new New York like to my old: four boxes. Sitting like dead bodies waiting to be identified and tagged.

Box #1: Evidence of my broken body. Like I need to look at x-rays. Wait. I wonder if the x-ray of my left hand will show where my knuckle went. Maybe it's lodged in my wrist. Oh there are my pictures of my broken nose recuperations. Oh. Hard to look at yourself with Dixie straws stuffed up your nose, fastened with dental floss. And there is my former friend and neighbor, Alison's book I borrowed. *New Age Doctor: The Emotional Causes of Physical Disorders.* All you have to do is look up the affected body part and it will give you an emotional explanation for why that body part is being negatively affected. Under "nose," which I broke in two different places on separate occasions in my acting class, it simply reads, *"Self Realization". What does that mean? That I am supposed to realize that acting is not for me or just the opposite?* The book is not very explicit. *Hmmmph.* No mention of "Wedding Ring Finger" so I look up "hand" under which it reads: *"Those experiencing injuries to the hand are likely experiencing some arrested development. If it's the left hand, paranoia can manifest itself."* The right hand, on the other hand, says: *"Spiritual awakening."* Clearly whoever wrote this was left-handed. Oh and there's the letter from Farmer's Insurance deeming my car a total loss. No kidding. And there's all I have left to show for it, my dented, personalized California license plate: THXFILM.

Box #2: Evidence of an acting career cut short. Skip. Too depressing.

Box #3: Evidence of college debt. Oh, yes. That sounds fun!

Box #4: Evidence of a broken engagement. I could actually open that one. It has my *Men are from Mars, Women are from Venus* book which Dylan, my ex-fiancé, gave to me to read so I could learn what our issues were and recover from my "I don't want to marry you" disorder. Dylan thought it was a temporary disorder. The book may have in fact sped up the undoing. I tried to read it, but it struck me that the male author was essentially saying men won't change and women would have to accept that. *Accept bad behavior?* And then when I read *"Men are like rubber bands"* I put the book under the bed where it remained until we'd both moved out, having gone our separate ways, our differences irreconcilable. And there is a lilac envelope addressed "to my future wife" handwritten by Dylan. Speaking of which, Dylan still owes me $123.61 for the phone bill. Oh and there's my *The Road Less Traveled* book. Funny enough, an ex-boyfriend, Craig, recommended that I read that one. And I did. Hmmm. I wonder if Pavlos is like a rubber band and he's just pulled away but will come back.

Ok, that's enough memory lanes for me. I'll just put them in the walk-in closet and try not to disrupt their slumber, lest they infiltrate my fragile, New York State of mind.

"AYMAN, I'm going to get coffee at Timothy's, do you want anything?"

"Yes, please. Would you mind getting me some coffee from Al's on your way back?"

"You sure you don't want Timothy's coffee?"

"No, Al's the man for me! I'm a one-man kind of guy." Ayman hands me money.

"No, no, I got it."

Fifteen minutes later, I return with a *We're Happy To Serve You* paper cup of coffee from Al's for Ayman (which I couldn't help but notice is written in Greek letters above three steaming cups of Greek coffee in between two Greek pillars, next to a Greek Vase), and Venezia coffee from Timothy's (in a Timothy logo'd paper cup) for me. "Piping hot coffee at your service," I tell Ayman.

"And I have something for you," says Ayman, walking towards a large box to the side of the lobby. "Another box came after you left." He drags a box to the elevator. "I guess they missed it. Better late than never."

I take the box #5 up to the apartment and hoist it up onto a shelf in the closet when a lone book thumps me on the head. I sink onto the floor to retrieve it. It's my Syracuse University Freshman Register – a yearbook – and it's open to Jake. The Roman God. We met in the first month of the school year when he moved onto our coed floor where I lived in a room built for one, intended for two, but shared by three. I thought I had met my destiny. In fact, I marveled at how effortlessly it had found me, in just the first few months of college. I had expected it to take at least a year.

The only thing good about the University was the Italian, Jake. He had black curly hair, a chiseled jawline, perfectly white teeth, and upswept topaz eyes. I was in love. The immediate kind. The kind that flutters. So when he fell in line behind me in the cafeteria, the sparks (well, mine) were palpable. I let my mind go where it wanted into daydreams of our future. I had visions of us as star-crossed lovers finding joy in the most mundane daily rituals like grocery shopping together, going to movies together, and percolating coffee grounds together. Meanwhile I had not collected anything on my tray. "How is the Jell-O?" I asked the waiting cashier. She suggested a mixed salad. I grabbed a hot plate of French fries instead.

I don't recall ever having been so fortuitous, but somehow we ended up taking seats across from one another at the window by ourselves, with his back to the corner and my back to the rest of the world. We must have acknowledged we recognized each other from our floor, one of only two coed floors in all of University-owned housing. We probably introduced ourselves. I had a hard time with his eyes. His gaze zeroed in on my pupils like lasers and I found myself unable to hold his gaze or extricate myself from it. When I could, I looked out the window or towards other tables but everything else was a blur.

"I just follow a few of my stocks," he said, when he took notice of me staring at the back of his *Wall Street Journal* which he was reading. There were only about a dozen subscriptions out of eight floors of seventy-five people each, and he had one of them.

At once, I was panicked by my ignorance of the stock market. *How could I make intelligent conversation?* I should have been more prepared. I should have been more prepared in worldly ways to seize worldly opportunities because he was a worldly opportunity.

And apparently I wasn't the only one who knew it. A few weeks later, as I returned from the library with *The Art of the Deal* by Donald Trump, and *The Fall of the Shearson Lehman Brothers* for the off chance me and Jake would meet again, he was busy dodging stalkers from Sorority Row who were hovering at the edge of the entry door to our rooms. They were giggling in that ridiculous Tri-Delta way. I eyed them curiously and condescendingly. What were they doing lurking and giggling in MY corridor? I had never seen them before.

"Jake," said Henry dryly, answering my evidently inquiring eyebrows. Henry was an International Relations major best known for wearing his shirt as underpants when the rest of his clothes were stolen from the bathroom by the Fifth Floor while he was taking a shower. He has never been amused with antics from non-floor members since. "They're looking for Jake. They followed him up here. He doesn't know them."

News of the competition shook my confidence. *If Jake had this affect on every X-chromosome, what chance did I have?* They were just the first of many stalkers I'd see traipse the-mile-long canopied stairs to our dorm room to see where Jake lived. "He lives with me," I wanted to tell them.

That was October when all of Syracuse came under a grey cloud such that it became clear why the façade of the University's main building (situated at the south entrance of campus), was used as the façade for *The Addams Family* house. My dorm floor had been dubbed the "hostility floor" and police had arrested an "art scholarship student" for stealing and then boiling the skull of one of the University founders on a stove in the communal kitchen because he wanted to study anatomy like the Masters (e.g. DaVinci). And other than running into Jake on the steps of the

University Church (where I'd hoped we'd have rice thrown at us) where he was filming a short (about the Greek system), fate had not moved Jake and me an inch towards eternal togetherness. And so when I returned to my floor to heat up some hearty vegetable soup to bring some warmth to the otherwise cold and dreary place and instead found a pile of human excrement next to the kitchen stove, I came to the realization that I had to leave and pursue my dream. The next day, I applied to transfer to the University of Southern California. I was going to pursue acting and let nothing get in my way. By March, the sun made an appearance and USC had accepted my application for the School of Drama. My exit interview with Syracuse's registrar was set and I would soon become a statistic among Syracuse's already plummeting retention rate.

With just one week before I was due to leave for good, I ran into Jake again in the Day Hall cafeteria. I felt more self-assured in this meeting. Fortunately, I had not been one of his obsessed crazed fans. I had not tried to create instances where we could run into each other. (I had given that up.) I had not attempted to ingratiate myself into his circle. (I didn't know his circle.) And now it was the end of the year, and I had left him alone. (I couldn't find him). It was important to me that I not be categorized like all the others with their pathetic adoration based solely on physical looks.(I wanted to keep my pathetic adoration a secret.) It had always been important for me to not behave like the other girls I was sure behaved: stupidly. (At least not outwardly.) As handsome as I thought he was, as beautiful as I thought the young women were who were fawning publicly around corners, I had too much pride to risk rejection.

"I think we've ran into each other only a few times this year," he said, smiling freely.

"Yeah, most times in the cafeteria," I said, smiling freely myself.

"I guess that proves we both have to eat," he said, gripping my shoulder. God that feels good. *Oh don't let go!* Oh shoot, he let go.

"Yeah I guess it does," I laughed, noticing his healthy salad and my French fry platter.

"Would you like to sit down?" he asked.

"Sure," I said, as we took the same seats we had the first time.

"Yeah, it's too bad so much of the year has gone by and we didn't get a chance to hang out," he said so earnestly and sincerely I was half prepared to change my mind about transferring.

"I know," I said, perhaps too downtrodden, "and this is my first and last year here. I'm transferring to the University of Southern California."

"Really? They have the best film school."

"Well that's why I'm going there. I hope to get into the School of Cinema-TV."

"Really? That's what I'm studying too," he said, as if seeing a kindred soul for the first time. "Well maybe I'll run into you in Los Angeles someday. I might end up there myself. You never know."

You never know.

I touch his photo as if to conjure up a genie and gain three wishes, as "you never know" echoes in my mind just like it had five years earlier.

But this time, I don't hesitate. I pick up the phone and dial 411.

"Information. What city?" the operator asks.

"Oh, um," I look at the "hometown" listed under Jake's photo. "Um. Union Circle, New Jersey. Jake Fanelli?"

"I just have one listing, Jake Fanelli Sr. on Lakeshore Drive?"

"Um, ok. Sure," I said, my hands ice cold and clammy. *Could he be Senior? Could he have a Junior?* I write the number down, draw a deep breath, fix my hair in the mirror, and dial, preparing for the voice of a wife or little Jake Jr..

On the third ring an adult male voice answers the phone, "Hello?"

"Hi. Is there a Jake Fanelli at this number?"

"Junior or Senior?"

"Oh. I'm not sure. I'm looking for one that went to Syracuse University?"

"That would be Junior," he laughs. "But he's not here right now. Can I take a message?"

"Well, I'm not sure he'll remember me but my name's Eve Foster. We lived on the same floor our freshman year at Syracuse. And I just moved to New York City from Los Angeles and came across my Syracuse yearbook, saw his picture and thought I'd try to look him up. But if you could tell him I have red hair and transferred to the University of Southern California. My number is 212-555-9550."

"Sure."

"O.K. Thanks."

We hang up and I hesitate to ever leave the apartment for fear I could miss Jake's call.

SIX HOURS LATER, the phone rings. My heart pounds.

"Hello? Eve?"

It's a man's voice.

"Yes?" I ask, anticipating the words *"It's Jake Fanelli."*

"What are you doing?" he asks.

Oh my God. Is it Pavlos? For the first time, I'm not thinking of him, and he's calling?

"It's Kristos."

"Oh. Kristos. Hey. How are you?" I ask as the soufflé in my chest flattens. I'm relieved it's not Pavlos but disappointed it's not Jake.

"Listen did you tell Liza about me and Sydney living together?" he asks, his voice on edge.

"No, of course not."

"Did you mention Sydney's name at all?"

"No. Positive."

"Are you sure you just didn't let it slip?" he probes, as if his brow-beating will get him a confession.

"No, absolutely not. I haven't even seen her. Why?" I ask, my heart racing from the possibility that a Polychronopolis family member will blame me once again for something I didn't do.

"Because for some reason she won't speak to me," he says. "She turns away from me anytime I come within a foot of her. Won't even look directly at me when she speaks to me."

"I don't know Kristos. Honestly, it can't be anything I've said because I've only seen her the one time at your office."

"O.K. Well there's my other line. Speak to ya. Ciao," he says and hangs up.

26. GARMENT DISTRICT
WEEK 4

It's now my fourth week at Mimi's. And I'm already taking the elevator up to the 21st floor with dread.

Coming towards Mimi's office is her 2 p.m. appointment: the crack lesbian PR team/lovers, Crispin & Dealer, who think they run the show, Mimi's show. When they arrived for an appointment last week, the first time I'd met them in person, I thought they were like any other guests who would be patient and wait in the reception area until Mimi could see them. I was wrong. They need no introduction, and they aren't to be kept waiting. They are longtime friends and the retained PR team of Mimi's. I am the newcomer (and don't forget it). And they'll outlast me. Long live the lesbian friends! They think I should know them, be as intimidated by them as we are by Mimi. After all, they came up with the words, "fashion for the modern woman." Trouble is, I hate them. They never have but a dour expression on their face, never say hello, please or thank you. Still, perhaps they hate coming here as much as I do.

"Can you tell Mimi we're here," they ask, as if in bereavement, standing in front of my desk.

"I'm sorry, I've forgotten your names..."

They say nothing. The question hangs in the air.

"Elaine, Susan!" shrieks Mimi in over-the-top glee as the women glide past me to reach Mimi's air kisses. She then ushers them inside but remains a fixture in the doorway. "Eve. Tell Fortuna, I wanted the nautical print. Not this one. And would you please come in and clean this office. It's filthy. An absolute mess!"

I follow her inside the office with the non-nautical print. "What's wrong?" I ask earnestly yet unamused by the insinuation that I had something to do with the mess or that I should follow a directive to clean up someone else's, and with particular irritation that she has unjustly accused me in front of her morbid guests.

"What's wrong?" she cries incredulously, squinting her beady Milanese eyes at me in hopelessness. "You need to straighten my office *throughout* the day."

"What do you mean? I do. I did. Just fifteen minutes ago," I say, defending myself under the glare of Elaine and Susan, who remind me of Cinderella's two ugly stepsisters who think wrapping their necks in Pashmina scarves will prettify them.

"You did?" she asks challengingly. "Where? I mean, look at this. The magazines are all over," she says, gesturing to the periodical spillover in the three-inch deep oak boxes on the floor behind her desk. We both know that they aren't in perfect alignment because the designers borrow from her stack and return haphazardly. "It's just a mess. Really. I can't work this way," she says, pressing her hands to her face, shaking her swingy hair. "Luigi!"

Luigi steps inside the oak door. Peculiar how he's always within earshot when she's yelling for him. "What? What's wrong Midi?" he asks paternally, using his pet name as if it has taming effects.

"This place is a mess and I have guests here!" she cries. Luigi looks at me and then consoles Midi like a spoiled child, his hands holding her shoulders.

I crouch to tidy the magazines again, begin to align their edges, but as I do, Mimi comes and pushes me away. "Just forget about those, look at my shawl, my closets, get some hangers, and take some of these out," she says, handing me empty hangers from her packed closet, as if summoning the ghost of Joan Crawford. "Look at that. Tens of thousands of dollars just crammed in there. Oh Eve. What am I going to do with you? This is a mess. I can't work like this. Get a rack and take some of these out."

While she catches up on the weekend excursions of Crispin & Dealer – the Hampton's, blah, blah, blah – I wonder why crazy women and hangers always go together. And I wonder why, when I've been here less than three weeks, I am the one blamed for a closet that was packed like sardines long before me.

"So, girls, what can I get you? Coffee, cappuccino?" asks Mimi, hanging her 10-pound wool coat on my shoulders (since my arms are already full carrying twenty pounds of clothes). She pushes her blond wisps from her forehead and tightens the sweater around her hips, a trademark that earned her an appearance an Oprah, all the while sneaking glances of herself in the mirror on the outside of the closet I'm trying to thin out. I'd like to trademark a third sweater around her neck.

"Yes," reply Crispin and Dealer to the beverage offer despite declining my offer earlier when my hands were free.

"Eve?" Mimi nudges me.

"How many cappuccinos?" I ask sans smile.

"Decaf - " says Mimi.

"A Snapple," says Crispin.

"Regular coffee and Equal," says Dealer.

"What kind of Snapple?" Mimi asks Crispin. "Eve, you should be the one asking her, not me."

"I didn't know there were different kinds, I don't drink them."

"It doesn't matter. Diet. Peach or orange. Peach," says Crispin decisively.

"O.K." I answer.

"Also, get the Milano cookies," says Mimi.

I exit the office with the order mentally in my head, set the clothes down and dial Tom at Sunrise Deli. Out of my peripheral vision I see the oak door opening. Fortuna pokes her head out. I hold up my finger to make her wait until I can relay the order lest

I forget it, but apparently that is code for "talk to me while I'm talking on the phone".

"Mimi wants you to make some popcorn too," she whispers as Tom finally answers.

"Fine," I say to Fortuna, at once forgetting everything I'm to order from Tom. After I manage to convey the order to Tom, I hang up. And then I stare at the clothing behind me wondering what I'm forgetting. *Popcorn!* Mimi wants popcorn. Great. Popcorn means running back and forth from my phone to the kitchen and making sure I check on the very last 30 seconds, which invariably holds the key to the degree of charcoaled popcorn she gets. Then my private line rings. "Hello?" I ask, taking an intolerant tone to whoever is on the other line. Abuse has a trickle-down effect.

"Jake Fanelli here for you," announces the receptionist.

"Who?"

"Jake – "

"OHMYGOD. Ok. Um. I'll be right out. Ask him to wait. Thanks," I say and hang up and scan my clothing. OHMYGOD. I call back Tom to add Milano cookies to the food order.

"Hello gorgeous, I get off at 2 p.m., you gonna meet me?" asks Tom.

"Heh. Heh. Can't," I say, no time to patronize Deli Tom for his daily 2 p.m. invitations to go off into the sunset together. "Gotta go."

I put the popcorn in the microwave on three and a half minutes (buzzz) and take my make-up bag into Mimi's private bathroom in the hallway between the kitchen and my desk. Oh man, I didn't take a shower this morning and I'm wearing this red ribbed Pierre Cardin knit top that I've had for years and hardly ever wear because it's simply not flattering. In fact, it's probably not even a real Pierre Cardin. And even if it were a real Pierre Cardin, he's not even a recognizable label anymore and it's still an unflattering top. Oh but everyone knows my Gap jeans. I look terrible. My heart is pounding a mile a minute, pissed that I am once again unprepared for Jake Fanelli. This could be my second strike. I had only just called back the other day to return his call, and to avoid playing more phone tag, I left my work number too. As I primp quickly, and reapply make-up, I hear my name being called just outside the doorway. It's Fortuna.

"Eve? No. I haven't seen her," answers Emilia, the 68-year-old German housekeeper for the 21st floor of Mimi de la Coco Inc..

"Well if you do, can you tell her that Mimi is looking for her?"

"O.K. If I see her," says Emilia.

"Do you know if she made popcorn?" asks Fortuna.

(Oh shit. The popcorn.)

"Eez dat vut eez burning?" asks Emilia.

I finish my mascara strokes with a barely steady hand, wait for the voices to disappear and then crack the door open to see if the coast is clear. I see Emilia. She sees me. I signal her to not say anything and she continues vacuuming. I drop my make-up bag on my desk and jog down the hallway toward reception, taking in a big breath when the door bursts open.

"Miss de la Coco call me?" says Michiko, the resident expert tailor, standing in the doorway with a green tape measure around her neck, straight pins poking out from a wrist pin-cushion, her other arm in a tunnel-carpel styled medical brace, and an eye patch over one eye. Michiko has worked for Mimi for twelve years, is loved by all, but still thinks she could lose her job any day.

"Hi Michiko."

"Miss de la Coco called me?" she inquires nervously. "I was at a doctor's appointment. For my eye." she says, apologetically.

"Don't worry. You can see her now," I tell her. "Is your eye O.K.?"

"Yes. Be fine. Surgery. Thank you Eve," she says, patting me on the shoulder. She points down the hallway for my approval for her to walk in that direction and I nod. I take another breath and open the door to the lobby where I see the back of a man in a yellow rain slicker and red baseball cap.

"Jake?"

"Eve!" he turns around, displaying the same dreamy smile I remember. "I was just in the neighborhood, thought I'd stop in and say hello," he says, his arms outstretched.

"Oh I'm glad you did. It's so good to see you," I hug him, feeling his chest feels so good, warm, I can barely pull myself away. He pulls back to get a good look at me, his arms still cupping my shoulders. God that feels good, don't let go.

"What has it been? Six years? I hope this is OK, me just showing up. I mean I hope I haven't caught you at a bad time," he says.

"No, no. It's fine," I say. *I've burnt the popcorn before.*

"You haven't changed," he says, which to me is a bad thing considering my beautification process began after my freshman year. "You look great."

"Thanks. And you have more hair," I say. And the same gorgeous *everything…*

"Yeah," he says, removing his baseball cap so that a mass of black tendrils cascade out like a sunburst in slow motion. My mind drifts until I hear a familiar voice I can't place.

"Eve? Oh Eve?"

I turn around to see Mimi standing in the doorway, the green tape measure around her neck. "There you are. I've been looking all over for you."

"Oh sorry, a college friend of mine just stopped in to say hello," I say as if it was a completely acceptable situation, pretending that this is a normal office, that this is a normal boss, that these are normal times, and that I have the freedom to come out to the lobby rather than be ball and chained to my desk.

"Hello," Mimi says to Jake.

"Jake, this is Mimi. Mimi, Jake Fanelli," I say, certain that Jake's handsome looks will reflect well upon me. "I went to college with him and I haven't seen him for six years."

"Nice to meet you Jake. Eve, take your time but when you're finished I need you."

"Sure," I say. *Did she just say, "take my time"?*

"Eve, did you order from Sunset Deli?" asks the receptionist.

"Oh yes," I say, turning around to see the delivery man Luis in his red and white striped shirt with my food. "Hi Luis."

"Hi Eve," Luis smiles as I sign the check.

"Well, I can see you're busy," says Jake. "I just wanted to say hi. It's great to see you. We'll have to have lunch or dinner sometime when you aren't working."

"Absolutely. I'd love to."

"I'm a little busy myself until my movie is finished. But we'll get together after."

"That'd be great. It's so great seeing you."

"You too." He pulls me in, kisses both cheeks, takes one last look, and exits onto the elevator as Don comes off of it carrying Mimi's lunch in a bag from Barney's which contains a Ziplock pouch of mixed greens with scallions, a slice of freshly butchered deli ham, a hardboiled egg and carrot sticks.

"Don, did you bring Mimi's sketchbook?"

"No, there's no sketchbook in the car. It's back at the house."

"Well can you go back and get it?" I ask. "She wants it."

"I can't. Luigi just asked me to take him downtown," says Don. "Besides, the time it would take me to go back to the house and return, it'd be 6 p.m.."

"Fine, I'll tell her," I say, inhaling as I grab the drinks and cookies from the receptionist countertop and take to the hallway as Don buzzes me in.

"If Luigi says it's OK for me to go back to the house instead of taking him downtown, then I'll go," says Don.

I walk into Mimi's office, but no one is there. Following the aroma of burnt popcorn, I find them in the design conference room. I place the drinks down and when Mimi is finished critiquing the "Sport Girls" Fall boards, I interject, "Mimi, Don said your sketchbook is back at the house."

"Well, run across the street and buy me a new one. And where is my lunch?"

"Coming."

"And where is the popcorn for the girls?" she asks as if I'm the negligent nanny.

"You have some there," I answer.

"I know. That's burnt," she replies.

"Sorry about that," I answer.

Fortuna comes in with a bowl of the popcorn. "Here it is." she says.

Mimi frowns. She disapproves that her hardworking and highly-paid designer has been doing my job. Making popcorn!

Mimi's phone rings. I run back to my desk to pick it up. It's a European male voice. "Valtno?" After he repeats his name a few times, I still cannot make it out. "I'm sorry can you spell that for me?" I ask.

"She knows," he says.

"O.K. let me see if she's available," I say, pressing hold before running into the conference room to tell her. "Mimi, a man by the name of "Valtno?" is on the phone.

She gets up from her Indian-style position on the floor and heads for the phone in her office, removing one of her gold earrings. "Hello?" Oh Valentino?" she exclaims giddily, and then speaks in Italian which I hear loudly until the oak door closes.

Great. I have asked the famous designer, how to spell his last name. I can't wait until she blasts me for this one. *Buzzzzz.* Great, she's pressed the buzzer - the buzzer that used to make me jump out of my skin (much like the electric shock that lobotomized some guy in *One Flew Over the Cuckoo's Nest* or was it *Clockwork Orange*?), but now sounds like any other office sound. In any case, it's my cue to see her. It seems she can't even wait until her call is over to let me have it. I walk in nervously, anticipating the worst. Instead, she hands me an empty coffee cup. She'd like it refilled. She's smiling. *Phew.*

27. GARMENT DISTRICT
WEEK 8

Mimi's returned from a week in Paris at *Premiere Vision*, the "farmer's market" of fashion and textile buying in Europe. Our honeymoon period is over.

She drops an envelope on my desk, stuffed with receipts from lunches, taxis, airfare, the Meurice Hotel, and samples from Au Printemps, Galleries Lafayette, Au Bain Marie, Marie Claire, Canovas, Kenzo, Descamp, Nina Jacob, Etamine, Un Jardin en Plus, Sonia Rykiel, Comoglio Parls, and Pierre Frey. All "business expenses" she assures me.

"Expense them," she says, wearing the Kenzo and Sonia Rykiel samples. "And I'm ready for my lunch."

I leave the receipts at my desk, loosely, hoping they'll blow away in some extraordinary confetti fashion, and head for the kitchen to prepare her lunch, or rather, shake out the mixed greens from the ziplock bag that her Fifth Avenue servant has carefully packaged, and unfold the deli slices of ham, position the carrot sticks just so.

Every day at this time I hate my job more than ever. Answering phones and jumping at the sound of a buzzer is servile and remedial enough, but to also "serve" the Queen of Knitwear her food is so upstairs/downstairs demeaning. And, today, Mimi has decided to exacerbate the ritual by joining me in the kitchen (otherwise known as the "servant's quarters").

She stands one foot away from me at the counter, fluffing the mixed greens on the plate while I mix the oil and vinegar out of her peripheral so that I can still triple the amount of oil. If there are indeed 24 grams of fat to 1 tablespoon of oil, she is getting 72 grams of fat with one serving of salad. But when I reach for the oil, I panic. She's never come into the kitchen before. Maybe she's onto me. Maybe she knows I've been tripling the fat grams. Maybe she's hovering to inspect my oil to vinegar proportion. I contemplate righting the proportion just this once but decide to just go for the triple and then quickly put the bottles back into the cupboard, so she doesn't see how uneven the once equal volumes have become.

But now she's pissing me off. She is in my way, still fluffing the greens I loaded onto the plate. *What is she doing? Redecorating? Inspecting my plate decor?* If I'm expected to prepare her lunch because she's "so busy" deliberating over which print to steal from the graphic designer of the week, then she certainly better not idle beside me picking at the *frisée*. If she has time to do that, she should be fixing it herself. What a friggin' Milanese Prima Donna.

"I'll bring it into you," I insist, trying to squeeze her out but she doesn't budge.

"You know, Eve," she says, primping the arugula, repositioning the ham as if she were unrolling a cashmere blanket, altering the composition of the plate as if it were a Fauvian landscape, "It's all in the presentation. You see," she says, stepping away from the plate to present her masterpiece.

I look into her beady green eyes, the ones that initially seemed so sensitive and loving like Grandma's but now imbue Satan, and I think about the weeks of abuse I've endured, the kind that wears you down, robs you of any regular heart rate, induces chronic paranoia because all you want to do is please this person. You become so invested at pleasing them and trying to be impenetrable to their inhumane treatment, only to find that their demands increase exponentially as well as their dissatisfaction, only to see it boil down to this: food preparation. *If I can't even prepare lunch correctly, how can I possibly be employable?*

"Well, Mimi," I say, finished with apologizing or attempting to overcompensate for all the imperfections she points out on an hourly basis, "I guess that's why I'm not a waitress."

"Oh… well of course you're not," she says, surprised that I have feelings. "I didn't mean to imply you were," she says as she resumes her plate-scaping.

I yank open the freezer door to get ice cubes for her water and it nearly collides with her head, but she doesn't seem to notice or flinch.

"I just mean that, for instance," she continues, "if you were to throw a dinner party at your home, wouldn't you like it to look nice for your guests?"

"I live in a studio. I don't throw dinner parties."

"Well maybe not *formal* dinner parties," she says, "but when you have friends over for a casual meal."

"*And*, I eat alone," *Bam!* That's what you call *mic drop*. I muscle my way in to open the silverware drawer she's blocking. I remove a knife and fork and wrap it into a dinner napkin as the Fortuna locks eyes with me and then Mimi, and hastens her step out of the kitchen.

"Well, then when you cook for yourself," says Mimi, coming back for more!

"*And*, I order takeout." At that, I snatch the plate from her hands, position the salt and pepper shakers on the edge, take the glass of water into my left hand, clamp the silverware in my armpit, and leave Mimi in the kitchen alone without a plate to primp while I go about setting up her lunch in her office as is my job. While I recognize that Mimi's tone has actually been pleasant for a change, she only does that when she senses someone at their limit. She is the master of passive-aggressive and I am finally wise to her manipulation.

I pass Don and the designers in the hallway. They've obviously overheard the unprecedented exchange between me and Mimi and have followed Don's lead and retreated into the hallway where they now surreptitiously hover like family members awaiting the word on a loved one's life and death surgery. I connect eyes briefly with a bewildered Don who is no doubt worried about what will become of me. He rubs his eyebrows with nervous anticipation, as in "oh boy" what have you done now. Secretly, though, he's amused and delighted that it has been me of all people to put Mimi in her place. Unsuspecting Eve.

Inside Mimi's office, the lunch presentation is almost complete. I position her plate, glass, silverware and shakers just so, and realign her desktop *objets d'art*: the Pre-Columbian artifacts, antique magnifying glasses, ivory-tusk letter opener, miniature leather memo pads – to the ninety-degree formation I've been instructed to do. The configuration is so important to Mimi that Sophie, the 29th floor housekeeper and Emilia suggested I photograph the layout so that I can replicate it perfectly each time. Don opens the door, his expression worrisome.

"Don't even say it. I don't care. I've had it. She is nuts," I say pointing beyond the closed oak door.

"Shhh," he warns me.

"I don't care if she hears me. She can fire me. I don't care."

"She just likes to play Svengali, and you're like her little project."

"Not for long," I say.

"Look, before you get that lunch all situated, I just came in to say that she wants you to take her lunch over to Luigi's office. She's going to eat there."

"You are not serious," I say, eyeing my perfect ninety-degree angles.

He shakes his head. It's true.

"That bitch." I scoop up the plate, glass, salt and pepper, and silverware and kick the oak door, and head towards the elevator. When the elevator stops on the 29th floor, I descend, passing by

Sophie and Emilia, who jump back as if I were a runaway clothing rack.

"Is Mimi in there?" I ask Erin who's filing her nails at her desk outside Luigi's office.

"Yes, but they're having a private meeting with someone right now."

"Fine." I set down the plate and silverware for Erin to take care of it. "Can you –" I am interrupted by Erin's ringing phone.

"O.K.," says Erin, hanging up. "That was Luigi asking for Mimi's lunch to be brought in."

I sweep up the plate and condiments into my grasp for the third time and burst into Luigi's office so Mimi and Luigi see my irreverence. When I turn to leave, I don't see Mimi at all, but Alec Baldwin, their prospective Southampton home buyer to who I've just angled my bum at, thinking it was Mimi. I've almost escaped without Alec seeing my face when Luigi calls out, "Oh Eve, can you bring me some balsamic vinegar?"

"Sure." I close the door. "Erin, where is Mimi, she's not even in there. She had me bring her lunch here and she's not even here."

"I know. Luigi's going to eat her lunch."

"Well then what's Mimi going to eat?" I ask worried that Mimi will ask me to round up a second lunch for her.

"She's going to eat the food we ordered for Market."

"Well then would you mind getting Luigi balsamic vinegar?"

"No problem, I'll just page Jose and have him bring it up," she says, having long since mastered the art of delegation. She dials the phone while balancing her personal checkbook. "Oh, and if Luigi's looking for me in the next hour, tell him I had to go the bank. I'm actually going to get a manicure. I'm going to Italy the day after tomorrow and I have no time. You should come with me."

"That would be nice. I'd love to go, but I really can't leave my post," I say. I head for the elevator, passing the sales team who are showing the line to retailers who are buying (or not buying) next year's Summer line. Sophie is by the kitchen and silently with her forefinger, motioning me to follow her into the kitchen.

"Have you had lunch?"

"No."

"Well here, take a sandwich."

"Aren't they strictly for the sales team and retailers?" I ask, repeating the oft quoted rule that forbids non-sales team employees from eating food ordered for Market.

"Yes, but they've already eaten and otherwise they'll just go to waste, here, take, take."

I love Sophie and Emilia. I take a sandwich and cookies and fresh fruit and dart towards the elevator, hiding the food under a napkin until I get there, the home free zone. Jose bounds off the elevator with the balsamic vinegar for Luigi and there, trailing behind him.. is … Mimi who sees me with the Market food and casts a scornful look upon me. "Sophie told me to take it," I explain with a mouthful of lettuce and turkey and bread. Mimi shakes her double-processed blonde Frederic Fekkai head of hair and, not breaking elevator-dismount stride, plucks a sandwich off Sophie's platter just past me and rejoins the retailers.

I jump on the elevator and take it back to the 21st floor where there is no attending receptionist to buzz me inside, so I wait and wait, not wanting to break any more rules, but when I think of the calls I'm missing from being away from my post, I opt to climb over the empty reception desk to get through. No sooner do I swing around the corner when I run into Bebe and Tiffany who have their handbags over their arms and appear startled by my presence.

"Where's Mimi?" asks Tiffany, fearful.

"Up on twenty-nine. Why?" I ask, worried that I will have to go back to the 29th floor to fetch her for something they must "absolutely show her now".

"We're going to shop the stores" says Bebe. "Since it's 2:30 p.m. now, we probably won't be coming back afterwards."

"Fine," I answer.

Tiffany leans over to whisper in my ear, "It's Barney's semi-annual warehouse sale."

I nod knowingly. Being a designer is simply an excuse to shop during the workday. I want to say "have fun" because it's a nice 80-degree day out but my mouth won't form the upturn necessary to suggest sincerity. I can't stray five feet from my desk without getting buzzed to bus Prima Mimi's desk, but they can go shopping mid-afternoon. Life is so unfair. And I am one bitter garment girl.

Hmmm. I think I'll stop off at my corner El Cigaro newsstand on the way home and get some self-help magazines, something that will suggest ways to curb bitterness. Speaking of which, Jake has still not called.

"I AM LOOKING FOR A WOMAN TO MARRY.
IF YOU INTRODUCE ME TO THE WOMAN I MARRY,
I WILL PAY YOU ONE HUNDRED THOUSAND DOLLARS."

AS IT TURNS OUT, part of my self-help ritual has become reading about other people's desperate pleas for love in the *"Strictly Singles"* section of the *New York* magazine. I was going to give it up and start embracing Oprah's *"O"* more, but this week's cover story, illustrated with a Roy Lichtenstein-styled comic strip with a man and woman arguing, is titled, *"What New York Couples Fight About."* Naturally, it caught my eye.

But, even more entertaining than reading about people's desperation is listening to it, which I can do by calling their voice mailboxes to hear their bids for love. Many of the men, I've come to find out, sound a lot like Woody Allen. After a few dials, I yawn. It's closing in on midnight and I'm exhausted. I'm so tired that I almost went ahead and responded to this man's half page ad but am one inch short of his 5'7" height requirement. I count the lines he's written. There are thirty-five lines. At $34.50 a line, he spent $1207.50 to advertise for his future wife. And he'll pay $100,000 more for the person who finds her. Such desperate people. In any case, I wish I could think of someone for him and collect the money.

I reach to turn my bedside light off when the words, "Very handsome, self-made millionaire…" catch my eye. I flip the light back on.

VERY HANDSOME SELF-MADE MILLIONAIRE,
28, 6'2", 185 LBS., INTELLIGENT,
SLIGHTLY OFFBEAT SENSE OF HUMOR,
SEEKS A BEAUTIFUL, FREE-SPIRITED INTELLIGENT
WOMAN WITH A PASSION FOR LIFE THAT EQUALS MINE.

Oh my God, that's me! I'll just call and listen to his voice. I dial. He sounds attractive. Less Woody Allen, more Adam Sandler. Before I know it, I have left a message and my home number. Unfortunately, the carrot I've dangled feels like the same old pea under my mattress – if I had a mattress. I don't sleep well. *Why do I get the feeling I can't leave well enough alone?*

28. DEAD EVA

Tim, the *"Very handsome self-made millionaire"* from the pages of the *New York* magazine has called. I have still not heard from Jake.

Tim apologizes for returning my call so late, at 10:30 p.m. one week and one day after I left his mailbox #1109 a message, but as I can imagine, he's had so many calls. "There are a lot of desperate women out there," he says, laughing, "present company excluded of course."

We decide to meet thirty minutes later at the corner of my apartment, 44th and 2nd at the Nigerian Embassy, like two models on a go-see. He arrives in khaki shorts and a white t-shirt that has a "Staples" company logo and sneakers. He looks harmless. We decide we're both happily surprised that neither is aesthetically offensive, and he confides that he got wise to booking first dates involving more than just a quick hello. He's been stuck with too many dinners with women who were nice, professional, but not his type, and then he's blown $80 a pop and two hours of his life. He likes that I was so agreeable to meeting him impulsively like this.

"Well, I did pick a public corner, just in case…"

"In case I'm a mass murderer?" he nods then looks around. "Ahh. Nigerian Embassy. Good thinking," he says smiling, noting the dark and empty offices of the Embassy behind us.

"I almost had you meet me at the opposite corner. There's a cop posted there 24/7."

"Next time," he says, smiling.

Encouraged by the mention of a "next time," I ask him how many dates he's been on. He's lost count. "So how do you let them down?" I ask, wondering if he's the type to just suddenly never call again like someone else I know, the answer to which I'd like to find out beforehand.

"I just tell them that I got back together with my ex-girlfriend," he says.

"So you lie?" I ask, with a look that implies lying is a bad thing.

"Yeah, I mean, it could happen that way," says Tim. "And, I think it's a much kinder and gentler rejection. That way women don't go psycho."

"Psycho?"

"Present company excluded of course," he says, smiling and then ribbing me, then putting his arm around me jovially.

"NEXT TIME" turns out to be Halloween. Tim has invited me to a black-tie event. He's warned me that we're likely to be the youngest and only non-Jewish couple there, but it's a networking opportunity for him. He'll be marketing. It's our second date.

Tim arrives at my door bearing a wild bunch of posies, looking decidedly more handsome in his tuxedo than the Staples logo'd shirt from before. I let him in.

"So, just out of curiosity, why is there a cop by your elevator?" he asks as I try to create a makeshift vase out of the Choc Full 'o Nuts coffee canister.

"What do you mean there's a cop by my elevator?" I ask.

"I mean, there's a cop by your elevator. In full uniform."

"Oh, that's not a cop!" I laugh. "I can't believe you thought that's a cop. That's my doorman."

"No. It's a cop. Trust me. Unless of course your doormen wear NYPD uniforms."

"*Hmmph.* Oh, maybe for Halloween?"

"No. This isn't a uniform cut from a plastic bag. It's an official NYPD jacket."

"Maybe someone borrowed it for authenticity," I offer.

"No, it's a real cop. Real NYPD. Trust me. They don't let others wear their jackets. They can be thrown off the force for doing that," says Tim, checking out the view from my seventh story window just like Lars Thornwald did in *Rear Window* when he went looking to see who was onto his murderous deed: killing his wife.

"*Hmmm.* That's strange. I have no idea."

With the posies all situated in the coffee tin in front of the French windows, Tim and I are ready to leave.

We walk down the hall towards the elevator, and there, just as Tim said, is a policeman in a real, non-plastic NYPD jacket seated on a folding metal chair next to a can of Lysol. "Oh, you weren't kidding," I whisper to Tim.

"Good evening sir," says Tim, pressing the "down" button.

"Good evening," says the policeman.

I exchange a curious look with Tim as we hover nonchalantly, taking in our reflections in the mirror in between the elevators as if it's the most normal thing to have a cop seated in front of my elevator. After a fairly long wait for one of three elevators, the freight elevator arrives, with the custodian on it, announcing the other elevators aren't working. We step onto the elevator, joining a full load including Dr. Evil. As we descend the elevator, careful not to get caught up in Dr. Evil's lair, I break out of the elevator pack and head straight for my doorman.

"Ayman? Why is there a policeman sitting by the elevator on my floor?"

"Um… someone *died,*" he says quietly with a squeamish grimace, while nodding to incoming and outgoing tenants.

"Someone died?" I ask alarmed.

"Yes," he says, gesturing for me to keep it quiet.

"Who?" I whisper.

"The tenant in 714."

"Someone died on my floor?" I exclaim, my proximity to death revitalizing my fear that the black cloud over me has taken over the building.

He nods.

"Who?" I ask reluctantly, fearing it might be someone I know, like my seventy-year-old next-door neighbor who, come to think of it, hasn't picked up his daily *New York Post* in a week, or the eighty-three-year-old man, Frank, who always wears checkered shirts with suspenders and, when not in Paris on business, always greets me on the elevator by announcing to everyone else in it, how his heart has just revived from my joining the ride. God, I hope Frank's just in Paris.

"You know the young short, blond woman who was always walking her dog late at night in high heels? Eva Kowinsky?" asks Ayman.

"No…"

"Well she died," says Ayman, clearly sorry to break the news. He then excuses himself to retrieve dry-cleaning for the Penthouse tenant, Mrs. DiStephano who is waiting by the closet.

I follow him. "Ayman, you said she was young. How old was she?" I ask him.

"Oh not that young. Mid-thirties."

"Mid-thirties?" I exclaim, having expected her to be at least forty. "How'd she die?"

"Murder. Maybe suicide. Here you go Mrs. DiStephano," he says, handing off her Five Star dry-cleaning.

"Murder?" I ask shocked, having expected natural causes like a heart attack or something hereditary.

"Or suicide. Cops don't know. They're doing an autopsy. Apparently she's been dead for two weeks."

"Two weeks?! So how'd they finally discover her?" I ask.

"The smell," says Ayman as my jaw drops.

"Trick or treat," says a five-year old Mini-Me standing beside his dad Dr. Evil, holding a pumpkin pail.

"Sorry we don't have treats, but you can take a Poinsettia," he says pointing to one of the potted holiday arrangements dotting the lobby floor. The kid is not interested.

"The *smell?*" I ask, doing the math about what a dead person must smell like after two weeks, compared to what I might smell like after a day without a shower. Not good.

"Yeah. Tenants were complaining of the stench on the floor. In fact, everyone on your floor complained of the smell but you."

"Everyone but me?"

"Didn't you smell it?" asks Tim.

"No, I didn't smell anything. The only thing I've ever smelled in the hall is fried food."

Ayman and Tim exchange looks.

"You're saying I was smelling a body?"

Tim and Ayman exchange knowing glances.

"No. I know I wasn't smelling a dead body because I saw my neighbors cooking it, their food I mean, on the stove. They had their door ajar to let out the steam."

"So why do the cops think it could be suicide?" asks Tim.

"Well they don't know," says Ayman. "All they know is that she ordered takeout from eleven different places in one night two weeks ago and wasn't heard from until they found her today in her apartment."

"Where was the food from?" asks Tim.

"Oh yeah, maybe it was food poisoning," I say.

"Local places," says Ayman.

"Local?" I ask, alarmed, recalling the staple I found in the Chinese food I recently ordered from just down the street.

"She ordered a few times from the Szechwan place, Al's Deli and, um… Chinese from down the street. Cops are testing the food, but they think it's fine. They think the food was for the dog."

"Dog?" Tim and I ask at the same time.

Ayman nods squeamishly. "Her dog was in there."

"Alive?" I ask.

"Yes," says Ayman.

"So where exactly is 714 on my floor?" I ask.

"It's the apartment next to the elevator on your side of the hall."

"Oh," I nod knowingly, "so that's why the cop is sitting next to a can of Lysol."

"Yeah. The smell is pretty bad, and they have to guard the door to make sure no one goes in or out of the apartment. They're still treating it like a crime scene. And they've been interviewing the tenants."

"Well they haven't interviewed *me*..."

"Well is there something you want to tell us now? Without the presence of an attorney?" asks Tim, striking me as yet another man trying to implicate me in something I didn't do even if he is joking. Speaking of which, I hope her death is rendered a suicide because if word gets back to Pavlos that a woman was murdered in my building, he will, after the initial disappointment that it wasn't me, think my jinx aura was responsible.

"Well, on that note, we should go," I say. "We're going to a black-tie event," I tell Ayman.

"Me too," says Ayman, flipping his black tie, laughing at his own joke. "Have a good time and be careful out there," he says, and then whispers in my ear, "I hear she was meeting men on the Internet, so be careful, you never know who's out there."

"Ready?" asks Tim, holding the door open for me.

"Um, yeah," I say, walking towards Tim as a delivery man from Al's walks in carrying four bags of food.

"Food delivery coming up," I overhear Ayman say into the intercom just as we exit the double doors.

"Honestly, I wouldn't worry, Eve," says Tim, flanking my side, perhaps noticing my blanched face. "I'm sure it's just a murderer who's systematically killing young women, floor by floor."

"Thanks Tim. I feel so much better," I respond facetiously as he opens the car door for me. I am pulling on the seatbelt when my stomach sinks...err, drops to the baseboard.

"What's wrong?" asks Tim, getting into the car. "You look white as a ghost. I mean you're pale anyway, but right now you look really pale."

"I just…. realized… something. The woman who died was named EVA and she lived in 7-1-4, and I'm EVE and live in 7-0-4!"

"Oh. I see what you mean," he says, starting the engine. "It's a clear case of mistaken identity. The murderer meant to get you. To be safe, you'd better sleep at my place tonight. We'll order takeout."

"So is this what your ad meant by 'offbeat sense of humor?'" I ask.

WE WERE, as Tim expected, seated among elderly Jews at a table for twelve. Using the "Dead Eva" story, we basically became the life of the party. That is, until we all began to consider who might have murdered Eva, who would have had motive, and somehow, much to the delight of the elderly Jews, Tim began building a case around the idea that the murderer was actually after me.

I would have laughed too, if it wasn't beginning to sound more and more plausible. For, as they all laughed from the supposed implausibility of the theory, and unanimously concluded the joke with *'Who would want to kill Eve?,'* I was able to think of two people who would want me dead: Pavlos and the Chinese delivery man. And, although Pavlos would have seemed the more likely Prime Suspect, the fact is that Ayman had said Eva had ordered Chinese that night. Maybe the food – the poisoned food – was intended for me.

"Why would the Chinese delivery man want to kill you?" Tim asks as he drives me back to my apartment.

I tell him the story.

A few weeks earlier, I'd had a hankering for some Chinese food and so I ordered some from the restaurant just down the street. Twice, I made them deliver me a new order of food because something was invariably wrong with the order that was delivered.

Then just a week ago, the delivery man had to make two trips to my apartment because they got the order wrong. I thought he'd apologize. Instead, he yelled at me in the hallway, refusing to take my food because I'd eaten some of it (before realizing it was the wrong order). I called the restaurant manager and complained of his behavior, requesting never to have him as a delivery man again. So last week, I ordered Chinese again. I ordered mixed vegetables and shrimp. What I got was mixed vegetables, shrimp and a carpet-sized staple. I called the restaurant manager and implicated my delivery man. I think he wants to kill me.

With that, Tim drops me off at my apartment. I thank him for the evening. He sees me to the door, kisses my cheek and says he'll call me.

I enter the lobby, happy for the relatively subdued evening in which I remained alive, ready to plug my nose upon arriving at the 7th floor, when Sammy, the late shift doorman hands me a letter – a court summons.

"What is this?" I ask him.

He shrugs.

"Did the other tenants get one?"

"No, just you," he says.

I open the summons, nervously presuming I'm being called to enlighten the court about my whereabouts on the night Eva was murdered or killed herself with local Szechwan or Chinese, but I am mistaken. This is not the case of Manhattan vs. killer of Eva. It's the case of "City of Los Angeles and the State of California vs. Serena Yack." I am to appear in Malibu Court on November 16th.

Also called to testify: Pavlos Polychronopolis.

29. MALIBU RESTITUTION

PERSONS WEARING SHORTS,
BATHING SUITS OR
WITH BARE FEET
ARE NOT PERMITTED IN COURT

For a 60-degree October day in New York I'm dressed impeccably in black high-heeled loafer-front Mimi de la Coco shoes, black Ralph Lauren Lycra black leggings, a black Mimi de la Coco blazer and a black Gap crewneck lambswool sweater over my shoulders, a Mimi de la Coco trademark for which Mimi appeared on *Oprah*. But given it's 85-degrees in Malibu I appear lacking in judgment, which can't be a good precursor as a witness for the prosecution.

It's still hard to believe that the first time I will see Pavlos, in the five months since the accident, is not in New York where I live only five blocks north of him, but in Malibu 3000 miles away, just north of the scene of the crime. Many months ago, I thought only temporary emotions separated our permanent reunion. Instead, permanent emotions make this a temporary reunion.

My lawyer gives me the nod. It's now time to convene inside the court where I presume Pavlos is already sitting since I haven't seen him in the hallway just outside. I enter the court anticipating that inevitable moment when Pavlos turns to see me coming in. I try to focus only on finding a seat and see space in the fourth pew from the front. I slide in, and, as luck would have it, I am just a few feet down the pew from Pavlos. He smiles, the same kind of smile as when he told me he loved me. I smirk a wiser, confident, impervious smile, one that has none of the innocence or idealism I'd had when I first met him. A smile that has long since diminished my idealistic notions of men. Boy, I must look really attractive.

"PLEASE RAISE your right hand. Do you swear to tell the whole truth, nothing but the truth so helps you God?"

"I do."

"For the court please tell us your full name and address."

"Eve Foster, 310 East 44th Street, New York, New York, 10017." As luck would have it, I am the first called to testify.

"So, Miss Foster, how long have you lived in New York?"

"Three and half months."

"And, why did you move to New York?"

"Because L.A.'s a deathtrap."

The courtroom laughs. "What do you mean L.A.'s a deathtrap?" asks the Judge.

"Let's see… fires, floods, earthquakes, drunk drivers, riots…" I stop myself, suddenly concerned that I may be offending the Judge with my condemnation of his city.

The Judge, however, is laughing, and blowing his nose. He asks a few more questions to establish to what extent the accident changed my life. *Had I been considering moving to New York City before the accident?* Not at all. What were the conditions of my life just prior to the accident? I had the lead in a play - Rhonda Reuben the lesbian casting director, I had just got new headshots which had elicited four calls the night of the accident. *And employment?* I had been laid off earlier in the day. I was working for an interior decorating firm that lost it's main client - a baseball player - due to the baseball strike and they couldn't afford me.

The judge raises his brows. "What are you doing now in New York?"

"I'm a personal assistant to a fashion designer," I answer.

"Sounds fun. Do you like it?"

"Um…"

"Do you get a lot of clothes for free?" he inquires coquettishly as if he has a private fetish.

His question, however, is a sore spot, for it once again reminds me of the fact that I don't get a clothing allowance but Erin, who files her nails and dispatches Jose to do everything, does. Surely if the assistant to the President gets an allowance, the assistant to the CEO and namesake of the company, the Visionary, should get an allowance. "No, I don't get a clothing allowance," I answer.

"Is that her design, what you're wearing now?"

"Um, some of it."

"That's nice. Well. *Ahem.* I suppose we should get back to business," he says, abruptly catching his fashion digression.

He sums up the case and then asks if there is anything I'd like to add.

"Well, I would just like to add, that in all this time, I have never received an apology. Not once." Not from Pavlos the Greek, not from Serena the Drunk.

"Miss Yack, it would please the court and this Judge if you would kindly apologize to Miss Foster. Are you sorry for what you've done?"

"Yes, my whole life has been ruined by – "

"Miss Yack, your whole life? What about this young woman's? You're the one who took the wheel of a car while intoxicated and slammed into this girl. Are you sorry for that?"

"Yes – "

"Well then why the Lord have you not apologized?"

"I am sorry Your Honor."

"Don't tell me you're sorry, tell her!"

"I am sorry," she says, looking at me.

"Is that apology satisfactory to you?" the Judge asks me.

"It's O.K.," I answer, hoping he'll now instruct Pavlos to do the same.

"Now, Mr. Polychronopolis," says the Judge, "I understand you have filed your own suit?"

I eye Pavlos curiously from the stand. The defense attorney interrupts, approaches the Judge's bench and then I am ordered out of the court for the remainder of the proceedings. As I wait out in the hall, alone, I wonder why Pavlos could listen to my testimony, but I can't listen to his. *Could he be testifying against me?* I sneak a glance through the window. Pavlos is up in the chair, answering questions, gesturing Greekily as he answers.

My lawyer comes out of the court and tells me I cannot look through the window.

I take a seat on the bench, my mind swirling with the possibilities of what Pavlos could be saying. And I can't think of what it would be. Ten minutes later, the court spills out into the hallway and my lawyer informs me that Pavlos filed his own civil lawsuit against the drunk driver and I may be called to testify so I cannot listen to prior testimony lest I be unduly swayed.

Then, the handsome young defense attorney asks permission to speak to me privately. He tells me that Pavlos is seeking a significant amount in lost wages for the weeks he was "incapacitated" to work. He tells me that he doesn't like Pavlos and thinks that Pavlos is lying but feels for me and thinks I should be compensated. He asks me if I'll accept a $3000 cash settlement, that Serena doesn't have anymore than that, and has hocked her wedding ring to come up with that much. "Her husband is divorcing her," he adds. He tells me about her community service, the AA meetings she has to attend. "Her life has been completely turned upside down from this."

"Uh, I'm sorry, but I don't have much sympathy for her… but I'll consider the offer. "

And then court is adjourned. The Judge will review the cases and render his judgment later.

"Do you need a ride?" asks Pavlos, as we exit the courthouse.

"Um, yes, I could use a ride back to my hotel," I answer, having hoped for this opportunity for months, to finally find out what happened in the weeks after the accident, straight from the horse's mouth, as to why he would jettison without a word. Given his invite, I am of the mind he wants to clear the air himself.

But I am wrong. The only discussion occurring in the car is the one Pavlos is having with whomever is on the other end of his cell phone. I cannot believe he's doing it to me again. This is not the way it's supposed to happen.

"Do you want to stop for coffee?" he asks.

"Um, sure," I answer, hopeful once again that we'll go inside a coffee house and have that discussion, obtain that closure.

We pull up to a Starbucks. I wait for him to finish his call before going in. Instead he hands me $5 and asks me to get him an espresso. He then resumes his phone conversation.

I cannot believe I'm here again, fetching, not Tylenol now, but coffee. I look out the window at him, thinking he might finish the call and join me inside, but he doesn't. I make the purchase and return to the car with our drinks. He hangs up the phone, takes his espresso and resumes the drive to my hotel. I can't get over the irony that after all this time of not seeing each other, we are once again heading south on Pacific Coast Highway but this time, he's driving.

"The judge really liked you," he says.

"Why do you say that?" I ask, staring out the window at the ocean.

"Because you were adorable... what you said about L.A.?

"That it's a deathtrap?"

"Yeah."

"It is. So how's your eyebrow?"

"I think there's still glass in it."

I nod, unsympathetically, not taking my eyes off the ocean when it occurs to me that the Pacific Coast Highway has often provided the backdrop for climactic Hitchcock finales, particularly for his heroines. There was vertigo in San Juan Battista, and birds in

Bodega Bay. Maybe Pavlos is going to push me out of the car. Maybe I'm going to push him. "So why isn't it that I could hear your testimony?"

"Because I have a lawsuit against the girl."

The words of the prosecuting lawyer hover: that Pavlos is a *"liar"* and *"Borderline scum."*

"So did they offer you a settlement?" Pavlos asks me.

"Yes," I answer, suddenly of the mind that this is all he wants from me, the whole reason he's offered a ride.

"How much?"

"Not much," I answered, wondering if he's trying to gauge how much he could stand to gain by accepting a settlement. "How much are you asking for?" I asked aloofly, feigning disinterest.

"A significant amount. Is that your hotel?"

"Yep. That's it."

Pavlos pulls into the hotel circular and keeps the engine running.

I sit there in disbelief. I can't really believe that he's really just going to drop me off and have that be the end of it. I can't believe that he wouldn't make an overture to apologize, explain or inquire about anything. I move slowly, waiting for him to take his last opportunity to clear the air, or try to summon the words myself. I disengage the seatbelt. The air feels suffocatingly thick. The words don't come.

"O.K. thanks for the ride. Bye," I say.

"Bye," he says.

I get out of the car, close the door and head for the double doors. I hear his car heading for the highway.

I head to my room in disbelief. *How did the last half hour just pass without a word about the prior three and a half months?* As little as I expected from this interaction, I got even less. *How could I have overestimated him, again!* I search for the card of the defense attorney. I'm going to accept their settlement offer of $3000. It's not what I'd hoped for, nor what I think I'm due, but I believe she has no more money and I can't stomach any more losing.

"So, how much can she offer?" I ask, making one last attempt to coerce more from the lawyer.

"Three-thousand. That's it. I'm not low-balling you Eve. I like you. I know it's not a lot of money, but that's just all she has. If you accept it, I can pick you up now and take you to my office and write you the check"

"O.K. Then, I'll take it."

DREW, THE DEFENSE ATTORNEY, arrives to pick me up in a red Porsche. The top is down.

"So what's happening with Pavlos' case?" I ask him.

"Well no one believes him, not even his own lawyer, but will the judge believe him, that's the question."

"Well, how much is he asking for?"

"One-hundred-thousand dollars."

"What?!" I exclaim. I'd just assumed that Pavlos' case involved a paltry sum. I was certain he'd gain no more financial restitution than me given I lost far more than him.

"For medical bills – "

"One hundred thousand? He cut his eyebrow!"

"The medical's just part of it. He said he's missed work."

"But he's self-employed."

"Well he's allowed to submit lost wages. Anyway, everyone knows he's lying but we just can't nail him."

"How do you know?"

"The doctor bill he submitted is dated *before* the accident."

"Well then you have him."

"The medical is only $38,000 of it. He's claiming $62,000 in lost wages and contracts for the six weeks he was out of work immediately following the accident. What kind of work does he do? I mean what does he import and export?"

"I don't know. But six weeks out of work? That's what he said?"

"Yes."

"Well that's not true. I was with him almost every day for most of the weeks following the accident, and he never stopped working.

He was working deals on the phone all the time. He even took a trip to San Diego to flesh out a deal the following weekend and then he was back in his office in New York."

"How do you know he was in the office in New York?"

"Because I called him there."

"He testified that he wasn't physically able to travel."

"Well he did. I saw him. Believe me, nothing slowed down his deal-making. Don't get me wrong. I hate this girl Yack and I'm not discounting our injuries, but do I think a 24-year-old should be paying for it the rest of her life based on lies? No."

"Would you be willing to tell the judge what you just told me?"

"OH BY THE WAY, I had to tell your lawyer what we're up to," says Drew as we head back along PCH in the red Porsche to see the Judge privately.

"What?" I ask alarmed.

"It's professional courtesy."

"But won't he be upset to lose a case?" I ask as we pull into a Balinese restaurant near the Court to eat until the Judge is ready to see us.

"No, he thinks Pavlos is a lying scumbag too. Besides, he doesn't have anything to do with Pavlos' civil case and that's the only case your testimony is going to impact. Of course the same judge is presiding over both."

"HE'S A LYING scumbag," says my lawyer Phil. "I knew he was scum the moment you walked into the courtroom and didn't sit next to him. We knew something was up. We were relieved. We thought you were such a nice girl. We couldn't understand why you were with such an asshole."

I confess to Phil that I'm worried there might be retribution should Pavlos discover I testified against him. While not mentioning the Greek Mafia by name, I manage to convey the tightness of the Polychronopolis family.

"Well we have to mention it in the official court records, but don't worry, Pavlos will never see it."

"How do you know he'll never see it?" I ask.

"Because I'll never show it to him."

"WE WON'T SWEAR you in formally again," the Judge says to me, still wiping his mouth with a napkin when we enter the courtroom. He hands his plate to security. "But I remind you that the first swearing-in is still effective. You must tell the truth so help you God."

The judge asks me to characterize how much Pavlos worked in the days following the accident. I tell him exactly what I witnessed and with that he dismisses the case of *Polychronopolis v. Yack.*

"Now, I understand you accepted a settlement of $3000 for the State's case against Ms. Yack? Is that correct," the judge asks me.

"Yes."

"Is that satisfactory to you?"

"I was informed there was no more to get."

"That's probably true. You were smart to take it," he says and then winks at me.

"So, what are you going to tell Pavlos when he asks why he didn't get any money?" I ask Phil as he gives me a ride to my hotel in his black Porsche.

"The truth. That the judge just didn't believe him."

I ARRIVE home via another one-way plane to Manhattan, just before Midnight, to three messages. I have three chances that Jake called. *Three!* Message one is from Tim. He says he's sorry he hasn't called me back from the message I left a week ago, but he's gotten back together with his ex-girlfriend. The second message is from

Olive. She's got a new apartment and can see Mount Hood from it and it's gorgeous and she's eating cheese and wine and wishes I was there and asks what I've eaten today. The last message is from Mimi. She's mortified that I forgot to tell Don to pick up a pomegranate for her dinner before I left for California. *What is she going to do with me?!*

I go to bed (or should I say, "I go to floor?" since I don't have a bed yet) recalling a conversation I had with Tim, wherein he told me how he "lets women down gently" by telling them he "got back together with his ex-girlfriend." This leaves me highly amused. Better to find out sooner than later that you're dating a liar. And then my mind turns to the pomegranate, and all the recipes that call for pomegranates, and conclude that Mimi's maid must be making pomegranate soup… and this puts me to sleep.

30. GARMENT DISTRICT
WEEK 12

"Eve, what am I going to do with you?" cries Mimi at the end of my first day back in the office since California. I walk into her office expressionless. I was five minutes away from leaving the "pomegranate day" of abuse behind me. (As it turned out, Mimi was going to start a pomegranate fast to rid herself of some inexplicable weight gain.) "What's wrong?"

"We are going to the AIDS Benefit tonight and we don't have tickets. You were supposed to have purchased them, remember?" she cries.

There's nothing that angers me more than being blamed for something I didn't do. "Well, no. I wasn't supposed to purchase tickets. It's not my job to purchase tickets. It's never been my job to purchase tickets," I say, hesitant to point out it's the job of PR, specifically Noreen to decide which events Mimi must make an appearance at, which ones she must give money to, and then get a check requisitioned to pay for the tickets.

Noreen is called in. The PR firm is dialed. Everyone is upset. Everyone, including Panic Peter, the editorial props guy, deflects blame. And one thing is clear. I am being railroaded. I seem to be the only one who recalls that the Official Routing Process of Invitations instituted weeks ago at a formal meeting, handed the "Invitation" reigns over to Luigi's office and PR. The only function I was to serve was as mail carrier, not Check Requisitionist.

I leave Mimi's office only to overhear my name lobbed around as the culprit. Once everyone has cleared, and I've heard my name muttered quite long enough, I exhale and march back into Mimi's office.

"Mimi?"

Mimi turns towards me, her eyes preying on me with bewilderment and disappointment, the oak door still swinging back and forth. "Yes Missy?" she asks, signifying she's not quite finished unjustly berating me for this.

"I… *quit*. I can't take it anymore. I can't do anything right for you. I don't have another job lined up. I don't know how I'm going to pay my rent. But no job's worth *this*."

She stands there, her jaw agape, the valium neutralized(?). She appears genuinely shocked that anyone has leveled an appropriate reaction for her inappropriate behavior. As she reaches for a tissue among the tribal artifacts on her desk – ones that I so painstakingly situate at perfect right degree angles – she messes them up with her Cartier bracelet.

"Oh, dear. You know it's not you," she says, repositioning the tribal knife to a right degree angle. "I'm just under so much stress. Here," she tries to dab my running mascara, my snot. "Is there anything I can do?"

"Change?" I ask.

She draws a blank expression.

I blow my nose. "If you want, I'll stay until you find someone." I need the money.

"Oh would you?" she asks tenderly, rubbing her hand down my arm, her eyes gazing into mine as if perplexed by how human I am.

Perplexed by the humanness visiting her office. What a phenomenon. Such realness rarely rears its ugly head in the Garment District. In fact, until Hilary Clinton marched through the district to champion national healthcare, one only spoke of "trends, trends, trends," and what was selling on the main floor of Barney's.

On the way home from being skewered, I pick up a voicemail from Olive. "Hey. Wassup? Oh man, you wouldn't believe my day. I am so stressed. And I've just eaten a pound of cheese. What'd you eat today? Oh yeah, have you asked your boss for time off from work to come home for Thanksgiving? Or maybe I could come there. Call me."

31. THANKSGIVING AT TIFFANY'S

Olive has sent me "The Perfect Man" for Thanksgiving. He is wearing three white buttons and a red bow tie and is lying flat on a white plate. The perfect man, according to *American Greetings*, is a Gingerbread Man.

Inside the card is the same well-dressed Gingerbread Man missing his head. *"He's quiet. He's sweet. And if he gives you any crap, you can bite his head off."*

Hmmm. Olive didn't care enough to send the very best. Wait. Olive's also enclosed an article from *Self magazine*, titled, *"The Man Who Disappears"* by Maggie Scarf.

While families come together across the nation to eat and give thanks on this national holiday, I sit down to read about the psychology of relationship deserters. Can't wait till Christmas. Still, it is a compelling headline:

"THE RELATIONSHIP WAS GOING WONDERFULLY,
THE FUTURE LOOKED BRIGHT. THEN ONE DAY HE STOPPED CALLING.
THE ONLY WAY TO PROTECT YOURSELF FROM HIM
IS TO RECOGNIZE THE WARNING SIGNS."

Hmmm. It's a tough call. Watch the big cartoon figures floating down Fifth Avenue for the Macy's Thanksgiving Day parade on TV, or read about *"The Structure of Evil,"* according to the article's sub-heading. I flip on the TV to see Mickey Mouse and then return to the article, paying close attention to words applicable to Pavlos *("serial seducer, evil, emotionally impotent, comparisons to a serial killer, cruel, sadistic, heartless, Don Juan")* and me *("victim, perceived vulnerability ready to be exploited")*, and to the inevitable denouement when combining the two *("evil seduction turning to shocking betrayal, sudden desertion")*.

> *"As the Don Juan sees it," reports Hannah Fox,*
> *a clinician in private practice in NYC,*
> *"there's not really anyone out there to say goodbye to,*
> *because he lacks the concept of a self in the first place."*

Wow. Holy…

The phone rings. "Hi Sissy." It's Olive.

"Hi."

"Whatcha doing?"

"Nothing, what are you doing?"

"We just finished eating turkey, mashed potatoes, gosh so much stuff. I'm so full. I had three pieces of pie. Did you have turkey?"

"Yeah." I answer.

"Oh good – "

"On a bagel," I add.

"Oh. Well guess what we're doing?"

"Digesting?"

"Heh, heh. Yes, and we're watching the Macy's Parade on TV. Mom was looking for you in the crowd. I wish I could've gone. How was it? Was it packed?"

"I didn't go."

"You're right there and you didn't go? What mom? Oh, yeah. Mom said to tell you that she saw a woman get hit by the Mickey Mouse balloon and she thought it was you because the woman had red hair."

"Great. See it's better that I didn't go?"

"Well… so did you get my card?" she asks.

"Yeah. Thanks. Cracked me up."

"Did you read that article?"

"Yeah, it was dead-on... except for suggesting there were "warning signs." Because that's the thing. There weren't any warning signs. There was no way for me to know Pavlos would do this."

"Really?"

"Really."

"Hmmm. Well, I gotta go. We're going to watch *It's a Wonderful Life*. I wish you were here! What are you going to do for the rest of the evening?"

"Pull Mickey from my head."

"What? Oh! The balloon!" Olive laughs. "That's funny. I'll tell mom you said that. She'll laugh. What mom? No, I didn't eat all the cheese. There's still brie in the − oh the gruyere? Yeah, I ate that days ago."

"O.K. bye," I say.

"Alright bye-eee."

⌒◡◠

As I step out from under the Belle Arts awning and breathe in the brisk holiday air, I feel remarkably happy and refreshed. No longer will I waste my thoughts thinking about Pavlos and what signals I did or didn't miss.

"Hey there."

I turn around to find my neighbor Brad behind me with his dog, Gerald. When I ran into him and Gerald last Thursday, he filled me in on his love life, or the end of it. He broke up with a woman because as he put it, "She licked a part of me I don't think is supposed to be licked." And, then he segued(?) with telling me he was converting to Orthodox Judaism, a much more conservative form than he'd previously practiced. After we exchange "Happy Thanksgiving," he announces that he has found his wife.

"Wow, since Thursday?" I ask.

"Well, no, it's someone I met last February."

As we walk up Second Avenue he tells me that last February he went on a mission to find his wife. And that since then he's dated eighty-two women, no exaggeration. He logged them.

"So she was number 82?" I ask.

"No, she was #2 and #3." But he just wasn't sure, so he moved on to #4. Seventy-eight women later, he was sure. He had a third date with her last night and he's going to ask her to marry him and she's going to say "yes" because they already discussed it.

"Wow, congratulations Brad. What a great story!"

"So how 'bout you?" he asks me." You moved here to be with someone right?"

"No, not exactly." I tell him the story of my Manhattan arrival.

"I was dating this guy Pavlos, he's Greek and – "

"You know what?" he interrupts me, "You don't have to tell me he's Greek. 'Pavlos the Greek' is kind of like saying 'Abdullah the Egyptian,' or 'Mohammed the Muslim.' You kind of already know."

We laugh and I finish the story about how I came to be ditched.

"Well were there any warning signs or was this guy just that smooth?" he asks me, eerily echoing the article's supposition.

"He was just that smooth."

"Really?" he asks almost disbelieving before stopping in front of the window at Tiffany's.

I peer in too. And as I contemplate the signs I may have missed, I catch my reflection among the sparkly solitaires.

"Look at this one. The clarity is amazing," says Brad, pointing to one of the solitaires.

"Yes, it is, isn't it? So, I guess this is what you'd call Thanksgiving at Tiffany's?"

～⌐

I ARRIVE home to a message from Don. He says to tell everyone I'm spending Thanksgiving in Brooklyn with the most handsome Italian family. He's got turkey in Brooklyn for me and he's coming to pick me up in the Town Car. All I have to prepare is a salad. "And remember," he adds, "presentation is everything."

32. GIFT EXCHANGE

"Friday will be my last day," I happily inform Mimi, seconds after getting the call that, after submitting to a rigorous 15-minute interview last week, I am one of the lucky ten selected from a pool of 75 applicants to start work at Jekyll & Hyde, a theme restaurant in Greenwich, and all it took was a little embellishment on my resumé. I said I had been a waitress at Johnny Rockets on Melrose in Los Angeles for four years. (It had only been 2 months.) *Still, how hard can waitressing be?* At last, my life as an actress begins anew.

And, despite being at work at my desk, barricaded in a corner surrounded by racks of samples, answering to the gluttonous buzzers instigated from behind the Oak door, I'm in a great mood. And what's more, Dominic the Donkey is playing on the radio.

"Santa's got a little friend, his name is Dominic…"

I'm singing it as Emilia comes by to vacuum. I do an impression of Dominic the Donkey for her, "Eee-aw, eee-aw."

She raises her eyebrow in mock horror, turns off the vacuum, and asks in her native Germanic lilt, "What dis dat?"

"Dominic the Donkey."

She sizes me up. "Yeah. You're a donkey all right." She starts up the vacuum again, betraying a rarely seen smile. Then we both laugh.

Don comes by, delivering the Barney's bag of lunch to 23-year-old Becky, my replacement-in-training, now sitting beside me having just enjoyed her last meal out of the office. I do my Dominic the Donkey impression for him. He smiles, "That's good, really, that's very good."

"You think?" I ask, wondering if I could develop it into material for a one-woman show.

"Yeah, 'cause if I didn't know any better, I'd swear I was talking to a jackass."

We laugh.

"I can't believe you're leaving. I'm really going to miss you," he says after Becky requests to be excused for a bathroom break, her last.

"I know. I'll miss you too." And I really, truly will.

"You have to promise to call me. I'll come pick you up in the car anytime. We'll go for pizza. Whatever you want. And if you ever need a haircut, I'll take you to my brother-in-law's salon in Brooklyn. He gives the best haircuts. People come from Manhattan for haircuts. Elliot Gould is a customer. Just call me."

"I will."

"Oh and I almost forgot. Did you bring the coat? She's asking for it."

"Oh *that*." Mimi had left her Max Mara pea coat in the town car and Don gave it to me to return to her since Don was going on vacation for a few days. "Well, um, it was a really cold weekend. So I kinda wore it."

Don cringes.

"It is seriously the most comfortable, beautiful coat I've ever worn. I feel like Audrey Hepburn. In a pea coat. I wouldn't have thought I'd like navy blue on me, but it looks great."

"O.K. but did you bring it in? That's a $5500 coat."

"Well, it's here but I don't have another coat and it's going to be in the '40s tonight. I'll freeze."

"Alright. Keep it till I ask for it again. I'll tell her I left it at my house," he says, smiling and shaking his head.

"Don, Mr. de la Coco wants you to bring the car around," says the receptionist.

"On my way." Don steps away and then does a doubletake. "This place won't be the same without you." Don shakes his head in disbelief and disappears around the corner, leaving me teary-eyed.

But, I return to the final task at hand: forging Mimi's signature to 400 headshots for the fans they're expecting at the perfume launch at the Short Hills Mall in New Jersey over the weekend. Only then will the PR team unveil what name was selected for the perfume. I submitted five ideas (Mimi D, MDLC, I.M. Coco, Midi, and under "anonymous" I submitted Me Me Me) but have already been told I'm ineligible to win now that I've quit.

"Eve?" asks Becky, "Mimi wants me to place a call to Bergdorf Goodman, but I can't find him anywhere in the rolodex."

I clutch my stomach with laughter.

"What?" asks Becky. "What's so funny?"

"Bergdorf Goodman?"

"Did I say his name wrong? She said it so fast I didn't hear her. Is it Bergman Guman?"

I laugh… *harder.*

"What?" She cries, beside herself.

"Bergdorf Goodman is not a man," I tell her. "It's a store. A high-end department store."

"Oh, I didn't know. I'm from Ohio! You're not going to tell Mimi are you?"

"No, no, don't worry. I'm sorry. It was just funny. But, just one question."

"Sure…"

"Do you know Barney and Tiffany?"

"Huh?" She looks stressed and ready to throw in the towel.

"You know, Barney's and Tiffany's?"

"Huh?"

"Never mind."

"I'm from Ohio. We don't have Bergman Goodorf's there."

"I know. I'm from Oregon, and we don't have Bergman Goodorf's there either." I laugh.

"I said it wrong, didn't I?" she asks, her forehead creasing.

"Eve?" Mimi calls from behind the oak door.

"Yes?" I ask, following into her office.

"So what do you think? Do you think she can handle the job?" Mimi asks me.

"Sure."

"I think so too. I just have one worry."

"What's that?"

"Her penmanship. It's not very good. What am I going to do without you!"

I shrug. Funny thing is that since I quit, she's much easier to work for. Nice even.

⌒‿⌒

GIVEN THAT Mimi and Luigi are heading to the Upper West Side and I am heading to Macy's to partake in the holiday spirit (window-shop on 34th Street), Mimi insists that Don drop me off along the way. Mimi's insistence that I hitch a ride with them in the town car is gracious but creates a problem: *How am I to get out of the car with her pea coat without her noticing?* Don said leave it to him, so I sit uncomfortably in the car as we slowly move along in traffic.

After an exchange with Luigi in Italian, Mimi asks me if I submitted any names for the perfume.

"Yes, a few," I answer.

"Someone submitted 'Me Me Me.' Do you know who?"

"No, sorry," I answer.

"I thought maybe it was you," she says.

"No, not me," I submitted some other names." I answer.

"So Eve. Tell me. How's your love life?" Luigi asks me. "You seeing anyone?"

"No."

"Whatever happened with that young man Jake who came by the office?" asks Mimi. "He was very handsome."

249

"Um well, I haven't heard from him since then." Wow she remembers his name.

"Who is this Jake?" Luigi asks Mimi with a show of paternal curiosity.

"Did you call him?" asks Mimi, disregarding Luigi's question.

"Once."

"He never called back," adds Don.

"Thanks Don."

"So call him again," insists Luigi.

Don cringes.

"What?" demands Luigi. "Is there something wrong about a woman calling a man? What could be wrong?"

Mimi explains the "The Rules" to Luigi in Italian. At least that's what it sounds like.

"If you ask me," says Don, "it's his loss. Look at you. You're gorgeous. And I'm not just saying that 'cause I want to sleep with a girl half my age before I die."

I laugh, and then Mimi pipes up, "He'll call you. I can tell."

Silence. Don eyeballs Mimi in the rear-view window.

"Really? You think so?" I ask.

Mimi nods knowingly.

———

AS WE NEAR my drop off, Luigi mentions that his son is moving to Paris and has a couch he needs to get rid of. Before I know it, Mimi has designated Don to deliver the couch to me. She suggests I get it slipcovered.

As I finish thanking them in advance for the couch, Don pulls up to 34th Street where he insists on opening the door for me, chauffeur style. When he comes around the side, he hands me a Bendel's bag that contains the pea coat. Mimi rolls down the window and frowns.

"Missy. Don't you have a coat?" she asks.

"No, I'm fine. I'm just taxiing home anyway."

Don and I exchange nervous glances.

Mimi and Luigi slowly lift their parental frowns and wave goodbye.

A few hours later, after enjoying time with holiday shoppers, I embark on a long walk home in Mimi's pea coat. At around 9 p.m., I greet Ayman with a gift. "Happy to serve you," I say to Ayman as I hand him Al's holiday brew.

"Why thank you," he says, as he curtseys an imaginary dress.

"And, I have something for you." He walks to the closet where the dry-cleaning is kept and returns with an envelope. "You remember the woman who died in #714? Eva Kowinsky? Well, this was found among her personal effects."

It's an envelope addressed to "Eve in #704." Inside is a card with a picture of a woman walking on a cable that's suspended from atop a skyscraper on the west side of Manhattan to a skyscraper on the east side of Manhattan. The card is from Jake Fanelli. He says he's been busy with post-production on his movie but has been thinking about me and wants to know if I'll have lunch with him – ten weeks ago. I turn the card over. It's a *Hallmark* card.

33. MISTAKEN IDENTITY

I called Jake the next day to tell him the funny story: the case of mistaken identity. That his note was mistakenly given to a woman named Eva who, after receiving the wrong envelope, died, although I was sure one had nothing to do with the other.

"That's good to hear. Not the death of course," he said.

We are meeting for lunch today at Jekyll & Hyde, just ten weeks after he invited me.

ALTHOUGH I applied at the downtown Jekyll & Hyde in Greenwich, I have been assigned to the just opened, midtown J & H, a four-story pre-war at Avenue of the Americas and 56th Street. It has an incredible view of… Sam Goody, for all your home entertainment needs. I have five redeye shifts a week from 5 p.m. to 2 a.m.. Tonight will be my first night and tomorrow, Mimi will officially be on her own – with Becky.

It's raining hard as I wait for Jake outside the eatery in a manufactured line to make it appear as if all of Manhattan can't wait to get in. Meanwhile, Mimi's pea coat is getting soaked and it strikes me as the don't-get-soaked-kind-of-coat. Twenty minutes later, just when I begin to consider the notion that Jake won't show, he shows.

"Hi there," he says warmly, enthusiastically, all smiles as he approaches in a hooded yellow rain slicker, holding a large umbrella.

"Hi," I smile. He gives me a bear hug, kisses one cheek, then the other. Oh, don't' let go.

"You look great," he says, eyeing the soaked pea coat. "So sorry I'm late. It was rough getting a taxi."

"No, no it's fine, I just got here myself."

"It's great to see you," he says. "I was afraid I'd never hear from you again."

I nod. "Me too."

"Oh. Here," he says, handing me an envelope.

"What's this?"

"I'm giving you your Christmas Card now. I wouldn't want your apartment building to suffer another loss."

He smiles. I laugh as I look down at the card. It says, "Don't Open Until XMAS." Once again, my thoughts turn to daydreams as I think of Christmas. I picture me and Jake by the tree sipping eggnog as the aroma of cinnamon and pine fills the air, just like the non-homeless people I saw through the windows on Second Avenue when I first arrived.

"Welcome unfortunate souls," announces the "Decaying Butler" from within a dungeon-like elevator, waving us in. Once inside, the doors of the elevator close, a spiked ceiling descends and the elevator becomes a human tenderizer/compressor all-in-one. As the spikes get closer and a toddler wraps both arms around my leg, a sinister laugh comes over the sound system, and then a voice. "In 1931, Dr. Jekyll fled London for New York City, a new city filled with outcasts and wanderers. He soon found others like him – daring men and women whose exploits into science and adventure were deemed too unorthodox by society – and together they formed the Jekyll & Hyde club. Dr. Jekyll, most of all, was fascinated by man's two separate natures; good and evil, good and evil…."

"Maybe we should've met somewhere else for lunch," I whisper to Jake.

"Good and evil. Good and evil…"

"I guess the sound system needs fixed." I add.

"But the spikes appear to be in perfect working order," Jake adds, noting the impending impale.

Finally, the spikes as well as the child wrapped around my leg, retract, and the vaulted door opens to the restaurant where a Nurse wearing a blood-soaked uniform greets us, "Brave diners can visit the Slaughtered Lamb Pub."

"No one recognizes me as an employee yet," I mention to Jake as we near the hostess, "so I'm getting the customer treatment."

"Eve, is that you?"

"Um, yes," slow to recognize Frank, the Assistant Manager behind the hostess podium.

"Why aren't you dressed?" he asks as Jake helps me remove my, err Mimi's, soaked pea coat.

"Um, because I'm early. I'm just here – "

"Kevin, Eve's here." yells Frank.

"Eve, thank God, I was afraid you weren't going to show," says Kevin, the Manager who, at the interview, asked me if my red hair was natural.

"Huh?"

"We need you to do the Frankenstein Bride re-animation until Five o'clock, then you can join the late shift at Nine, so that will give you a little break," says Kevin.

"But my shift doesn't start until Five. And I'm a waitress not a bride."

"The schedule changed."

"Oh well no one told me – "

"Eve, it's your responsibility to call in every morning to see if it has changed."

"But this is my first day of work."

"Better get to it then. The bride's costume is upstairs, Gene will show you the way. I need you to pull double duty until I can get another bride."

I turn to Jake. I am speechless and anguished that I have to disengage from this physical and mental proximity to him so soon after our ten-week separation.

"I guess I'll have to take a raincheck," says Jake.

"I'm *so* sorry."

"No, no. It's ok. I understand," he says gazing into my eyes.

"I'm sure you'll make a lovely Frankenstein bride."

"Eve? Follow Gene please," yells Kevin.

I stare at Jake. I can't move.

"Eve?" repeats Kevin.

"I'll call you," says Jake, retreating into the elevator.

I'll call you later today, my car is waiting.

The vaulted doors close and the elevator descends.

"Eve, would you please go with Gene?"

"Gene who?" I snap.

"The guy with the hole in his head. Over there."

That's why I'm not a waitress… That's why I'm not a waitress…

AFTER REPEATING this over and over for two hours from within the casket-like Frankenstein "Re-Animator" where I am lying in state until the doctor-prescribed levitation (to the tune of terrified shrieks from adults and kids alike), and taking a one-hour break (not the four hours that Kevin had promised) in which I scarfed down a bloody Batty Burger, I began a late shift (still wearing the latest in Frankenstein Bridal-wear) in a barricaded area of the restaurant, the corner surrounding the bar, aka the Slaughtered Lamb Pub.

"We have 200 varieties of beer," I inform the couple seated below the paintings with the roving eyes, as the talking Great Sphinx (a *papier-mâché* of the real thing) drowns me out with his live barbs. As it turns out the midtown horror-themed eatery is not much different than the midtown horror-themed garment district.

"What's the difference between an ale, stout and porter?" asks the woman, her own husband offering no clues.

"Umm, the ale?" I look around for more senior help. "Rodney?"

Rodney, the MVW (Most Valuable Waiter) recruit from downtown, signals he'll be right over just after he closes the deal on his customers. Kevin, the manager, currently dressed as a Count of Transylvania witnesses the teamwork and comes over to tell me that I have to get my beers memorized, that it's not fair to pull Rodney off of his customers when he brings in more money than anyone else here. (Well Rodney also has central air conditioning in his section as well as twice the seating capacity, but I guess my four years at Johnny Rockets is insufficient to get priority seating. That's what I want to say.) Kevin recommends that I stay after closing and taste-test ten beers. Any more, he says, would dull my senses. "It's like testing perfumes," he adds.

After Rodney explains the difference in the beers, inciting awe in the eyes of my customers for how knowledgeable Rodney is, the customers are ready to order.

"We'll have the Old Devil, a Lucifer Belgian Golden Ale, a Rogue Dead Guy Ale, a Nightmare Porter, two Monster Burgers, and one Batty Burger. Did you get that?"

"Yes, I got it." Clearly they've taken Rodney's usual suggestion that they sample several beers.

"Could you just repeat it back, so we're sure you got it," they say with detectable condescension. It's as if they've tattooed their foreheads with *"I love Rodney."* I repeat it back. They reluctantly give their approval.

I play out the remainder of my shift pretty much comparable to the beginning, repeating "that's why I'm not a waitress" as I continue to manifest beer trivia meltdown, mosh my way through the human pile-up at the bar in order to quickly deliver spilled drinks and incorrect orders to my customers, or simply arrive empty-handed altogether having dropped everything to come "running" to their page (which is always a mistake; invariably they didn't know that the button looped around the table lamp, when pressed, would page me to their table immediately). Then, they either say that they didn't press the button (a lie), or look at me dumbstruck, in disbelief that the button they pressed wasn't to turn on the lamp.

"Well, did it come on? The light?" I ask.

"Oh, I guess not," they'd acquiesce.

FINALLY, AT 2 A.M., I am permitted to clock out without doing my taste-testing, primarily, I imagine, because my body is covered with at least 60 of the 200 beers and I can therefore taste test on my own time.

I'm so tired I don't have the energy to change. I just want to pull on the pea coat, get in a taxi and get home. If only it were that easy. It's absolutely freezing and Mimi's pea coat is still soaked, and while it's inconceivable that I'm going to walk all the way home at 2 a.m. looking like the Bride of Frankenstein, carrying a sopping wet pea coat, through intermittent sprinkles, that's exactly what I'm doing. I'm walking and hailing but failing at the latter. I didn't even know it was possible to walk two(?) miles at 2 a.m. in Manhattan without finding one single vacant taxi. I guess this is the difference between summer and winter, and day and night. Fifty minutes later, my mouth chattering, my ears, legs, and hands red from 40(?) degree air, I turn the corner. Now onto Second Avenue with just thirteen blocks to go, I set a personal goal to get there by 3 a.m.. That's good Eve. Goal setting. Not planning, but goal setting.

It is at this time that I surreptitiously discover that chanting "That's why I'm not a waitress," raises my body heat index. I keep chanting.

At 2:55 a.m., I pass by the corner magazine stand, catching sight of *Backstage* through the window, and think of the acting possibilities now that I'm a full-fledged waitress/bride. The thought takes some bite off my ears.

In the home stretch with just one more block to go, I catch sight of movement at the Nigerian Embassy. It's a homeless man inside a cardboard box, his dark coat and socks visible, his snore audible, draped in *New York Observer* newspapers. I must be out of my mind to complain about anything. I remove from my pocket, my tips from nine hours of work ($12) and place it in the Choc Full 'O Nuts (The Heavenly Coffee) tin beside him. And, as my mind considers his circumstances instead of my own, I don't feel the chill anymore. What an unexpected placebo effect. And the message is clear. For all the consideration I'd given to those better off than me, I haven't given equal time to those worse off.

At 2:57 a.m., I walk through the pine-wreathed door of the Belle Arts lobby where Norm, a night shift doorman, is sleeping while seated on a stool, his socked feet at a space heater. He wakes up as I pass, saying "Hi," before his head falls forward again.

I take the elevator up to seven, walk the hallway to the end and step inside my apartment, never so happy to see it, never so happy to fall asleep in the middle of the bare studio on grey shag carpet. Never so grateful. Never so much hairspray in my blue hair.

OLIVE HAS LEFT a message saying how pissed she is that I have to work during Christmas. "I wish you were coming home," she says. "It's crazy of you to be alone on Christmas in Manhattan."

After attempting to go to work today, I am turned away. I am not on the schedule today or tomorrow, but I'm told to check back with them on Monday when the new schedule is drawn up.

I return home to a message from Jake. He's going out of town for the holidays but will call when he returns. He hopes I have a great holiday with my family.

I enjoy my free time off by walking the city. Seeing it in a way I haven't seen it before: leisurely. And it's stunning. Saks Fifth Avenue even has a big red bow around it, around the building itself.

Rockefeller is rollicking with ice skaters skating to Elvis' Christmas Album. I sit on the steps of St. Patrick's watching the traffic, the shoppers, and the Christmas lights. And then doors open as a late mass exits to the tune of Ave Maria.

I walk home and hang up the pea coat.

⌒⌒⌒

ON MONDAY, as instructed, I call into J&H for the schedule. There is a recording. Only the downtown J&H will remain open during the holidays. "See you in the New Year, from all of us at Jekyll & Hyde." *What?* I call back repeatedly and can't get transferred out of a recording. I call the downtown J&H and Kevin's on vacation with his family and they don't see me on their schedule.

"But I'm supposed to have five shifts between now and New Year's."

"Sorry."

"Can you check to see if I'm on the schedule for the Re-Animator?"

"Nope, not there either. Sorry, but it's really busy here…"

"Ok, thanks."

We hang up.

Am I unemployed? What does that mean? Does that mean I can stop trying to memorize 200 beers?

⌒⌒⌒

"ARE YOU READY? Write this down," says Olive, who has taken the news of my potential unemployment the best.

I write down a series of numbers and letters.

"That's your e-ticket. You are reserved for a roundtrip."

"Olive, this is crazy, it will cost too much," I say.

"Forget about it. Mom and grandma are paying for it. Just tell me if those times are fine and I'll book it right now."

"Yeah, they're fine."

"Ohmygod. I can't wait to see you. I feel so much better that you're coming. I hated thinking of you alone in Manhattan. Especially on the holidays. And your birthday."

34. HOLIDAYS GO LIGHTLY

~Christmas Eve

"We're expecting a smooth flight for the most part. Portland is reporting good weather, just rain in the forecast.

"Good evening Miss. Would you care for some peanuts?"

I look up to see a male flight attendant. No sign of Doris Day anywhere. "Are they honey roasted?" I ask.

"Indeed they are" he responds, handing me the packet and a green holiday napkin. "I see you've flown with us before."

SIX HOURS LATER, I've landed. Olive drives up to the curbside of United baggage claim to pick me up. We laugh that we're dressed exactly the same in jeans, black jacket and a camel scarf. After a hug, she hurls my luggage into her much-improved car, a used Audi. And then we're off to grandma's house where she says, "everyone is waiting".

"So is there any cheeseball left for me?" I ask as we drive, anxious to eat my two all time favorites: Grandma's cheeseball and Christmas cookies.

"Yes, Grandma put some away for you. I already ate mine. Can I have some of yours?"

"No."

"No?"

We laugh.

"SWEET PEA!" exclaims my aunt Sherry as I'm greeted by a trail of aunts, uncles, and cousins.

And then, the song: "Happy Birthday to Eve" is sung by all as my mother presents a cheeseball with a lit candle.

"Make a wish!" says my mom.

I make a wish and blow out the candle as Olive dips a Wheat Thin into my cheeseball.

In short order, everyone is either playing cards, sleeping, playing ping pong in the garage, watching TV, or just talking and drinking.

And then Olive reads from a book, *The Secret Language of Birthdays*, "Those born on December 24 cannot expect to have an easy life – "

"Come on," I smirk with disbelief.

"That's what it says," she insists, handing me the book to read for myself. She wasn't kidding:

Those born on December 24 cannot expect to have an easy life.
Their joys, sorrows, rewards and disappointments are generally of a
greater order of magnitude than those around them, who indeed may think that
those born on this day put themselves through
unnecessary stress and tribulations.
The key to those born on this day improving themselves lies in recognizing
certain patterns in their lives, studying them and resolving not to
repeat those actions that didn't work.

That night, as I climb into bed at my mom's house, vowing not to repeat actions that don't work – which rules out a lot – I retrieve a voicemail from my new iPhone.

"Hi Eve. It's Jake. I just wanted to give you a call and wish you a happy holiday. What with a sudden snowstorm, I didn't go out of town with my family as planned, so I'm here in New Jersey just about to sit down with my family to eat but I just wanted to make sure you weren't alone for the holidays. I forgot to ask what your plans were, and what with the snow, I thought maybe you were stuck in the city. If you are, you are more than welcome to join us here in New Jersey. I could come pick you up. No one should be alone on Christmas, or Christmas Eve. If you are with your family, then God Bless and happy holidays."

I fall asleep smiling, trying to picture Christmas in New Jersey.

~ Christmas

"Wake up sissy."

"Don't call me that."

"Oh, I forgot. Wake up."

Santa has arrived.

As we open presents (including the Mimi-logo'd gifts I'm giving out), Santa (my mother) presents me with a gift from Olive: my very own pashmina scarf.

"Isn't that gorgeous?" says Olive. "I read that's what everyone's wearing in New York."

"You're right," I tell her, as visions of the lesbian PR duo and their pashmina scarves dance in my head. "Thanks!"

"OK Olive, now you can open this," says my mother handing Olive a box that says, "Don't open till XMAS," which nearly causes me to choke on my eighth Christmas cookie.

I get up and run to my bedroom, to the pea coat. Inside the left pocket is the "Don't open till XMAS" card from Jake. I open it. And although the ink has spread from a certain downpour, I am able to make it out:

Dear Eve, I can't believe you're leaving this
subzero weather in Syracuse for what? Sunny L.A.?

*Sorry to see you go so soon. I was looking to running into
you so some more. Best of luck in L.A.. I'm sure it will be great.
Who knows, maybe I'll see you there someday!
Stay in touch, Jake Fanelli
p.s. If you're not too busy your last week, maybe we can meet for lunch?*

"What is it?" asks my mom, poking her head in, then reading the envelope.

"Oh, just a Christmas card," I say, "from six years ago."

I return to the living room, my smile wider, card in hand, where the unwrapping continues.

"There she is," says my stepfather Harold.

"So Grandma wants to know what you've seen in New York," says my aunt Marilyn.

"Have you seen the Statue of Liberty?" my six-year-old cousin Jessica asks.

"No, not yet." I answer.

"No?" exclaims Olive.

"No, I've been a little busy," I answer.

"Gosh that's one of the first things I'd do," she says.

"Me too," says Jessica.

I was about to share in the list of things that have prevented me from seeing the Statue of Liberty when I sniff something ominously familiar. "Is someone wearing perfume?"

"I am. You like it?" asks my mother. "Harold got it for me. Do I smell good?" she asks, leaning her neck into me for me to sniff. "It's called *Me Me Me.*"

"Noooo! That's Mimi's perfume and that's the name I picked!" I shriek.

"You picked that? That's a good name," says Harold.

⌒‿⌒

~New Year's Eve
AFTER MY very own pre-flight huddle with loved ones, I said my goodbyes and boarded the red-eye flight back to New York.

"Happy Ball Drop Day," said the taxi driver as we began the drive to Manhattan.

"Same to you," I said, fighting off a yawn.

Within a few hours of arriving home and falling asleep on the couch from Luigi's son (my first non-carpeted bed in four months) I am awakened by the buzzing of my intercom. Deliveries that have been held over for me while I was away, are now coming up. One is direct from Givoudan Roure, the perfume manufacturer. For having won the naming of the perfume, I have won a year or a lifetime supply of *Me Me Me* perfume by Mimi de La Coco, whichever comes first. There's a note from Mimi. It reads:

Dear Missy, I know your penmanship.

She also writes that the new girl is not too bright and if I can just work a few hours a day for her, she'll pay me a full day's wage.

Another box is from Don. Inside it is a winter coat. It's his wife's but, he's bought her a new one, so he is giving me her old one. He says he'll pick up the pea coat "next year." No sooner do I finish spritzing on the perfume and trying on the coat when the intercom rings again.

"Another delivery coming up," says Ayman.

I hold the door open awaiting the delivery. Off the freight elevator comes head custodian Sammy with a delivery man carrying a Euro-plush top Serta Mattress and box spring. The card reads:

Dear Sleepless in Manhattan, Sleep well.
Love mom, Harold and Lulu

"Hi Eve, Jake here…"

I frantically start looking for my cell phone to take the call from Jake, excited and nervous and anxious, but he's not on the phone. He's on the other side of the box spring.

"Oh! Hi."

"Hi," he says, smiling as he makes his way into my apartment. "So you *are* here. I just came to check on you. Did you get my message?"

"Yes, I did… I just got back from Oregon."

"Well I was little concerned when I didn't hear from you, and I was coming into the city anyway."

Sammy winks at me. It's his thumbs up for Jake.

"Can you sign for this please?" asks the delivery man.

"Sure, thanks." I sign. "Thanks Sammy," I say as he leaves with the delivery man while Jake and the bed – stay.

The intercom rings again. "Jake's coming up…happy new year," says Ayman with a smile I can hear in his voice.

"Thanks Ayman, happy new year to you too," I say before releasing the button.

"Thank you for the Christmas card," I tell Jake. While we both know it was not a Christmas card in the conventional sense, it still had Santa written all over it.

"Sorry it's a little late," he smiles.

"Better late than never," I smile.

"Have you eaten? I'm pretty sure that I owe you a meal and I'd like to cash in on my raincheck."

JAKE DRIVES me back to New Jersey for dinner at a hangar where a pilot readies a twin-engine aircraft for flight. Minutes after finishing a nice meal, we are out on a farmland runway like in *North by Northwest*, and I am unnerved that the pilot needs Jake's assistance with the propeller. But, seconds later, we are up in the bitterly cold sky.

"See now *this* is the way to see Manhattan," says Jake.

"*So* much better," I say, as we view the top of the Empire State Building without having to look up.

After the flight, Jake escorts me to his car and reaches to open my door. "Here let me unzip that for you," he says. "Uh, I mean *unlock.*" We laugh all the way to Manhattan, so much so that he mistakenly blazes through a red light as we cross Ninth Avenue. But, my luck has changed for the better: no broken metacarpals!

As Jake parks his Pathfinder in front of my building, I hear my name called out. I turn to see Sydney with a girl our age with red hair. Sydney introduces us to Catherine who has just moved here from Paris, Texas. Her moving van arrives tomorrow.

"Oh, you must be dating Pavlos?" I say to her.

"Yes. I'm moving in with him, although he's in Los Angeles right now. How did you know?" It was the answer to the riddle of the Sphinx. I now know what Pavlos imports and exports.

JAKE SEES me up to my apartment before returning to New Jersey. As we say our goodbyes and make plans to see each other "next year," Jake takes a last look out my French windows. "Wow look at that snow," he says.

I join him at the window and take a look. It's a light snowfall. Won't even stick to the pavement. "That's going to stick," I say.

"Yep," he agrees. "Way too dangerous to go home just yet." We laugh.

Jake gazes intently into my eyes, takes my left hand into his, gently rubs his hand over my fourth metacarpal, and says, "You know what?"

"What?" I ask, bracing myself – a knee jerk reaction I hope to break free of someday.

"I hope you don't mind me saying this but… I'm glad you had the accident."

The warmth of his hands seeps into my skin. In his smiling, twinkling eyes, I melt. "Me too," I say in a long-awaited exhale, ignoring a tear pooling in my lid (because I switched to Waterproof Lancôme Black Noir mascara).

There is a thin line between mishap and miracle…

ACKNOWLEDGMENTS

Special thanks to…

Fellini, my fur baby.

My mom who first suggested that I write down "ever crazy thing" that had happened to me. I think she just expected a list.

My first literary agent, Edward Jay Acton, who read the first three chapters on the train home from Manhattan and thrilled me with his encouraging words. Discovering later that he once represented James Baldwin and Barack Obama was icing. (But seriously, when can I meet Michelle?)

My friends and family…. Tracy Steward, Michelle Hartmann, Butch Parker, and Leta Baysinger who have listened to so many of my stories, sometimes falling asleep (Leta). Jane Welch-Westgate, Chris Littrell and so many other cheerleaders. Alisha Gaddis, Tish Cohen, Joyce Yarrow, Debbie Markley, and all my fellow creatives for the steady stream of inspiration. Kristen Tennant for help in the final lap!

The late Frank McCourt, author of *Angela's Ashes*, for the literary inspiration. No one does gallows humor like him.

Last but not least, Manhattan. You are magical and madcap, and I dig that about you!

270